BOOKS BY WILLIAM HUMPHREY

The Last Husband and Other Stories
Home from the Hill
The Ordways
A Time and a Place
The Spawning Run
Proud Flesh

PROUD FLESH

PROUD FLESH

WILLIAM HUMPHREY

 *Alfred A. Knopf*
NEW YORK · 1973

This is a Borzoi Book
Published by Alfred A. Knopf, Inc.

Copyright © 1969, 1973 by William Humphrey
All rights reserved under International and Pan-American
Copyright Conventions. Published in the United States
by Alfred A. Knopf, Inc., New York, and
simultaneously in Canada by Random House of
Canada Limited, Toronto. Distributed by
Random House, Inc., New York.
A portion of this book appeared originally in
Esquire Magazine.

Library of Congress Cataloging in Publication Data:
Humphrey, William, 1969.
Proud Flesh.
I. Title.
PZ4.H927Pr   [PS3558.U464]   813'.5'4   72–11017
ISBN 0–394–46637–3

Manufactured in the United States of America
FIRST EDITION

■■■ **ONE** ■■■■■■■■■■■■

After forty years as their family physician, Dr. Metcalf—"Doc" to all the world—knows the Renshaws better than anybody else. Which means only that Doc knows even less than anybody what ever to expect of them. Expect the worst: everybody who knows the Renshaws knows that. Having brought them all into the world, having cured their illnesses and healed their hurts, having come when summoned to their every call, in all seasons, at any hour, Doc has a larger claim than anybody else upon the Renshaws' gratitude, but Doc is not relying on this now to save him from blame, from threats, from who knows what Renshaw unreasonableness, when he breaks his news to them.

For even in a place where every man's first loyalty is to his own clan, with the state of Texas coming a distant second and the South a still more distant third (and there it ends; even as a schoolboy, at morning assembly, the Texan men-

tally invokes the doctrine of interposition upon his pledge
of allegiance to the United States of America one nation
indivisible), the Renshaws are known, are notorious, for
their clannishness. Being Renshaw is a state of mind. They
are not a family, they are a nationality and a cult—pharisaical,
fanatical. The Renshaws are like a colony of bees, just as exclusive, just as singlemindedly self-intent, and just as ready,
each and every one of them, to sting its sting and die should
the hive be attacked. And it is Doc's duty now to tell them
that the queen bee, their mother, Edwina, is dying.

The Renshaws are unprepared for this. "Ma's heart
condition" is something they have known about for a long
time, but they have been led to believe, by none other than
Doc himself, that it is a mild one. Now Doc is in a dilemma.
Shall he reveal that, like the court physician to an aging
monarch tenacious of her power and mistrustful of her waiting heirs and successors, he has watched her condition worsen
for years but has kept it from them on orders from her, not
being allowed to tell even her daughter Amy, the nurse, and
the most devoted of her children, its seriousness? Or shall he
let them think it is as sudden a shock to him as it is to them,
and risk having the Renshaws suspect him of incompetence,
or negligence, or both? The sigh with which Doc prepares to
break his news is as detached as he can make it, professional,
philosophical, fellow-human. There comes a time, he says,
when all the advancements of science are to no avail. Which
to anybody else would convey the message that he, Ben
Metcalf, MD, is up on all the latest advancements of science;
but with these Renshaws you never know.

They stand in the shade of the pear tree where generations of Renshaw men have stood to receive such news, have
squatted and kept vigil whenever there was sickness in the
house. In their sweat-soaked clothes, panting for breath, they

look like survivors from a capsized boat just washed ashore, especially as one of them is dressed in a sailor's white suit. The sailor's eyes brim with tears. The three older men only swallow hard, their Adam's apples working audibly. Three of the fruit from the tree they stand beneath are not more alike than they, so strong is the family resemblance among them. They do not look griefstricken at Doc's news; their resentful expression is habitual, it is the Renshaw look, with which they confront all of life; it is a family feature, like the Renshaw brow, the Renshaw jaw. They say nothing. They level at Doc three identical sets of eyes, or rather of shadowed eye-sockets, which are like the muzzles of three double-barreled shotguns. If there is a difference of temper among the three brothers it is this: that like the three stops made by the hammer of a gun as it is cocked to be fired, Clyde's is at the first stop, Clifford's at the second, and Ballard's at the third, ready to go off at any moment. The silence is filled with the drone of wasps among the fallen and liquefying pears—for the old tree can no longer hold its fruit until ripe—and the stridulation of a locust like a telephone ringing insistently in an empty house. Up from the fields comes the mournful chant of Negroes picking cotton.

Their mother—grandmother—is a strong-willed woman, as they well know, Doc says, and one with a tight hold on life. But she is also a sick woman and one no longer young, and knowing them as he does, how close a family theirs is, he feels they will want to be told his worst fears now so they can call the others home to her side. Hope for the best still, he tells them, but—and he draws another sigh—be prepared now for the worst. He has done all he can do for her.

—All anybody can do, he hastily amends. All anybody can do. For you never know what is going on behind those

5

slits of eyes. Only that they think as one, if they stop to think, then they act as one. She may be sick and old, but when Edwina Renshaw dies her sons and grandsons, not to mention those daughters of hers, are going to want somebody to blame. Then Doc's white hairs and the fact that he brought them all into the world will count for nothing. These four here: they would not seriously suspect him of leaving anything untried; but they are perfectly capable of believing it a duty to the old lady, to the absent members of the clan, and to themselves, to accuse him of it just the same.

At last one of them speaks. It is Clyde. He says it is just like Ma never to let them know how really sick she was so as to spare them worry, even to mislead her doctor, suffer in silence and all alone. Doc heaves another sigh, this one of relief, and saying that he must not be away from his patient any longer, makes his escape. He turns and steps out of the shade into the blaze of day. At the touch of the sun his head appears to flare into incandescent white ash like the mantle of a lamp. Head down, he wades through the shimmering heat waves on the far shore of which stands the house. The porch runs the width of the house, casting a shadow as straight as a ruled line which divides it into layers of black and yellow. In the upper story the windowpanes glint darkly, all but the one in the corner room, with its day-drawn shade.

Ballard volunteers to go to the telegraph office.

Derwent, wiping his tears on his sleeve, offers to drive him. It was Derwent who drove the doctor out from town, fifteen miles in just over ten minutes.

Clifford reminds them that somebody will have to go after Uncle Howard and Aunt Estelle and them; they cannot be reached by wire.

There is a silence during which each man stares off in a different direction. Finally Clyde says what all are thinking:

"They're not the only ones."

There follows another silence.

"Well," says Clifford, "you can't go after him."

There follows another, deeper, longer silence. The wasps drone, the locust repeats its ring, up from the fields floats the Negroes' melodious moan.

Then in a tone of dreamy defiance, "Can't?" says Ballard.

I

Of Edwina Renshaw's ten children only Clifford, her eldest son, was left at home; the rest were scattered and gone. But with one exception they had not gone far, and their fixed orbits within their mother's strong gravitational field brought them home regularly and often. In recent years they had rallied still closer around their mother to close that one gap in their ranks. It was always open house at Edwina's. None of the children ever wrote or phoned ahead to announce a homecoming. None of the boys would have dreamed of giving his mother warning that he was on his way out bringing five or six hunting companions with him to spend the weekend. Bring as many as they pleased and arrive just at mealtime, they would find places set and the table heaped high.

Her table was set in the old-fashioned farmhouse style, with the plates turned bottom side up waiting for grace to be said over them, the spoons in a pewter stand in the center, cone-rolled yellowed linen napkins as supple as chamois in cracked and yellowed ivory rings, toothpicks in a holder of Bohemian ruby glass. She served the old country-style recipes: chess pie, chowchow, fruit and berry cobblers; at hog-killing time in the fall, backbone and baked sweet potatoes, cracklin' bread. A great deal of game birds in, as well as out of, season: quail, woodcock, doves, tangy black-meated wild duck.

Eulalie, the cook, had an antique boy's coaster wagon with removable sideboards, the envy of every little boy in the neighborhood, which sat outside the kitchen door, and every morning at seven, as soon as the cream had been separated, the breakfast dishes washed and the milk utensils scoured, the two women would jam on their sunbonnets and Eulalie would take up her old sliver of a knife and they would trundle off together to the garden or to the root cellar, silent, synchronized, like one woman and her shadow. When they came back, wagon creaking beneath pecks of tomatoes, three or four dozen roasting ears, heads and heads of lettuce and bunches upon bunches of carrots and onions, it would be an hour later; for each ear of corn had to be tested, the shucks peeled back below the tassel, a kernel punctured by thumbnail, the ear selected only if it spurted milk. Down the rows of watermelons they would go, Eulalie thumping each one with her yellow nail, the two of them huddled down, heads cocked, listening: the one over which they nodded together would, when cut, split with a loud crack running ahead of the blade and part with a smack like two red lips. Then out to the smokehouse, where hams hung from the blackened beams for three years were adjudged ripe when they had attained the color and the texture of a mossy stone. Or out to the chickenyard where soon they might be seen surrounded by half a dozen headless pullets flopping on the ground in successive stages of death while Edwina pointed out and Eulalie enticed yet another with a handful of grain, then swooped and grabbed and wrung its head off in mid-squawk, execrating it and its whole race so as to work herself up against it and excuse her cruelty. By late morning the air of the back yard was spiced and sugared by the aroma of pies set out rim to rim to cool on the kitchen window ledges, and outside the door stood a queue of neighbor children waiting for pots and pans to lick. Hulls and shells and pods and peels and feathers and shucks and bones went out of that kitchen by the cartload—and with them went about half of the food. For the Renshaws admired nothing so much as bounty, lavishness, waste, despised nothing so much as "chinchiness"—their word for thrift. Everything Renshaw was overfed. The turkeys, chickens and geese rendered buckets when cooked. The pigs were so larded they scarcely opened their eyes when their evening trough was filled. The only lean creature on the place was Edwina. Tall and spare, she ate like a hummingbird: a shirred egg, the pullybone of a cold fried chicken, a dish of clabber. Ten cups of blistering black coffee per day, despite doctor's orders. And at night before bed a hot toddy, the ingredients for which stood on her night table, for she trusted no one to make it to her taste—that is, to put in such a dollop of bootleg Old Overholt as, for the sake of her heart, she spiked it with.

Until that day in September when she was brought back from the garden in Eulalie's wagon, unconscious, blue in the face, her feet dangling over the sides and her heels scratching furrows in the dirt, the flaw in her heart had been Edwina Renshaw's close-kept, open secret. Whenever Doc Metcalf was called in to treat her for an attack he was made to swear to tell none of the children about it. Edwina's heart had been like a broken vase, so placed that the crack did not show, on a high shelf, out of her children's reach. To them only its good side was ever turned. The break, had they seen it, they would have blamed on their baby brother. They would have been right, and Edwina herself did blame him; but to allow the others to do so would have been to acknowledge the wrong she had done them, as well as the mistake she had made, in favoring that one child over all his brothers and sisters.

In September with the first touch of the sun the fields of cotton threw back heat into the air like a bed of white-hot coals. The breath came short and even sound hearts labored. And so Edwina had not waited for Eulalie that day but had gone down to the garden alone in the cool of the morning while there was still some shade. Derwent, her favorite grandson, was coming home on leave. Now in his second hitch (how those blackland prairie boys, born beyond all memory of the sea, all made for the Navy whenever there was any enlisting to be done! And how often the motive for enlisting was not patriotism but paternity!), Derwent remained an apprentice seaman in rank, and he always would. He had been promoted more than once; but always after a few weeks he was busted for insubordination or for a lead part in some shoreside brawl. Derwent never minded these demotions; on the contrary, they kept him young, a perennial boot, and they satisfied that rank-and-file pride in low, manly station of which Derwent had a large share. They kept him popular with the kind of girl he liked. The kind who preferred a tar, feeling too much on her good behavior with petty officers. He would come bringing his grandmother some doodad from some outlandish port which would have to be hidden from sight, and a shipload of dirty stories which she would squeal in protest against and laugh at until she cried. He would squire her downtown in his middy blouse and bell-bottomed trousers, his little white hat cocked on his brow, his rolling gait converting the square with its hunkering farmers into the deck of a gunboat in a running sea. It was to pick Derwent a mess of the butterbeans which were his favorite dish, and which he never got fresh on shipboard, that Edwina had gone down to the garden that morning. She was clutching a fistful of them when Eulalie found her an hour later lying pitched face down in the dirt.

II

Her reign had been Victorian in length, her sovereignty absolute, claiming allegiance at birth from all in whose veins a drop of her blood flowed. Whenever any of her sons foregathered away from home their first words were of her, like British colonial officers with their toast, "Gentlemen, the Queen. God bless her!" Spoiled, capricious, contrary, she had but to snap her fingers and those great unruly boys of hers, the terror of six counties, sprang to serve her like acolytes. To all her progeny in every generation she was "Ma"; that was a name which none of the grandchildren was permitted to call his own mother, just as none of her sons, no matter how long he might have lived in his own house or how many children had been born to him there, ever came to call the place "home." Ma was Ma, and home was Ma's house.

Dutifully, unquestioningly, like offering them up to a religious order or to a draft call, her sons and daughters turned over their children to her—woe to the daughter-in-law who demurred! Beginning when they reached six and lasting through sixteen, the grandchildren each spent three weeks every summer with Ma down home on the farm. Cousins came to seem like brothers and sisters in the Renshaw family. They went as to a summer camp, with uniforms tailored to Ma's rigid taste and the unvarying season of outings she had planned, and her determination that none should feel any inequality in their parents' financial positions. For the girls, pinafores and shirtwaists cut to the pattern of her own distant childhood: two pink, two blue; skirts with hemlines precisely fifteen inches off the ground. And such was her domination that boys in the first hot flush of long trousers meekly suffered themselves to be put back into kneepants: two pairs white flannel, two of blue serge. At the County Fair on Labor Day, the summer's last excursion, they looked like a select, well-endowed orphanage, and she its directress, or, nunlike in her own habit-shaped black or gray dress, and nunlike in her severity—at least toward the girls—like its mother superior.

And so the farm came to be home for the grandchildren as well. It did not lack a man. There was unmarried Uncle Cliff, the one the whole family looked up to—though in middle-age he was a child, backward and tonguetied and countryfied, childishly good-natured when not in the throes of some childish tantrum and off somewhere pouting, who spent all his time with a pack of hounds and who knew where to find wild honey and the biggest blackberries and the best baits for catfish and when the bream were biting, but nothing more—because he was the one who had stayed with Ma and never left home.

But it was not in the summertime only that Edwina's daughters and daughters-in-law relinquished their sons to her.

In the independence, the impudence, the sassiness which she fostered in a boy (her favorite endearment was "rascal"), they felt her between their sons and them the year round. With their daughters they were free to do pretty much as they pleased. Girls had only to meet certain negative requirements: to be chaste, demure, silent, and when the time came, long-suffering and uncomplaining toward some vagrant man of their own, preferably one chosen, certainly one approved, by Ma. It was boys Edwina cared about, and that they should grow into men. She knew what made a man. He must be braggardly and bold, touchy, trifling, headstrong, wild—obedient to no one in the world but her. They were glad to obey her. Pretending to disapprove, she egged on her grandsons as she had their fathers before them by winking at their escapades with girls, their recklessness with cars and horses and guns. She wanted them vigorous but idle. Polite but bawdy. Chivalrous but predatory. In a word: men.

Although widowhood now seemed her lifelong vocation, there had been a husband once . . . dust and a handful of anecdotes for twenty years: Lonzo (Alonzo), known behind his back as old Dot-and-Carry because of the hitch in his gait, not congenital but from a crippled big toe, broken, then disowned and neglected, grown gnarled as a brier root, in a kick he had given a calf that persisted in wishing to suck its mamma whom he was trying at the time to milk. Tame as a tabby cat with his wife, with all the rest of the world he had been quarrelsome, self-opinionated, abrasive. This tale was told of one fistfight he had gotten himself into. One day in a cafe in town he had hailed a man sitting on a stool at the far end of the counter as his long-lost friend Lew Pearsall, and stumped down to shake old Lew by the hand. The fat was in the fire when the stranger failed to lay down his knife and fork. Said he was afraid there was some mistake. His name was Selby, and he did not remember to have had the honor. Lonzo stood there with his empty hand stuck out. Perhaps one or more of the other diners snickered. Lonzo swore he never forgot a face, and reminded Lew of that night in Texarkana when together they— The stranger said he was afraid there was some mistake. Then Lonzo accused him of thinking he was too good for his old friends, said now that he came to think of it that was the sort he had always been, and called him by six or eight names which the stranger found even less acceptable than Pearsall, and which could only lead to the backalley behind the cafe, where finally the spectators had had to disarm Lonzo of the brass knuckles he happened to be carrying in his hip pocket at the time.

This readiness to fight a man over his own name was something the Renshaw boys had all inherited.

Perhaps old Dot-and-Carry had had to let off such an excess of steam outside the house because of being so bottled up at home, looking already in their faded sepia-toned wedding photograph which hung over the parlor mantelpiece— she enthroned upon a stiff ladder-backed chair and wearing not a bridal gown but one of those gray soutanes such as she was wearing on the day a half century later when struck down by illness—like the consort to a queen. Unremembered now in the lineaments of his offspring, in all of whom down to the fourth generation her pattern was distinct and assertive as the tartan of a clan: brown, almost black eyes, round-lidded, deep-set under shelving brows, a high ridged forehead, reddish-blond hair highly resistant to graying and balding, long sharp nose with narrow nostrils, short upper lip, overfull pouting lower one, the jaw heavy and a trifle undershot, and in the men a thick neck, thickly corded, with a gaunt Adam's apple like a knot in a rope. That, with allowances (though not many) for the difference in sex, was the image of her who now lay behind day-drawn shades in the upstairs bedroom of the big rambling yellow house on the hill.

People were inclined to feel that Alonzo Renshaw had been dead even longer than he had. In conversation his widow managed to convey the impression that she had raised, if not conceived, her ten children singlehanded. And it was true that even during her husband's lifetime she had been both mother and father to their boys, leaving to him the girls. She it was who regularly on the third Saturday of the month brought in her brood to be barbered. They would arrive punctually on the stroke of ten, and the barbershop would be emptied in expectation; for she sat through the entire shearing and her presence put such a damper on the customary male conviviality of the place that the customers, and even the shoeshine boy, retired to the backalley until her departure. They would line up in order of age: Clifford, Clyde, Ross, Ballard and Lester. At Mr. Birdwell's hands they all received the same monkish tonsure, but this never discouraged their mother from issuing a stream of directives for trimming each of her boys in such a way as to soften and flatter what she alone could discern as his individual features. On climbing down from the chair each had to submit to her running her hand through his hair to muss it up and give it a less newly-clipped look. He was then free to go outside and stand by the peppermint pole with his hands in his pockets until the rest of his brothers were done. A favorite Saturday morning pastime of other boys proud of their shagginess was to stroll past the barbershop and whisper something taunting, having reference to cueballs and peeled onions, to the accumulated Renshaw brothers around the pole, who, unable to respond beneath their mother's all-seeing eye, like so many Samsons shorn of their force, could only hiss an invitation to meet them later, an invitation seldom accepted, as the Renshaw boys fought all for one and one for all, and did not scruple to fight all five against one.

Anyone who bore the name Renshaw, no matter how remote the connection, could count on Ma's boys for help in time of trouble. Likewise he could count on hearing from them should he do anything to besmirch the name.

Once word reached the boys that Conway Renshaw, who lived in the neighboring county, had been dragging their proud name in the dirt. They called him Uncle though none knew exactly how he was related to them. Uncle Conway had recently opened a grocery store in a Negro neighborhood in his town. Through a sharp credit system he had in no time at all made such a good thing of it that already they were calling him "Nig" Renshaw, and a local wit had tagged him "the black man's burden."

The Renshaw boys disapproved of this reputation for sharp practice which their kinsman had earned. However, it was not only that. And they could have lived with the notion of a Renshaw's living deriving wholly from Negroes, if only it had derived a little more indirectly. Association with Negroes was all right. They themselves passed time with Negroes, under certain outdoor sporting conditions. They all liked Negroes, liked some of them better than lots of white men they knew, and brother Clyde was even then evincing that preference for the company of Negroes which was to end by making him almost an alien from his own race. What stung was the thought of a Renshaw waiting on Negroes, serving them, taking orders from them, clerking to them, selling them intimate household items for petty cash, hand to hand, retail. And so a little vigilante party of Renshaw boys dropped in unannounced at the grocery store one busy Saturday afternoon. It was a hot summer day and Uncle Conway was doing a carnival-stand trade in RC Colas at seven cents a bottle (a nickel was the going price at the time). Black, or rather, work-worn, blackish-yellow, horny hands clamored for gingersnaps and vanilla wafers and bananas and canned sardines, all paid for with fistfuls of sweaty small change laboriously counted out of snap-top pocketbooks the length and the shape of socks—it looked, when they drew one out of their overalls pockets, as if they were extracting a vital body gland —and consumed on the premises while Uncle Conway filled their orders for the week's provisions, off-brand goods at marked-up prices to which was further added a carrying charge for credit. Uncle Conway professed himself mighty pleased to see the boys, and asked automatically after Ma. But the blood flew to his cheeks and he suddenly adopted a more distant manner toward his customers and they a more respectful one toward him. That was on a Saturday; the following Monday morning Renshaw's grocery failed to open its doors for business. Uncle Conway sold out that same week. Shortly afterward he re-emerged in the business world on a more genteel plane, taking on the local franchise for bottling a new brand of strawberry pop. This did not go over so he went into the feed and grain business, was set up in it by Ma's boys, said those who sided with them in this dispute.

Not everybody did. They were criticized for their high-handed interference in their uncle's affairs, and for that family pride which made them do it. Still, the same ones who blamed them had to concede that whenever any Renshaw was in trouble, or under outside attack, Ma's boys were there johnny-on-the-spot to help him out. The Renshaws were like hornets: tangle with one of them and you had the whole nest down upon you. Better be prepared to look the other way, turn the other cheek. For the Renshaws were never so quick to defend or avenge one of theirs as when he was in the wrong.

Whether they actually laid hands on Malcolm Beatty to avenge their cousin Claude (who certainly started the trouble that led to that bloody Saturday afternoon on the town's public square) was never known. It was generally accepted that Beatty had meant as part of his plan from the start to leap those four stories to his death. Be that as it may, he must certainly have been strengthened in his desperate resolve by the noise of those five lawless Renshaw brothers pounding on his office door.

Cousin Claude Renshaw, like all farmboys, was a shade-tree mechanic, only Claude was better than most, a mechanical wizard, and left the farm on the strength of it, within a year was foreman of a garage in town and within another year owned it, within two more had bought out his nearest competitor, taken over the local Ford distributorship, then hired town people to do all the paper-work out front while he went back to what he loved: greasemonkeying. He had been seen once to lift an old roadster with one hand and slip the already jacked-up jack under the axle all for the admiration of one passing nameless wide-eyed little boy. A philanderer, he would have been astonished to hear a word of reproach from his wife, almost as astonished as she would have been at herself.

That Saturday afternoon—it was during another September, ginning season, and about a month since Malcolm Beatty had served public warning on him to stay away from Mrs. Beatty—Claude Renshaw came into the crowded square lying along the hood of a slowly moving car listening to the engine as a doctor listens to a sick man's heart. He would raise one black grimy hand and slow the driver, the owner of the car, to a walk, ignoring the gabble of horns—like a file of impatient geese—of the cars in the rear, then signal again to accelerate just a bit, directing with the finesse of an orchestra conductor. In this way, sounding like a wedding cortege, the file of cars progressed down the west side of the square headed south and came to the corner where along the curbstone the usual Saturday group of men squatted talking. The noise caused them all to look up, and the sight of Claude Renshaw lying along the hood prompted one of them to remark, as was later remembered, "I didn't know the season was open yet."

At the corner the car turned and started up along the south side, enabling the traffic trailing behind to exit from the square, which it did with a parting angry hooting of horns. In the ensuing silence a sound broke overhead, light-ninglike, crackling: a shot, a rifle shot, the sharp thin bark—unmistakable to all those vets, gun cranks, hunters, many of whom had themselves brought one back from the Pacific—of a Japanese Arisaka, oriental as a brass gong or the twang of a zither string. Down on the street an engine roared as if in pain. The car on the hood of which Claude Renshaw lay, shot forward, swerved, leaped the curb, flinging Claude into the air, hurtled across the sidewalk and through the throng of pedestrians and charged head-on through the plate glass window of the Piggly-Wiggly. Emerging from the spray of glass, the car hit the checkout counter, queues of shoppers falling over one another like bowling pins. It bounced hard and rocked back, then the horn began to moan as the driver slumped over the wheel. The air went out of the two front tires and the front end sank as a dying animal sinks to its knees. The horn trailed off in hoarse diminuendo, died. Then it was seen that in the hood of the car was a blood-ringed bullethole. The hush strained and broke and the wounded and the shocked inside the store and outside on the walk groaned and wailed in chorus. So many people were bleeding from cuts about the head and arms, face and legs, that they appeared to have been caught in a sprinkle of bright red rain. The only person apparently unhurt was the driver of the car. They pulled him out, whimpering. Then it was recalled that as the car struck the curb the man riding on the hood, Claude Renshaw, had been thrown off. But Claude had not felt his fall. Entering behind the ear, the bullet had passed through his head and through the hood of the car, and the almost faceless thing that lay in the gutter amid the peanut hulls and the hot tamale shucks and tobacco juice was no longer Claude Renshaw, hardly seemed ever to have been.

Already one of Ma's boys, Ross, was on the scene. After one horrified look the crowd had sucked back with a gasp, and the corpse now lay in a pool of sunlight. Ross Renshaw crossed this space and stood looking down at the body of his kinsman. There he was joined by his brothers Ballard and Clyde. The fire siren could be heard starting to unwind in the distance, while from the nickelodeon in the deserted confectionery down the block came the whine of a balladier and the whang of a steel guitar. Shrieks and sobs rent the air as the injured were coaxed and led away. Now the crowd surged in once more, those in front clawing back but pushed forward despite themselves by those behind, the late arrivals who had yet to get their look.

The town's day constable arrived and made everybody stand back. Thus, luckily, no one was in the way when the second victim of the afternoon fell from the skies and broke on the paving stones six feet from the original corpse. Heads snapped up in outraged disbelief, and people saw hanging out the fourth floor windows across the panes of which was lettered in gold MALCOLM O. BEATTY, GEN'L INSURANCE, and peering impassively down upon the scene below, the faces of Clyde, Ross, Ballard, Clifford and Lester Renshaw.

III

MA IN CRITICAL CONDITION FOLLOWING HEART ATTACK
HURRY HOME

Ernest Bates, the Western Union operator, read the message back across the counter in his toneless official voice. Then overhearing himself he looked over his glasses and said, "Oh! Ballard! I'm awful sorry, Son!"

Ballard Renshaw nodded briefly, scowling. "Here," he said. "Here's the list of names to send it to," laying down another sheet of paper and shooting a glare at old Will Mahaffey, busy composing a message at the far end of the counter.

Ernest read the list back to Ballard:

"Mrs. Ira Renshaw Parker, 4722 Eisenhower Drive, Waxahachie

Mrs. Laverne A. Goodman, 103 Harmony Lane, Nacogdoches

2 3

Mrs. B. T. Rideout, Mineola

Mrs. Lois Renshaw Baker, 227 John Birch Boulevard, Dallas

Mr. Ross Renshaw, % Tower Hotel, Mineral Wells

Mr. Lester Renshaw, % Blankenship, Grand Saline."

Ernest looked up, and before he knew it, asked, "Is that all?"

"And was that all?" Will Mahaffey was asked.

Will nodded. "Ne'er a one of them wires," he said, "went outside of the state of Texas."

"How long is it since that one left home?"

"It's ten years."

"Naw, it ain't. It's more like five."

"It's more than five."

"And he's never come back in all that while? Not even on Christmas?"

"Maybe he died."

"They never have give it out that he did."

"Maybe he died in some way they would sooner wasn't known."

"He's not dead."

"How do you know he's not?"

"You can tell."

"How can you tell?"

"Tell by looking. You ever asked any of them how he's making out? The look they give you? He's alive, all right."

"Maybe he is in the penitentiary. That would explain why they didn't wire him to come home to his mother. And why they don't much care to be asked about him."

"He could be. Yes, that boy might very well have wound up in the penitentiary somewhere."

"I always thought he would make out right well. If he would ever just put his mind to it."

"Maybe he has. Maybe that explains it. Maybe he's risen to think he's too good for his folks, for his old home-town."

"He would think he was too good for the town whether he made out well or not. He always thought that. They all think that."

"Well, I can't say I liked that one any more than the rest of them, but still he ought to be told now about his ma. He has a right to know. Whoever's fault it was that he left home, that he's stayed away all these years, he's still a son, and even the worst son ought to be told when his ma is sick and like to die. Not to let him know is a sin and a shame. I would say the same to them, mean a bunch as they are. I would."

"I would wait till they asked me if I was you."

"Umh, and not hold my breath while I waited."

So by the time Ballard and Derwent got back from town, neighbors and old friends of the family, some of whom had been among the men in town with cotton at the gins, others summoned no one knew how save through that instinct of country people for impending death, had begun to arrive. The men, in clean overalls and khakis, fresh, faded blue workshirts spotting darkly with sweat, squatted in the shade of the pear tree like frogs around a pond. Grave and decorous, they got slowly to their feet at the approach of the men of the family. Will Mahaffey was there and Will's boy Brother and Brother's twin boys Billybob and Billyjim. Prentiss Partloe was there; he doted on Mrs. Edwina, though she had decided once and for all thirty and more years ago, on the basis probably of a single harebrained boyhood prank, that Prentiss was not quite all there (his two terms' service in the State Legislature down in Austin was not calculated to alter her judgment), and had treated him accordingly ever since. Curtis Roberts, too, had come over, and even as they stood to greet the Renshaw men, another truck and another passenger sedan were heard rattling to a stop down the road. Tall, lean men, all of them, with brick-colored necks and faces, with pale, sun-bleached lashes and brows.

Ballard Renshaw greeted the men with a scowl and a wordless nod.

Curtis Roberts, speaking for all, said, "Boys, we are just as sorry as we can be to hear this terrible news. Youall know how we feel about Mrs. Edwina." From the others came a murmur of agreement.

Ballard said, "Haven't youall got cotton to pick?"

"Never mind about our cotton," said Prentiss. "It'll get picked when it gets picked. What does the doctor say, Bal?"

By way of answer Ballard turned his back and struck across the yard to the house. Derwent followed him, his white suit unendurably bright in the glare.

The men settled down to their vigil. More came. John Bywaters, Clifton Terry joined the group. John's wife went up the driveway toward the kitchen door carrying a roasting pan from under the cover of which, as it bounced to her step, a roll of steam escaped.

"Yes, yes," sighed Calvin Sykes. "When their time comes the women have to go, same as the rest of us."

The party line would be busy by now. The neighbor

women came bringing the suppers they had been preparing for their own families when they heard the news. For it was their place to provide the evening's meal for their troubled neighbors, whether they liked them or not, as someday others would do for them. From the kitchen came no sound, yet on that very silence was borne the sense of solemn bustle, of a sorority of kindly, capable witches stirring pots, performing their traditional rites. Outside the kitchen door, around the chinaberry tree, the neighborhood Negroes, back-door beneficiaries of all that food that went out of the kitchen, had begun to gather.

"The Lord is no gentleman, that's a fact," said old man Tom Westfall, just arrived. "He cracks His whip over one and all alike, irregardless of sex."

"In my opinion," said Will Mahaffey, "the women do it better than us men. I have buried three, and I don't expect to go as graceful as e'er one of them when my turn comes, old as I am and living on borrowed time."

"Edwina Renshaw won't go ladylike. She'll go, I reckon, if she just has to, but she won't like it."

"Like it or lump it," said old man Westfall, lowering himself creakily to his hunkers, "when your time is up you've got to go. Youth nor beauty nor tears nor all the money in the world nor five times five fighting sons can't buy nor bully nor wheedle you one minute more than your allotted span. Keep your satchel packed at all times and ready for the call. For the great day of reckoning will surely come, and then the Lord God Almighty will hold us each and every one up to the strong light and cull the bad from the good like candling eggs. He takes grannies and blushing brides, boys in first reader and young men at the plow, them still at the breast, them with their full set of teeth and them left to gum it as best they can. He can call you on Sunday or any day of the week, so be ready at all times. Be packed and ready to go. Be sure of today and you're sure of eternity, for none of us can be sure of tomorrow."

"Amen."

"Amen."

"Amen."

IV

By August the cottonfields have whitened as if the sun has reduced the earth to ashes. In September come the migrant workers and settle on them in a swarm. Bent black figures in clothes darkened and colorless with sweat, dragging their long bolster-shaped sacks behind them, they eat their way across the fields, white ahead of them, stripped bare and brown in their wake, like some plague of great white-bodied, black-headed caterpillars. Even the little children pick, emptying their towsacks and patched pillowcases into their mothers' and fathers' sacks at the end of the row, at the weighing-up.

They pick from dawn to dark, and while they pick they chant. It is like a broken record left to spin in the same worn groove. When finally a voice is raised in a new tune it is like when the phonograph needle is lifted and advanced beyond the break. After a while another break is reached. They inch along the rows more and more slowly as their sacks swell. Bit by bit black hands and arms, sticky with sweat, turn white from the lint that fills the air, clogs the nostrils, chokes the breath, sprouts white moustaches on sweaty lips, turns hair and eyebrows grizzled; and soon all of them, bent as they are, look hoary and stooped with age.

Trucks or trailers sit in the field, with extra-tall sideboards or with sides of stretched hogwire, and near each one stands a tripod of poles from which hangs the scale. There the sacks are dragged, doubled and hung by the ends to be weighed, the boss entering the figure in his daybook alongside the picker's name, and the picker himself, or herself, entering the figure in his sweat-dampened daybook—one of those given away to advertise snuff or farina or patent medicines. On Saturday afternoon after the final weighing-up they are paid their week's wages. Only on Sunday—and sometimes not then—does that lament of theirs cease, and then stillness settles upon the empty, glaring fields.

Yet such a stillness fell now, in mid-morning of a week-day, upon the ears of the men squatting in the shade of the pear tree. That chant which was so much a part of the season and the place that the cessation of it was momentarily like a failure of hearing, stopped, voice by voice, like the ending of a roundsong. Clyde had gone down to the fields and told the pickers to quit work in observance of Ma's condition, and upon the still air the silence throbbed like the tolling of a knell. The wasps droned among the pears, and from somewhere came the sob of a mourning dove:

coo-oo   coo coo coo

coo-oo   coo coo coo

V

Clyde was the one who, although he lived in town and had to drive out and back every day, ran the farm. Clifford, being the eldest son and the one who had never left home, might have been expected to be the one, but Clifford had done few of the things that were expected of him. He not only never took a wife and raised a family, he had never taken any interest in running the farm or in any other steady employment. It could not be said that Clifford had never worked a day in his life, just that he could never be counted on to work two days in succession. Yet Clifford was not shiftless, and he was anything but extravagant. He was moody and unpredictable, a mixture of boy, backwoodsman and old maid, a mystery even to himself. Never articulate, almost tonguetied in fact, and dangerous when in moments of feeling the words boiled inside him, his leaden tongue like a plug, a stuck safety valve, he would sometimes let days go by without a sound passing his lips, a sullen, half-tamed bear of a man. He did not have any speech defect, did not stammer, he just choked, and then he turned red—purple—apoplectic. Then he took himself off and was gone no one knew where for a week, two weeks, then returned with never a word of explanation nor even a greeting for anybody, he just reappeared, filthy, bearded, looking more like a bear than ever. The sight of money made him blush and scowl. He associated money with pleasure, pleasure with sin. It had been evident early that someone other than Clifford would have to manage the farm.

Managing the Renshaws' farm still meant bossing Negroes. For although many farmers in the county had switched from cotton to cattle as pickers got harder and harder to find, Clyde Renshaw stuck with cotton. Clyde liked cotton, but more than cotton Clyde liked cottonpickers. He looked forward all year to their coming. Or rather, he had always done so until this year.

Clyde liked Negroes. In fact, Clyde liked only Negroes. Not that Clyde's notions about Negroes were any different from those of people who disliked, even despised them; in fact, they were the same. Like the rest, Clyde too imputed to Negroes, especially the migrant cottonpicking kind, the sexual socialism of the barnlot. He too believed that unless you watched them every minute they would steal you blind. That they were lazy, lying, lawless, settling their disputes among themselves with an icepick or a straight razor. But these traits which others despised them for were just what Clyde liked about Negroes. He himself thought of nothing but what he called poontang from waking to sleeping. He knew honesty did not pay, that hard work got you nothing but more of the same, that the law was always on the other fellow's side, that the only law was the law of the jungle, eat or be eaten, screw or get screwed.

People said of the migrant workers that they lived like animals. Clyde said the same. But when Clyde said it he meant they lived the free, untrammeled lives of animals, without shame, without hypocrisy. Being outcasts from society, they were free from its restrictions. They lived. When the crop was gathered and they piled into their battered cars and hit the road north toward their next squalid campsite, leaving him behind with the profits from their labors, Clyde Renshaw watched them out of sight and longed to be one of them. Meanwhile it was Clyde's boast, as some men vaunt themselves on their knowledge of horseflesh or their affinity with dogs, that he knew how to handle Negroes. He spoke their language. The language he spoke after a day in the field made his wife Eunice say when he came home from work in the evening, "You can turn off the Amos 'n Andy now."

Clyde Renshaw had expected to have to fight a war in his time. Clyde had been determined to fight his war in his own way, with a minimum of interference from the U.S. Army. That the United States would win its war Clyde never questioned; his concern was to make sure he won his. To ensure his survival Clyde chose with care his branch of the armed service: the infantry; his rank: private; his strategy: that of the lone sniper, unencumbered by comrades in arms. Clyde was not hoping to escape the enemy's notice by getting lost in the anonymous ranks. The enemy was not what worried Clyde. What worried him was his own brave, patriotic or just plain stupid officers, and the brave, patriotic, stupid GI's alongside him.

Clyde chose to be an infantryman because that was where he was at home, on the ground, not in the air or on the water. He was a farmboy. What the army training manuals called "terrain" was what he had known all his life as fields, thickets, swamps. A hunter, a rifleman, as all farmboys are, he knew how to practice stealth, concealment. Germans and Japs were merely a more wily and more dangerous game than any he had hunted before. But mainly Clyde chose to be an infantry-man because he did not believe in teamwork; he believed in nobody but himself, and in the infantry a man was on his own. As he would later explain, "In the air corps or the tank corps, say, you're only as good as your machine. And who made your machine? Bunch of 4-F's in some defense plant out in California interested in just one thing: their pay envelopes— hell with the safety of the poor son of a bitch that's going to have to pilot the thing. And who serviced your machine? Bunch of goof-off ground-crew 'mechanics' that before being drafted were jerking sodas or delivering telegrams. In the Navy there you are out there in a tub slapped together by a bunch of Rosy-the-Riveters waiting like a sitting duck for a submarine to torpedo you or one of your Ivy League college graduate officers to steer you onto an a-toll or whatever you call them. In the infantry you're dependent for your survival on just yourself. Yourself and your rifle. Your enemy is just another man with his rifle. If you know how to shoot, how to stalk your game, how to read the signs he gives himself away by, how to lay low, you'll come through. There weren't many old country boys who didn't make it back. The ones we lost were those city boys raised on concrete that never held a gun in their hands before they were issued one in training camp."

Private Clyde Renshaw won so many citations there would not have been room on his broad chest for all his rib-bons if he had kept them instead of throwing them away, but he refused every promotion. This was thought by his superiors and his fellow-soldiers to be modesty; it was not. Clyde wanted no responsibility for anybody's life but his own. Not for nothing, Clyde reasoned, was a private called a private. A private had only himself to save. Officers, commissioned and noncommissioned, got killed through the cowardice or the inexperience or the bone-headed bravery of the men in their charge, those town boys who did not know how to take care of themselves. As to Clyde's strategy, it was simple: to kill as many of the enemy as possible. This was misinterpreted also. It was not patriotism. Clyde Renshaw had about as much patriotism as a green pepper. The way Clyde figured, the more of the enemy he killed the fewer of them there would be to kill him.

The result of Clyde Renshaw's victorious one-man campaign to survive and get home again was that he was the most decorated buck private in his theater of the war, and the last man there to get back home. He was too good a soldier to be let go, and when the war was over and all those ex-golf caddies and barbers' college students whose dumb luck had brought them safely through were home getting the good jobs and the girls, Clyde was kept on, as an old billygoat is kept among stallions, to stabilize the herd of beardless high-school kids with permanent hard-ons sent out to be the army of occupation.

To Ma war was a game of hookey played by grown boys to get away from women and work. "Well!" she greeted the conquering hero on his return. "Where have you been all this while? The others have all been back for ages. What kept you as if I didn't know?"

Clyde married. He told his wife his Army adventures—those that could be told to a wife. She listened avidly. Flattered, he expanded. The telling drew them together as they had not been before. Both sensed this and drew closer still. Until both realized that what they were enjoying was the memory of the time when they had not been married.

Bitter and bored, Clyde Renshaw longed for the lawlessness of wartime, for the license that had been his during the postwar occupation. Clyde craved a conquered country all his own, where he might be a one-man army of occupation, accountable for his conduct to nobody but himself. He found one right in his own back yard. For the beast that paced inside him restlessly, Clyde Renshaw found a jungle, his own private preserve, where by seignorial right he was the king of the beasts. Right in his own back yard where it had been all along, in the camp of the migrant Negroes who came each year to work his crops, Clyde Renshaw found not just another country but another world.

He went on baiting them, bullying them, teasing them, sicking them onto one another as he always had. Never a sack of cotton was weighed but Clyde provoked an argument over the weight. The sack weighed and emptied into the trailer, pencil stub poised above his daybook, Clyde would say, "Clovis Dodds. Semty-nine pounds."

"Semty-nine!" Clovis Dodds would screech, her flat face like a piece of water-worn fountain statuary, dripping sweat. "Semty-nine? Nuh-uh! *Nineny-sebm!* Not semty-nine: nineny-sebm. Yawl was lisnin. Yawl heard him say it, din't yawl? Din't none of yawl hear the man say nineny-sebm?"

"Well, Auntie, I can't take just yours out of there and weigh it again now," Clyde would say. "Can I?"

Thereupon she would set to keening. Then Clyde would heave a sigh and say, well, damn her old black hide, she was robbing him, but all right, ninety-seven. Then she loved him. She wrung his hand with her own two twisted claws that were scaly and fleshless as a chicken's foot. By then she believed she had cheated Clyde out of fifteen pounds she had never picked. Another trick of his: to slip a large rock into a picker's sack and let him drag it up and down the rows all afternoon, then at the weighing-up to voice his suspicion, have the sack dumped out (sometimes discovering in the process three or four more-recently-added rocks in addition to his) and relish their embarrassment.

He went on cursing them as he always had, as he might have spoken to a dog or some dependent and childlike creature that had engaged his rough affections. But he also began hanging around their camp after work, drinking with them, dicing with them, boxing and wrestling with them. In imitation of them he took to wearing a straight razor beneath his shirt on a string, a piece of butcher's twine—quickly snapped —around his neck. He reminded himself frequently that whenever one of them presumed too far, got out of line, he could always put him in his place. But he began to live for the time of year that brought them back. The first contingent, those who came to chop the cotton, came with the spring, and to Clyde they brought with them a quickening of self-renewal, like the surge of sap in the trees.

People said—and not just whites but also the settled Negroes of the community—sniffing at the squalor they made of their camp, that they didn't care how they lived. Clyde knew better. They cared how they lived, they just didn't much care where. They were a race of nomads, and indifferent to their surroundings, which were always changing. Respectability, security, a fixed place in society—all the things they lacked and which some despised them for not even wanting and a few bleeding hearts pitied them for being denied: they had rejected all that. Those who said scornfully that they could not be helped because they liked to live as they did were right in a way they would never know. Those people knew a secret. They alone, the despised, the outcast, were free. The prisoners of life were their lords and masters, hostages to their possessions and their reputations. The life they lived down there was one of continual riot, of flashes of temper as sudden as switchblades, of lust as casual and unrestrained as dogs meeting on streetcorners. Nobody cared what they did among themselves, so they were free to do as they pleased. The worst was expected of them: why not do their worst? Lawless as gypsies, lusty as goats, violent, vital, strangers to guilt and regret, they crammed more living into each day than most people accumulated in a lifetime.

No satisfaction so sweet as the secret enjoyment of a thing despised by the multitude, to have it all to yourself.

So began Clyde Renshaw's double life, and with it a black-and-white paradox of the mind. How could a man like, even admire, imitate, even envy those whom all the world, himself included, despised? How could the master envy the slave, and envy him precisely his freedom? And finally, how could a man love what was his without paying the awful price of love, without paying any price at all?

All men have their secrets from the world. Clyde Renshaw's was his liking for his despised black field hands. Among his other shifts for keeping his secret from the world, Clyde, when among white men, was the handiest of them all with the epithet he himself most dreaded: niggerlover. Clyde Renshaw also had a secret from himself: his more than liking for a black woman. To keep this from himself Clyde called what he felt for her by another name, or rather a variety of names, of which his favorite was poontang.

VI

When he was little, Clyde Renshaw had thought that the family that staffed his mother's kitchen had acquired their color there through their generations of service, as the skillets and the pans had acquired their coats of soot. They had been with the Renshaws "always"; thus for the Renshaws it was natural to assume that they always would. They traced themselves back to their ancestors Tip and Nell, the first of their line to have any name other than their given names. Tip and Nell had stayed on after their emancipation to work for the Renshaws for wages. The reigning Renshaw of that day decreed that as they now enjoyed the rights of citizenship they must also observe its rules; no longer two head of stock, they must no longer live together like beasts, their union must be legitimized. For this they needed names; thus Renshaws' Tip became Tip Renshaw and the former Renshaws' Nell became Mrs. Tip. Of this Nell, Clyde had once heard his grandmother say she was the finest woman *and* the finest Christian she ever knew. That if there was a heaven then Nell was surely there. And that when *she* got there the very first thing she was going to do was go straight out to the kitchen and see Nell. The present-day Renshaws smiled when they told that story, but they too accepted their black namesakes out in their kitchen as part of themselves, like their own shadows.

Idled by their mistress's illness and not yet evicted from the kitchen by the neighbor women, they were there now: Eulalie, Archie, Rowena—all of them but the one Clyde longed to see. Throughout the morning he had gone there on various pretexts meant to mislead only himself, though he knew that just because he wanted her to be she would not be there, and though to go there was to expose himself to one or the other of two torments—this morning it was both: the sullen silence of those of her family who knew about him and her, and the mere sight of that other one, her grandmother, old Rowena, who did not know what the others knew but knew what they did not. For Clyde alone, Eulalie and her son Archie seemed to have a third eyelid, like the one dogs have, which they drew over their eyes whenever he came in sight. That had never bothered him before, but today it really did make Clyde feel like a dirty pane of glass. But what bothered him more than this, much more, was to look into Rowena's sorrowful old eyes. In their depths Clyde saw darkly what she alone had seen and which her merely hinting at to him had destroyed his peace of mind. Yet he had gone to the kitchen repeatedly, as often as he dared—when he ought not to have dared at all—and now on his way out of the house to go down to the fields, still with no hope of finding her there, would go again. On his way out of the house which after half a lifetime in one of his own he still called home and where upstairs his mother had lain unconscious, maybe dying,

while he ranged the halls and peeked into every room, perishing with shame at each chance encounter, especially at each
encounter with himself in any reflecting surface, pretending
whenever he met anyone—and once it was his own son, with
tears in his eyes—to be exclusively concerned with what ought
to have concerned him exclusively, and pulling a stricken
face, or rather allowing his stricken face to be interpreted as
being solely for Ma, the flames of his jealousy and his desire
mounting higher by the moment, a jealousy that had constantly to be dissembled, hidden from every eye living and
dead and most of all from his own, desire that could no longer
be hidden from any eye, least of all his own. Today of all
days, when all other thoughts ought to have been driven from
his mind by concern for his mother, and especially such
thoughts as he was thinking, he was in a state like a horny
high-school boy forced to carry his satchel in front of him to
hide his shame from the world. No high-school boy, he was,
as those reflecting surfaces all told him, a middle-aged married man with grown children of his own. But in that visible
state he was, and in it he went through the kitchen one last
time on his way out of the house to go down to the fields and
give the cottonpickers the day off out of consideration for
his mother's grave illness.

Only to endure again the pain of not finding her there,
to endure again that look, or rather nonlook, of Eulalie's and
Archie's for him, and this time on top of the rest to endure
the sight of Jug, though he did not know until he saw him
how much he wished not to see Jug. Never to be found when
he was wanted, Jug could be counted on to show up when
he was not, looking as always as though he had slept in his
clothes and slept on the sidewalk or in the gutter, a mold of
gray whiskers sprouting on his gray face, his bleary blood-
shot eyes blinking and watering at the light of day. He sat

drinking coffee at the kitchen table surrounded by the isolation in which his in-laws kept him. It angered Clyde to have to defend Jug, for he despised Jug as much as they did, but as Jug was his choice, he had to defend him in self-defense. What did they expect? Just what did they expect? Jug served the purpose for which he was meant. Served it as well as another. He preserved appearances. Just who did they expect him to find, to take the job, Harry Belafonte?

"Either make yourself presentable," Clyde told Jug, "or else make yourself scarce. Go straight while my mother is sick. You bring a drop onto this place, you so much as smell the cork of a bottle, and all Texas won't be big enough for you to hide in."

Going down through the thicket, almost at a run despite the heat as soon as he was out of sight of the house, he took off his straw hat and passed his hand over his head, feeling the damp feverish skin of his scalp through his damp hair. I'm too old for this, he thought. On top of everything else I'm just plain too old to be carrying on like this. He came out of the thicket into the white glare of the lane, thick with dust as fine as fresh wood ashes and just as hot, spurting from under foot as the foot was set down, and he heard the moan of the cottonpickers. All morning long it had sounded inside his head, there was no escaping it. It was like the concerted groan of all the separate aches crying in his heart.

His grief might not be pure, might be foully adulterated in that slop-pail he called his heart, but it was real, it was unfeigned. He loved his mother as much as any of them—excepting only his sister Amy, and she was not human, Amy was an angel. He loved his mother as much as any of the rest, maybe more, just because of knowing how tainted the love was that he had to offer her. And even as she lay unconscious, maybe drawing her last breath, he could carry on as he had today, as he was doing now. Like a beast. Like the beast he was. And even now, even as his heart was breaking for her, still his thoughts were straining at the leash after the other woman in his life (his wife had long ago ceased to count). He paused for breath, and wondered in impersonal perplexity how it was possible for a man to bear in his heart at one and the same time a feeling as pure as his love for Ma and along with it—

He was being watched. He hunched himself, his neck stiffening and his senses straining alert. He located his observer directly. Perched on a limb of a tree and watching him wide-eyed as an owl was one of the children from the work camp. But for Clyde it was an imp from hell, and a great sadness came over him at the thought that his depravity had been judged to merit no bigger a devil than a mere cub like this one. And when it grinned at him, baring not fangs but rows of small white milk teeth, as much as to say, "You are not as bad as you would like to think," Clyde's soul shriveled inside him like the kernel of a nut gone bitter.

The child leapt to the ground and ran away and Clyde caught his breath with a sob and gathered strength to recommence running, and he heard someone calling him. Turning, though he hardly needed to turn, for he knew who it was, who it would be, even knew, God help him, what she would say, he saw a short black figure in skirts down to the ground toddling after him along the lane, calling in a voice exactly the same as the caw of a crow, "Mista Cly! Mista Cly! Mista Cly!"

Was it really so short a time ago that she had come to him with the tale which had destroyed forever the content-

ment he had not known was his until it was taken from him?
Could the misery he seemed now to have lived with always
really be still so fresh? She had come saying she hated to
bother him with problems when he had enough on his own,
but she had nobody else to turn to, and this was his problem,
too, in a way. He would not want any trouble on the place if
he could help it. He was the boss, and if he acted now to stop
it before it went any further, before it came out in the open,
he might be saving himself some unpleasantness and be saving
her and them a lot of real bad trouble.

She said she had always vowed and determined not to be
the kind of old woman who meddled in her daughter's way of
raising her children. How whenever she saw anything she
disapproved of, no matter how strong the temptation to inter-
fere, she would just close her eyes, keep her mouth shut. How
she had not said anything when Shug announced that she was
quitting school with only one more year to go before gradu-
ating and neither Eulalie nor Archie, who ought to have taken
a father's place when a little sister without a father and too
young to know what a mistake she was making, did nothing
to oppose it. How even on that terrible day when she announced that she was getting married and then named her
choice of a husband as if she expected them to forbid it and
then to despise them when they did not, she still had just bitten
her tongue and said nothing. It was not her place to speak
when those who were closest to Shug did not. That wedding
day had been the unhappiest day of her life—though she
could never thank Mr. Clyde enough for helping them make
the best of a bad situation, taking on Shug's husband (she
could never bring herself to utter his name, not to his face nor
in speaking about him) to work around the place (work! hah!
that worthless human wreck!) and fixing them up that nice
little house all for their own—but so was it the unhappiest day

in her life for poor Eulalie, and for her to have said anything would only have made it all the harder on her.

He had been about to show his impatience with all this when he sensed that it must be leading somewhere and that it might concern him to know where. Instantly it concerned him deeply. She said she hated to meddle, to spy and tell tales, and she had held off from coming to him for just as long as she could, hoping things would work out by themselves. How long was that? he wondered, his heart racing. Long enough for what to have happened? She apologized for bothering him. She knew he had enough on his mind already without getting involved in . . .

That was all right, he said patiently, stifling a scream of impatience. She had done right in coming to him. If there was anything he could do to help prevent trouble, family differences . . .

That marriage had been a terrible mistake, a tragedy, she said, tears coming to her eyes. She would never understand how a young girl, nice-looking, popular, smart in school, with a good chance to be somebody in life, could throw herself away like that. But Shug had made her bed and now she must lie in it. She herself had been against that marriage with her whole heart and soul, but she was determined now to do what she could to see that it did not end in scandal. And that was what was fixing to happen unless something was done before her husband woke up to what was going on. When a young girl married an old man (Clyde winced; though a lot older than his wife, Jug was not much older than he) trouble was bound to come of it sooner or later. When it was an old man in love with the bottle, sooner than later.

He succeeded somehow in asking what it was that she had seen to make her think . . . ?

Over her eyes she had drawn that film, like that membranous inner eyelid that dogs have, as though to shut out the sight, and she shook her head, as though she could not bring herself to say it, as though to deny to herself what she had seen.

Left to imagine the details, he imagined the worst. The worst was, images, scenes of Shug doing with some other man the things he had taught her to do with him. Faceless that man was, but otherwise the details were all there, and once painted upon the surface of his mind they penetrated to its bottommost layer, like fresco on a wall.

In the midst of the blackness that engulfed him a light sprang on. The man in the picture in his mind assumed his own features. What she had seen, what she was reporting to him without knowing it, was a meeting she had witnessed from afar between Shug and him. In his relief, his elation, he almost told her so.

"And when you got a bunch like them cottonpickers right on the place," she had said, "trouble don't got far to come."

Now she caught up with him, panting, old face puckered as a prune, and had this to say:

"Mista Cly, you going down to the field? Do me a favor, would you? Shug never has come up this morning and she not in her house either. If you see her hanging around down there please tell her to come on up to the house. Don't tell her I said so. She don't pay me no more mind than she do her mother. *You* tell her to. Will you do that for me, please, Mista Cly? I be much obliged."

. . .

The row of workers' shanties—rusty quonset huts and peeling sheetrock barracks bought at the disbandment of the nearby prisoner of war camp after the Italians had been repatriated—stood with their forefeet in the dusty lane and their backs in the cotton. In front of each one now stood a car, always a big model, sometimes a Cadillac, some of them not more than three or four years old. Those were what they liked, they got them cheap second- and third-hand, and in them they could transport their teeming families: Clyde had counted as many as ten come tumbling out of one. In front of the biggest building sat an ex-school bus with a Louisiana license plate. As soon now as Clyde had laid them off for the day they would pile into their cars and head for town where by midnight half a dozen of them would be in jail for drunkenness and disturbing the peace, carrying a dangerous weapon, maybe for assault with intent to kill. Clyde, a roll of bail money in his pocket, made a regular call at the jail each Monday during ginning season, looking into every cell, like a doctor going his hospital rounds.

In front of the first shack, one of the barracks, he stood for a moment listening, watching. There was no sound save for the everlasting work chant, and the lane was as bare as a dry creek bed. He stepped quickly and noiselessly onto the sagging porch and listened to the interior for a moment. He opened the kicked-in screen door and stepped inside. Occupied but four weeks of the year, standing vacant all the rest, and ventilated the year round by cracks and broken windowpanes and doors that would not shut, it smelled nonetheless of Negroes, an effluvium that worked on Clyde Renshaw like a musk, equally repugnant and exciting, a smell compounded of hair pomade and bitter, cheap roll-your-own tobacco, of corrosive, violently scented soap and coal oil and rancid lard, of singed heat-straightened hair and the sweat of labor and of

love, of fatmeat and Poke salad and buttermilk and again of
stale intermingled sweat, of poverty and promiscuity, of un-
privacy as rampant as a beehive's. The room he found himself
in was nothing but beds, three sagging sheetless unmade iron
Army cots in a row, touching, and on the floor two overlap-
ping tattered quilt pallets. Clyde knew it well. It, or any one
of the others, served out of croptime as their love-nest, his and
his bittersweet-chocolate-colored, unfaithful and indiscrimi-
nate mistress's. That musty odor smote his brain like drugged
fumes, and the memory of their embraces enacted there
flashed upon the screen of his mind, drawing from him a sob
of mingled desire and self-disgust.

The third in the row was one of the quonset huts. A gust
of fetid air flew in his face on his opening the door. On the
bed lay not she and some lover her own color but a row of
half a dozen pinky-brown children, napping, covered with
flies like raisin-sprinkled gingerbread men. Beside the bed in
an armchair the entrails of which hung out in loops, a
withered and shriveled black woman slumped asleep, her open
mouth exposing one long yellow tooth in each bright pink
gum. Always there was one like her, delegated to look after
the infants. One eye fell open. "Looking for somebody?" she
asked. "All out yonder picking yore cotton."

In the last shack he entered and passed through the
kitchen where on the table lay the remains of breakfast—
blackened banana skins and fish bones and Vienna sausage
tins—and stepped into another bedroom where memories of
their assignations again inflamed him. The air was unbreath-
able. He could hear the pickers' dirge, recalling him to his
errand. His heart choked with self-loathing and self-pity. It
cried out for purity—if not for unadulterated sorrow then
for pure unmixed lechery. But the loneliness of his spirit only
whetted the craving of his flesh.

Where was she? Where was that two-timing bitch? Suddenly he knew, and crazed with jealousy and longing he lunged across the room to the clothes closet. With one hand he grasped the doorknob, with the other the razor underneath his shirt. He visualized her, or rather them, crouching on the floor behind the hanging clothes, naked together and black together, black as the darkness that enveloped them, waiting for the sound of his departing footsteps. Blindly he yanked open the door. On the rod hung three bent and empty clothes hangers. Stirred by the wind they tinkled together like distant laughter. Along the floor the gray dustmice scurried toward the corners.

VII

In their younger years the Renshaw boys had run together in a pack—on Saturday afternoon when they
came swaggering into the public square five abreast
taking up the entire sidewalk people had flown out of their
way like chickens—and they were still close; but, left more
to their own devices in growing up, the sisters were more individual, and each had been conscious at an earlier age of the
instinct to leave home and set up for herself. There were
greater differences among them, and more differences arose
between them, differences which they learned to settle themselves without appeal to Ma, whose impartiality amounted almost to indifference. Not so with the boys. With them too
her verdict was impartial; but after the dispute was settled,
the private comfort she gave to the one who had been in the
wrong amounted almost to preference. When it came to boys,
Ma was apt to equate being in the wrong with being the
underdog.

On one thing, though, in opposition to their brothers, the Renshaw girls were united, or had been until all were married and gone from home. This was precisely the question of their getting married, and accounted for their being so widely scattered now, compared to the boys. The Renshaw boys had positively Sicilian notions about a brother's duty to his sisters' reputations, and were all the more vigilant after the death of their father. Local boys had been rather unforward in coming to court any of the girls, and as the girls said in complaining to Ma, you could hardly blame the fellows. A fellow does not want to be made to feel obligated to propose after taking a girl out a time or two, nor to be bullied by a gang of her brothers, maybe marched to the altar with a shotgun at his back, on bringing her home past midnight once. After calling and being watched, slit-eyed, by two or three, sometimes all five of the Renshaw boys, most suitors failed to call again. For unfortunately, though they were all what is called nice-looking girls, none of the sisters was quite handsome enough to inspire any local boy to run that gauntlet a second time. The girls charged that their brothers' concern for their reputations was incidental to the fun they got from scaring hell out of the various bouquet and bon-bon laden youths bold enough to come sniffing around their warren. There was ugly talk once, never fully substantiated, as the only witness was the alleged victim, of a premature kiss, a midnight ride, a beating. It began to look as if the girls might all be left to wither on the vine. All had ended by marrying beyond the adjacent counties, beyond the range of their brothers' notoriety, and in each case Ma's connivance had been needed in arranging clandestine meetings enough to bring the suitor to the desired point. In the case of one, namely Gladys, the young man had been backward, and him Ma brought round by disclosing to the boys that he was seeing their sister.

The first of the girls to arrive now was Hazel.

Admiring liberality and despising thrift as they did, the Renshaws found the sight of their sister Hazel—leaner, shabbier, more packrat-looking each time—always an embarrassment. Despite her upbringing in that prodigal family, Hazel was a miser, a true miser, and proud of it. Not just proud of her wealth, the size of which she alone (and least of all her husband, Troy) knew, nor just of her acumen in amassing it, but proud like a fanatic, a member of a cult, despising all those who do not know the truth. She relished the contradiction between the way she lived and looked and the way she might have lived and looked if she had wanted to. Hazel knew that people despised her for her stinginess. She relished that, too. She enjoyed being despised. It added to her sense of superiority.

Hazel loved money. Loved crisp crinkly new green bills, thick silver dollars with their milled and serrated edges that fell together with a ripe and solid *clunk;* her love of property took a mannish turn. Like her father before her (like her mother, too; for her mother too had the Southern country man's attitude in this) property meant to Hazel real property: houses, land. She had begun buying years ago: ramshackle rental bungalows, dilapidated duplexes in run-down neighborhoods, Negro shanties. She sold a few, traded a few, always turning a profit, and bought more. Meanwhile she grew leaner, shabbier, more secretive and apart, mistrustful, sly. She declined invitations so as not to have to return them. She scrimped her family, serving them stale and sometimes moldy bread bought in large lots from the back doors of bakeries; for meat served them the cheap inner organs, the lights of animals: the lungs, hearts, heads—after a while ceased serving them meat altogether. At thirteen, to teach them the value of money, her sons began paying for their keep; as their earnings rose so did their room and board. The house had the atmosphere of the meanest boardinghouse. A light left burning in an empty room or a faucet found dripping, a bar of soap left to melt on a wet dish could curdle the family atmosphere for an entire day.

Hazel had made herself the family's unfavorite. Her first spoken sentence had been a complaint. She was like a music box: the same tune every time she opened up. She did not quarrel, did not stand up for her rights, as members of a large family all must, and after a while she learned not even to assert them; she just looked done out of them, put-upon, orphaned. And she had a genius for contriving to be left out. It was she for whom at the last minute there was no room in the car. If at dinner there was one gristly or overdone or underdone portion of the meat Hazel got it, and declined all offers to exchange. The worm in the salad, the pebble in the peas, Hazel bit on them. In everything she made herself her sisters' unwanted drudge and second-fiddle. If originally this Cinderella manner of hers had been meant, consciously or unconsciously, to win affection and concessions, it had long ago become an end in itself. She found more enjoyment in being wronged than she found in having her wrongs righted. As her mother once said, to err is human, to be forgiven by Hazel is divine.

They came now in their ancient Dodge, she at the wheel, sacrificing the dilapidated old conveyance in her double haste —anxious for her mother but with her nose in the wind, scenting her mother's will. Leaving her husband outside with the men, she hurried into the house. And her brothers turned back to face their neighbors expressionless. They stuck together. She was one of theirs. And theirs was a clannishness remarkable even in a place noted for clannishness.

Next came Lois, alone, in the brave, too brave, desper-

ately gay weeds of her grass-widowhood, a fluffy little meringue of a hat, and in that new red convertible bought to
celebrate her divorce decree which made of her a show like
a float in a parade or like the entire navy of, say, Bolivia, and
she its sole admiral. Lois asked the same questions everyone
asked, as to what had been done for Ma, contriving somehow
to suggest that nothing could have been done right in her
absence. A chronic nag with a small insistent voice like a
mosquito's, tricked by life and unforgiving, she lived in a
state of unflagging resentment which even her divorce, that
condition for which she had lived as a life-term prisoner lives
for a parole, had failed to assuage.

Lois had married latest of all the sisters, at an age when
already she had been consigned to be the family's one old
maid, already an aunt many times over by then and seemingly
an aunt by nature and disposition, already by that time her
mother's principal confidante and destined by general sup-
position to be the companion of Ma's widowed years. She
had married after two weeks' acquaintance a good-natured,
unambitious, live-and-let-live boy some years her junior with
an hereditary tendency to drink and dominoes. Two weeks
later she presented for her mother's signature the bill of an-
nulment. To her mother, whose creed was that marriage was
a vow as unalterable as a nun's. One month later she stood
for the second time before the same justice of the peace with
the same slightly tipsy bridegroom and went through the same
spiel as before, this time making a cold furious mental reserva-
tion upon every word uttered, promising herself neither to
love, honor *nor* obey him but to make his life a daily bed of
nails, not till death did them part, but until a day (the exact
date she would know some eight months hence) sometime in
March of 1962, the child's eighteenth birthday—unless she
(the child, that is; for Lois was certain it would be a girl: that
too would be a part of her bad luck), unless she married be-

fore that time despite all her mother could do to poison her mind against that step.

She bore the child and weaned it—or rather, her; for it was a girl—and that was one year done. And nursed her through whooping cough followed by double pneumonia, learning in the process to forgive her her existence and to live for her and her alone, waiting on her hand and foot ever afterward and spoiling her so as to make her unfit to be any man's wife, which only made the man who married her all the more uxorious, and that was two years done. And bringing her safely through all the other childhood diseases, not one of which she was spared, and taking her to Sunday school and dancing and piano and elocution lessons and sending her off to kindergarten, and that was five years done, going on six. And found herself pregnant again by legal rape and had to start all over from scratch. This time she told him her plan, once, quietly, and endured his mumbled and confused self-apology and never mentioned it again but saw her daughter married and settled and the boy through school, or through as much of it as he could stick, then off to his military duty, and when he was discharged and immediately married, instructed the lawyer whom she had apprised of her intentions on the day of her remarriage, to proceed with her suit for divorce, looking at him as if he was crazy when he ventured to say he had forgotten about it and supposed she had too, when he said he would have thought she might have changed her mind after all these years, might have grown reconciled, might even have come to feel some attachment to the man with whom she had lived half her life.

That was three months ago and this homecoming was Lois's first since then. She had not dared face Ma's disapproval, and now, full of contrition, blaming herself for their mother's illness, she could hardly face her sisters and brothers.

After Lois came Gladys, with her husband Laverne, from

Nacogdoches. They were followed by Ross's girls and their husbands and babies, having done the hundred and fifty miles from Fort Worth in not much over two hours. Calls were received from others en route, but none from Amy. But it was known in the family that Amy's husband Ira was timid at the wheel and would not let Amy drive, complaining that she was worse than her Barney-Oldfielding brothers. And truly, to hit ninety-five or a hundred on a straightaway was nothing for white-haired Amy, the first-born child. Hazel's girls, April, May and June, all married and living in and around Corsicana, arrived, and her boys Ben and Arthur, in business together over in Terrell. Ross's Eugene, Harlan and Elwood came, the first two from Kerens, the other from Waco, where he was stationed. Clyde's Bryan came from Marshall. Lois's Gwyn arrived. Glenn and Hugh Childress came from Henderson. Uncle Fred, Aunt Inez and Uncle Seth came from Gladewater; Uncle Cameron and Aunt Beulah, Uncle Quincy, Uncle Monroe, Uncle Leon and Aunt Velma, Aunt Belle and Aunt Flora all came over from Carthage. Uncle Ed and Aunt Lillian came from Big Sandy. Cousin Herschell Kimbrough came from Clarksville, Cousin Calvin Renshaw from Commerce. The Cartwrights came, Duane, Ella and Mae, from Conroe. From Brenham came Cousins Bessie and Meade Vance and Cousins Raymond and Peggy Allen. From Temple came old Cousin Stacey Daingerfield and Uncle Roy Tayloe, who was certainly not an uncle whatever he was, but was too old to be called anything less. Cousin Travis Ledbetter came from Mabank, bringing Aunt Lola and Uncle Dave. But only last week poor crippled old Aunt Nan had taken to her bed for good. They would all be going down to Kilgore to bid her farewell soon.

And so one by one the Renshaws all came home, all but one, and that one was not going to come.

VIII

J unya Price," said the owner of the name, and doubling
his sack, hung it on the hook of the scale. He was
bare to the waist: prompt young muscles bunching
beneath a skin as glossy as an eggplant's.

Clyde found the name in his daybook. Was Junior Price
the one? Junior, the record showed, had picked a lot of
Clyde's cotton. What else of Clyde's, after hours, was Junior
picking? Given the day off with pay in observance of Ma's
condition, with money of Clyde's in the pockets of his im-
pudent skin-tight jeans while he, Clyde, sat tied to his own
shadow beneath the pear tree—where, how, with whom
would Junior spend his day?

"Fifty-four pounds," Junior called out. One of the new
breed coming up, Junior did not wait to be told by the boss
what the scale registered. At his waist Junior wore a pin
which proclaimed, "Black is beautiful." Oh, how Clyde
agreed!

Or was Joe Franklin the one? Would Joe—picking grapes later on this fall in California, or up a ladder in an apple tree in New York's Hudson Valley—say, "Talk about poon-tang, mmmmmmmmmmm, I know a little black gal down in east Texas . . ." And would his partner in the next row or on another ladder around on the other side of the tree say, "Yeah, what's her name?" "Nemmind that, but they call her Sugar—Shug for short—cause she's just as sweet as—" "Shug? Stays down on that big old cotton farm belonging to them Renshaws? Well, welcome to the club, friend!"

Why did he torment himself like this?

And if he knew? If he knew it was Junior Price, Joe Franklin? Knew it. Beyond doubt. Beyond hope of doubt. If he caught them at it? What would he do? Kill them. Slit their throats with the razor he could feel dangling against his chest. Hers, anyhow.

Yeah. He could see it now, the headline in the county weekly: LOCAL LANDOWNER KILLS NEGRO MISTRESS IN LOVE TRIANGLE. Fine reading that would make, wouldn't it? Be only one thing to do after that. With the same razor slit his own throat.

IX

Doves when they are flushed utter a squeak of complaint and tumble noisily out of the branches and, as though still gathering up their things, flounce away in awkward, off-balance flight. Alvah Tarrant, returning to his spot in the circle of men and squatting once again, dusts his hands from the clod he had thrown into the tree, and resumes:

"Talking to me the other day my boy says, Pa, it's time we thought of giving up cotton, planting soyabeans, kudzu. Plant them, says I, hell, I can't even pronounce them. Is that what they teach you down there at A & M? Soyabeans. I ask you. What kind of a bean is it that a man can't eat and a hog won't? Chinamen eat them, you may say, but you can't tell me even them commonists wouldn't sooner have black-eyed peas. What are they good for? What are they good for? good for durn near anything you can think of, says my boy to me. They make housepaint out of them and oleomargarine, and the Lord knows what all. Well, when folks leave off wearing clothes and take to painting theirselves instead, and when cows start giving grape juice, why then maybe I'll switch to soyabeans; meanwhile I'll stick with cotton, thank you. It was good enough for my old daddy and for his old daddy before him. Course didn't neither of them go off to college to learn how to farm. But cotton was good enough for them, and I reckon that's good enough for me."

The men have shifted, following the shade, but not Clifford. He sits out in the sunshine like a large, hollow-eyed terracotta idol set there to harden, staring at the house, hearing nothing, numb with grief, a dead smile baked on his lips. But Ballard hears everything, and he thinks, you like cotton so much why don't you go home and pick yours: you're not wanted here. Go home, all of you, and take your stinking pity with you, it and your stinking curiosity, your filthy nosiness. Ballard sits inside the shade but his face is flushed as dark as Clifford's. He hardly sweats, so tightly is he holding himself in, as if his very pores had closed in obedience to his will, his determination to reveal no emotion, no feeling, no sentience even, to give none of them that satisfaction. If Clifford's face is like baked clay, Ballard's is like cast bronze. He sits as still as his brother; meanwhile his mind ticks toward an explosion as steadily as the clockworks of a bomb. Whenever a new man begins to speak Ballard swivels on his heels and levels at the speaker eyes as cold and menacing as the muzzle of a double-barreled shotgun. What he sees with them is a ring of buzzards squatting round about him (and indeed, squatting in their baggy overalls, stoop-shouldered, stringy wrinkled leathery red necks protruding from their collars, they do resemble turkey buzzards, some of them), lifting their eyes at each fresh arrival, not to see who it is but to signify that they have remarked who it is not, which one it is who still remains absent as the family circle fills up, then blandly, innocently scanning the brothers' faces for signs of embarrassment, disappointment, apology. As more come in and take their places it is like turkey buzzards gathering for a feast. They have scented, or think they have, the death of a proud family's pride—long dead, long since putrefied, but until now kept hidden from exposure. They are thinking, what will you do now, you Renshaws? It will have to come out now, won't it? You've all carried your heads so high, scorned to render account of yourselves, but now you won't be able to say any more, "Oh, yes, we heard from him just the other day. He's making out just fine, thank you for asking." Now, if ever, you have to produce him. Produce him or else admit that one of yours is missing, has strayed beyond your ken, and that even now he can't or won't or doesn't even know to come home. Just hold your breath until I do, thinks Ballard. Just hold your breath until I do.

"Well," says Ollie Butcher, "they do say cotton is hard on the soil. Soybeans, they say, sort of pay for their keep, so to speak. Puts back in nitrogen and stuff. I wouldn't know, myself, and I haven't got but just a few acres in them, but that's what they tell me."

"Peanuts: there's a good crop now."

"Yessir! Peanuts *is* a dandy little crop. Only plant I know of that works for a man with both hands, as you might say: above ground and below. You take cotton, corn: the roots are roots, nothing more. Potatoes, on the other hand: all root, the tops just weeds for all practical purposes. But peanuts: root and branch a friend to man. Get me started on peanuts I can run on all day. Talk about a plant that you can do just about anything with. Youall must have heard about that nigger inventor that come up with a hundred and fifty-odd different ways of using peanuts? Peanut soap, peanut glue, peanut axle-grease—well, you name it, that booger had it. Spent his whole life messing around with peanuts. Regular peanut fool."

"Never was a nigger that didn't like peanuts. Why, I've seen them even eat the hulls."

Get two Yankees to talking, Clyde thinks, and it isn't long before the conversation turns to sex. Get two Southerners to talking and before long the subject is niggers.

"Well, they can have them. Me, I'll take cotton," says Alvah Tarrant. "You never heard of King Goober, did you? And cotton didn't get that name for nothing. What I like about cotton, it ain't perishable. You don't have to get shut of it as soon as it's picked like you do your melons or your tomatoes. You can hold on to it and wait for a change in the price."

"You can provided you've got something to eat while you're waiting. You can't eat cotton. At least, I can't—though they've been some years, let me tell you, when I was about ready to try."

All this talk about other matters was meant to take his and his brothers' minds off their situation, off Ma, with the understanding all around that not for a moment was it doing so. Certainly it was not doing so for him. His mind was not on Ma. If they and his brothers only knew where his truant mind was!

"I've held on to mine and waited for a change in the price. Good many times. It changed, all right. Went down. And then I've sold, fearing it would go down still some more, and seen it shoot right up the very next day. Seems like with cotton I'm like that nigger in the story: always zigging when I ought to have zagged and zagging when I ought to have zigged."

"You know what I'm thinking about as I squat here un-

able to stand up for fear it will show?" he heard himself ask
his neighbor Calvin Sykes. "The same thing I've been thinking about all day long. The same thing I think about all the
time. Right this very minute, while my mother lies unconscious on what may be her deathbed, I am mentally in bed
with that nigger wench of mine and giving it to her three
ways to Sunday. You never knew before that I kept me a
nigger wench right here on the place, did you? Now you
know. And when I ought to be thinking of my mother, as my
brothers and my boy there are all doing, she is what I am
thinking about. That's a loving son as well as a good husband and father for you, eh?"

"Why do you keep on with cotton then if that's the way
you feel about it? Why don't you plant them Chinese vege-
tables instead?"

"Cause I'm not a Chinaman, I reckon is the reason. Cotton is the only thang I know."

"Well, I like it!"

"Like the bo' weevils, too, do you, Alvah?"

"You can't blame cotton for the weevils any more than
you can blame a dog for its fleas."

He had not said that to Calvin, as he had not said it to
others previously when he thought he had heard himself saying it. But one day he was going to, it seemed, unless he died
first of fright while waiting to learn that he had not said it.
What was this mad urge to unmask himself that had come
upon him? It was as if he longed to destroy himself. To confess himself an adulterer, a niggerlover and a cuckold all in
one.

He used to enjoy having a secret life. To enjoy just
knowing he had one. Instead of a constant burden it had been
a constant satisfaction. He had enjoyed deceiving the world.
It made him more interesting to himself to think when he was

among other people, "You think you know me but you don't.
I am not what you think. What a shock I could give you with
just three or four words!" That his secret life was black made
it still more secret, still more exciting. It was not long since
the repeal of the old law which made cohabitation between
the races a criminal offense punishable by a prison sentence;
the unwritten law against it was as much in force as ever. The
consciousness of having another life that nobody knew about
had made him seem to himself like two people instead of just
one. It used to warm him with a steady glow of superiority
over others. He looked down upon them both for their ignor-
ance about him and for the meagerness of their single, known
lives. He used to amuse himself by doing what he now did
despite himself: sit talking trivia with somebody while in his
mind going at it with Shug hot and heavy. What had happened to change all that from delight and a sense of superiority to oppression and a sense of guilt, from sweet secrecy to
a compulsion to proclaim what he would sooner die than have
known?

It had gotten so he hardly ever knew what he was saying, had said, to anybody, so clearly could he hear himself
saying, having said, that one thing. It seemed to him that that
was the only thing he had to say to anybody. Anything else
was a waste of time. Anything else was beside the point.

In fact, he had ceased to lead a double life. He led a
single life: his secret one, the one he was not allowed to live
openly. And he had seen the fear that it might be discovered
change into the fear that he himself was going to give it away.
The fear that he was never going to get any relief from oppression until he had given himself away. And then after he
had, there would be nothing left but to slit his throat.

What had happened to the simple joy of banging his
chocolate-coated girl and saying—not in words, of course, but

saying to anybody he might suspect of suspecting him of it—
go screw yourself? Where had that untroubled pleasure gone?
Why? When? And how could he recover it? Why all this
torment? What did he care if she had other men, and if so,
what shade they were? He got his. He got all he wanted. You
can't wear one of those things out with use. And he didn't
know she had another man. He had only old Rowena's untrustworthy word for that, based on what she had seen, or
thought she had seen, with her old untrustworthy eyes. Some
witness! The one who professed to know that Shug was carrying on with some other man was the only one of her family
not to know that Shug had been carrying on for years with
him. Some witness to let upset you. And even if she was right,
so long as he had no confirmation that she was, what did it
matter? What you don't know won't hurt you. Why suffer?
Why get emotionally involved? He got what he wanted out
of Shug. What he felt for Shug was—hah!—no more than
met the eye.

He had become like one of those sexual derelicts who
spend all their time in round-the-clock movie houses watching blue movies. His nonstop blue movie house, that ran even
when his mother lay in danger of death, was his own mind.

The trouble with him—all this obsession with sex, this
mad urge to unmask himself—was, he was not well. Not well
at all. He had not been for some time. Today was just more
of the same, aggravated by worry over Ma and shame for the
unseemliness of feeling what he felt while Ma was sick. He
was not well. A constricted feeling in the chest, centering
around the heart, making breathing difficult. Ma's trouble was
heart, and those things could be hereditary. Loss of appetite.
Absentmindedness and inability to concentrate. Nerves. Unaccountable moments of nerves when for no reason at all his
eyes would suddenly fill with tears. Irritability. And always

that tight feeling in the chest, around the heart. Symptoms that, if you didn't know better, or in a young man, or if the woman had been white, you might almost have taken for lovesickness. He must see the doctor as soon as he got a chance, have a physical, a thorough check-up. Should do so regularly at his age. As for his obsession with sex, that too was something for a doctor. It was a physical thing. It was not personal. Even his feeling it today. The time was inappropriate, grossly inappropriate, but that was only an unfortunate coincidence. He always got hard-up at this season of the year when, with the workers occupying the cabins, there was nowhere that they could get together. It could happen to any man. A man was a man even when his mother was sick. It was something beyond his power to control. He was not to blame. And men had their change-of-life, too, the same as women. It made women less sexy but it made men more so. Certain chemical changes occurring in the body at this time. Hormones. Nothing to be ashamed of. He was not the first dog to be wagged by its tail. Not the first to experience the contrariness of that thing between his legs, how it wouldn't when you wanted it to and would when you didn't.

Watching himself constantly as he had to do for fear of giving himself away, he was all the more alarmed whenever others noticed something about him that he himself had not noticed. Thus when somebody remarked recently that he had lost weight, was looking thin, only then did he realize that he had had no appetite for weeks. Anybody who didn't know the facts of the case would have thought he was lovesick. How else could a man diagnose those symptoms when, being a man, he had suffered through them dozens of times in life, beginning when he was only a boy? That heaviness of breath, that pressure on the heart, that listlessness, that loss of interest in things, that ceaseless ache of body and mind, that longing.

And how could a man in those periods of self-absorption and absentmindedness hope to disguise the symptoms of his sickness? He remembered how his mother, and even more his sisters, had always known what was ailing him, had sometimes known even before he knew himself. "What's her name, Clyde?" they would ask. And although he denied everything, they had a way of guessing the girl's name and soon were teasing him with it mercilessly. Could they still smell out his condition? Could they still guess the woman's name? Or was it that the yearning to speak the name, to shape his lips around it, taste it on his tongue, had betrayed him into forming it with his lips unconsciously, divulging it to them, as he felt the compulsion to do now? As he wanted now to tell everybody he met about Shug and him? To utter her name, and link it publicly with his own.

Shee-it. What his sisters saw was what anybody could see, what showed, then as now. They knew where to look for it. That was what they had nudged one another and giggled together over.

Love: that was the one really dirty four-letter word. He could speak the other ones with no shame, that was the one that stuck in his craw. Love was the word the whole world used for a fig leaf. You could love your mother and your father, your brothers and sisters. A man could love another man and a woman another woman. But let sex come into it and love flew out the window. People spoke of loving couples. He had never seen one, and he had been around. He had seen couples not long married who were still hot for each other: that was called love. When that was gone what remained was mutual relief: that too was called love. He knew what he felt for his woman. He had only to look down to see. Just one thing bothered him. If that was all she was to him, wasn't he paying too high a price for it? Three billion people

on the face of the earth, more than half of them women: was
hers the only one he could find?

"Cotton's fine if you can just get you somebody to
pick it."

"Clyde, he gets them."

Yeah, he got them. How? By making an annual mid-
winter pilgrimage to Louisiana, sometimes two, to court the
gang boss, a bull of a man named Cheney, the color of cast-
iron, taking him to New Orleans and there for up to a week
wining and dining and wenching him and putting up with his
independence and his sass and pleading with him to come
back again next year, bringing with him that ex-schoolbus-
load of young black bucks in rut.

"Seen one of them mechanical cottonpickers at work
one day last week over near Winnsboro."

"Did you, Leonard. What did it look like?"

"About like a cross between a Hoover vacuum cleaner
and a hook-and-ladder firetruck. But I'll say this for it, it
out-picked any ten pickers I ever seen. Takes four rows at
a time, and that thang went across that field plucking the
bolls and spitting out the hulls like a dog shitting peach seeds."

They were the coming thing, Clyde knew. Already common in Mississippi and Alabama, and now beginning to reach
east Texas. His own pickers told of being turned away at
farms where they had worked for years, the planter having
rented or bought himself a machine.

"You got any idea what one of them thangs cost? And
they tell me you have to practically keep a fulltime mechanic
to tend to it."

"Yes, but you can make it pay for itself by renting it
out. Anythang'll do the work of that many hands you can
charge a good rental on it."

They did cost a lot of money and the upkeep on them

was high. But that would sure fix her wagon. She would find it hard to two-time him with something that looked like a cross between a vacuum cleaner and a firetruck.

"Left about half of the cotton in the field."

"Hah."

"Ah, well, we've seen some changes in our time, you and me, eh, Clar'nce? Seen mules go, and now the nigger'll go the way of the mule. It's just a matter of time."

X

The shadow of the pear tree contracted like a drying water stain until by noon it lay round and hard-edged directly underneath the branches, and there it stayed, as if seeking shade itself, until well past three o'clock. Then it began venturing slowly away from the trunk on the other side. The fallen and fermenting pears simmered in the sun.

At first the sound was like the hum a highwire makes when you lay your ear to the pole. The conversation sputtered and died as one by one, like grazing sheep, the men lifted their heads and listened toward the west. It was a car on the county road. They could place it, could clock it by ear. Within moments the volume had swelled to a loud buzz, causing one of the listeners to expel his breath in a low, unformed, dry-lipped whistle. Soon it attained the high fierce snarl of an outboard motor, the lead one in a boat race, and the men beneath the pear tree began unconsciously to lean forward, rising slightly on the balls of their feet. By the time the car neared the corner a mile away where the dirt road to the Renshaw place made a right angle junction with the paved road, the engine had the desperate pitch of a chain saw ripping through a knot. They waited, wincing. It went into the turn with a screech of tires that affected the hearers like a dentist's drill striking a nerve. Then followed a moment's silence . . .

By tradition, and by law, the right of way on Texas roads belongs at all times to livestock. The driver of a car coming upon a sow and her farrow wallowing in a mudhole or a hen and her brood taking a dustbath is expected to stop and get out and request them to yield. If he should happen to kill one, the Lord help him—the law won't. No kind of dressed meat comes as high-priced as that slaughtered on a radiator grill. To follow along for two or three miles behind a drove of hogs or a herd of plodding cattle down a dusty shadeless road on a Texas August afternoon can be trying; but the right of way is theirs, and even honking the horn can be risky: they might take fright and stampede and hurt themselves, or at the very least, in that melting heat, run a lot of actionable weight off their valuable carcasses.

Along the Renshaw road the pace of traffic was often set by a brindled milch cow called Trixie belonging to a widow woman by the name of Shumlin. Since her husband's death some years back, Mrs. Shumlin, in order to make ends meet, had been obliged to sell off the farmstead piece by piece

—it was not very big to start with—until now all she had left was the plot on which her cottage stood and a small kitchen garden, and another plot across the road on which her cowshed stood, or rather leaned. Her land all gone, Mrs. Shumlin had the problem of where to pasture her cow. She solved the problem by staking her out along the roadside to graze the narrow margins owned by the county highway department. These uncultivated roadbanks were capable, however, of producing but one thin crop of grass per year, so that as the season wore on, Trixie ate her way farther and farther from home, by late summer was grazing at a good two miles' distance. Through July, August and September Mrs. Shumlin had to get up earlier each morning to take Trixie to pasture, and had to set off earlier each afternoon to fetch her home for milking. She had to tote along two heavy pails of water for Trixie to drink when she got thirsty. And often when Mrs. Shumlin had walked the two miles to get her in the hot afternoon she found that Trixie had pulled up her stob and wandered another mile or more down the road—she always wandered away from home, ever in search of greener pastures and knowing that she had already eaten everything behind her. These inconveniences Mrs. Shumlin put up with not so much out of love for Trixie as for the sake of a dab of butter for her bread, or more probably for the sake of what the butter symbolized. Between buttered bread and dry bread lay the gulf separating respectability from penury.

Mrs. Shumlin called her a Jersey, and in part she was; but there was also a wide streak of Brahman, or Bramer as it is called, in Trixie. She had a lump on her shoulder like a Bramer, and down-turned ears and a large loose multifold dewlap, and her proprietary attitude toward the roadbed went beyond what even a Texas cow, conscious of her rights in law, might have been expected to show; in Trixie's serene, deaf, unhurried, unswerving appropriation of the exact crown and middle of the road was the sacred Hindu cow's consciousness of divine prerogative. Seen from the rear—and many a motorist had spent long sessions studying Trixie's rear—she resembled a four-footed washpot swinging between a pair of andirons. Having pulled up her stob and set off down the road, she never turned aside. Ruminating upon her bitter cud of dandelions, dock, plantain, chickory and Johnson grass, and seeing nothing alongside the road but more of the same, she moseyed on. So she was doing now, the rope trailing from around her neck, the stob tumbling end over end in the dirt. Meanwhile fate was closing in on Trixie from behind and before.

Behind her a truck loaded with cotton was chugging near. It ought not to have been there, it really ought to have been much farther down the road, for Hugo Mattox, the driver, and the owner of the cotton but not of the truck, had set off from home for town and the gin early that morning. He had been delayed by a series of mishaps.

Everything had gone all right until they (for Mrs. Mattox and the children were along) got to Canaan Corners. None of the breakdowns had occurred which the anxious owner of the truck, the neighbor from whom Hugo had borrowed it for the day, his own being laid up, had warned against, nor any of the equally large number which Hugo feared on his own. The radiator had not boiled, the fuel pump had not failed, the timer was working, the frayed fan belt had not broken, the springs appeared to be holding up under the load, she was burning no more oil than was to be expected. At Canaan Corners Hugo stopped and fed her another quart and went inside and bought himself a can of Prince Albert and a book of Riz la + papers—if only he had bought a can of tire patch instead! Why he hadn't he didn't know. Because even just sitting there, that left rear tire, the one with the boot, already looked like a flat. A retread, it was down to the cords for the second time. Hugo could hear it each time it turned over: it came down with a flat slap like a bare foot on a linoleum floor. He certainly ought to have bought a can of Monkey Grip. Because he knew that if that tire should go he would have to use the spare. As for it, well, he had, or his wife did, out in the front yard, flowerbeds growing in at least three better tires than that spare.

Worried about that left rear tire, Hugo drove so slowly that the engine began to overheat and the radiator to boil. About three miles beyond Canaan Corners he had to stop and dip some water from the ditch. Just as he was climbing back up the bank carrying the can, all of a sudden the left front tire heaved a sigh and went flat as a fallen cake. The truck bed tilted and cotton sloshed over the sideboards. Two extra-large bolls that seemed about to come spilling down appeared over the edge. These were the heads of Hugo's two boys.

Mistrust of that spare tire made Hugo bring the boys down to ride in the cab, and it was a good thing he did; for just as he feared, despite the fact that now he drove even slower, so slow he had to stop twice more and let the engine cool down, they had not gone five miles more when they had a blowout. Surprisingly enough, it was not the spare, nor even the left rear, but the right rear—probably the best tire he had. Then how Hugo wished for a patch kit! Not for that tire; for by the time he fought the truck to a stop the rim had chewed that tire to a rag; but for the first flat. So now he was worse off than ever. Now he would have to take the original flat and flag a ride into town and have it fixed and flag a ride back, and then he would still be riding, now without any spare, on the tire he had mistrusted from the start, plus the original spare, which if it had been his he would not have trusted for a swing to hang from a limb for his boys to swing in. Naturally there were no tire tools, so he had to carry rim, casing and all. Leaving his wife and kids Hugo set off down the road lugging the tire. It was then going on 8 a.m.

Hugo had gotten about two miles down the road when along came a car. It was Mrs. Sibley, who sold cosmetics door-to-door to the farmwives of the district. She stopped and offered Hugo a lift, saying after he had put his tire in the trunk and gotten in, that she supposed he wouldn't mind if she made a few calls along the way. They made ten or a dozen stops, at each of which Mrs. Sibley brought out her entire line of samples and gossiped with the customer and booked orders. While sitting in the car waiting for her, Hugo saw half a dozen cars go past headed for town, and he just wished he knew of some polite way of getting out of this ride Mrs. Sibley was giving him.

Around ten o'clock they were lurching along when all of a sudden there was a loud clatter and the motor gagged.

"Good night! What on earth was that?" Mrs. Sibley gasped. They bucked to a stop. "Did you ever hear anything like that before?"

"Yes'm," said Hugo in a weak voice. " 'Fraid I have."

"Have?"

"Yes'm."

"You believe you know what's the matter?"

Hugo nodded. "Yes'm," he said, swallowing. " 'Fraid I do."

"Well! Wasn't it a lucky thing I just happened to pick you up!" said Mrs. Sibley.

"Yes'm," said Hugo.

Having nothing to drain the crankcase into, he had to

take off the pan with the oil in it and not spill any in doing it. In it he found pieces of metal, as he had known he would. So he came out from underneath and raised the hood and went to work. He disconnected the distributor wires and took out the spark plugs. He disconnected the radiator hose. He took off the cylinder head and the cylinder head gasket. He took out the valves and, without the aid of a valve spring compressor, the valve spring rockers. Then he crawled underneath again and turned the crankshaft until he located the broken connecting rod and then turned it until the piston was in firing position. Then, black as a coal miner, he came up and drew out the piston and took off the rod. It was going on twelve noon.

"You sure," said Mrs. Sibley, fanning herself with one of the pasteboard fans she gave away to advertise her line of products, "that you know how to put all that back together again?"

"Yes'm," said Hugo.

There was only one thing to do. That was to leave Mrs. Sibley, take the rod, and his tire (unfortunately, though she had just about everything else, Mrs. Sibley had no tire tools in her kit either), to town and get a new one. Or rather, to Hogan's used car parts and automobile graveyard eight miles the other side of town, and just hope and pray that Hogan had down there among all the other wrecks in his apple orchard a 1954 Nash. So Hugo set off, and after about three miles flagged a ride into town, where he finally found a man at the compress going out Hogan's way as soon as his cotton was ginned and baled, and hitched a ride with him.

Hogan seemed to recollect a Nash somewhere around and Hugo finally located it down at the foot of the orchard, upside down in a gully and overgrown with creepers and vines. It was a '49 as near as he could make out. Did a '54 and a '49 take the same size connecting rod? Hugo wasn't sure. Neither was Hogan.

"Well, there's one way to find out," said Hugo with a sigh.

They brought down Hogan's old tractor and a towing chain and turned the wreck right side up. Then Hugo went to work and took off the pan, took out the plugs (a little harder in this case, as the car had been sitting there rusting for eight or ten years), took off the head, took out a piston, took off the rod. If it had once been the same size, it was worn down considerably now. Shimmed up with a little babbitt, however, it might do. So Hugo took it back to the shop and melted down some babbitt and babbitted it. By the time this was done Hugo had just about forgotten about his flat tire. Did Hogan have a pretty good 7.50–15 innertube? He did. It had just come in on a wreck. How much? Seventy-five dollars if he had to take it off himself on a day as hot as this, seventy-five cents if Hugo did it himself. For another half a dollar he could have the tire, rim and all. Just leave his in exchange.

That certainly would have saved a lot of time and work, but as luck would have it, the wreck was an International Harvester and Hugo's truck, or rather his neighbor's, was a Dodge and the rims were not interchangeable. So Hugo jacked up the wreck and took off the wheel and pried the casing off and pried his casing off the rim and put the inner-tube in his and pumped it up. Now he was ready to start back. He borrowed off of Hogan half a Dixie cup full of cylinder head gasket seal compound and set off down the road to flag a ride.

When Hugo finally got Mrs. Sibley going again it was four o'clock in the afternoon. She very kindly offered to drive him back to where his truck sat. "Boy, that sure took

you a while!" said Hugo's wife. "And us sitting here in the
heat all this while with no dinner nor nothing to eat."

Now at half past four, having overtaken and passed
Mrs. Shumlin herself some distance back, Hugo was chugging
down the road, still proceeding very cautiously on account
of that spare tire, not to mention the left rear, when there
ahead of him, ambling down the middle of the road, was
Trixie, Mrs. Shumlin's cow. Hugo pumped the brake pedal
and slowed up. He stuck his head out the window and
yelled, "Hoo, cow!" Trixie merely flicked one ear.

"Hop out and lead her off and tie her to a fence post
with that rope around her neck, Billy," said Hugo, "so I can
get around her."

"Don't you do any such thing, Billy," said his mother.
"She looks mean to me. She's one of them old Bramers. Honk
at her, Hugo, why don't you?"

"I honk at her and she jump that fence and rip her bag
on one of them bobwires we'd be in some fix, wouldn't we?"
said Hugo.

But when after about a quarter of a mile the radiator
recommenced to boil, Hugo decided to risk a little toot on
the horn. He pressed the button and nothing happened. He
knew he had no headlights—that was why he had had to
promise the owner of the truck to be back before nightfall;
but he never knew he had no horn.

Hugo stopped the truck to get out and lead the cow off
the road and tie her to a fence post himself. The glance Trixie
flung at him over her hump changed his mind. She did look
mean, and Hugo was just as glad his wife had forbidden Billy
to go near her.

Between the middle of the road, occupied by the cow,
and the deep ditch on either side of the road there was, Hugo
gauged, just about enough space to squeeze the truck through.

Drawing up close behind, he prepared to inch past. The cow sidled in front of him. He fell back, then started around her on the other side. She tacked that way. Again to the left, then again to the right he tried; each time she veered in front of him. While pretending not even to know he was there, the cow forestalled Hugo's every maneuver. This went on for three-quarters of a mile, bringing them to the junction with the paved road and to that moment when the men squatting beneath the pear tree up at the Renshaw place were rising on the balls of their feet and listening with clenched teeth and bated breath to the zoom of a speeding car.

Hugo heard it just seconds before he saw it, and even before it left the paved road and came into the turn he was already pressing instinctively, frantically and futilely on the horn. The moment caught him in yet another attempt to get around the cow, this time legally, which is to say on the left, or in other words, in the lane of oncoming traffic. It was this that saved him. For the other car was also in the wrong lane, and although Hugo swerved hard right and stomped the accelerator, the worn-out and overladen old truck responded sluggishly, thus the two vehicles passed safely if illegally, separated by exactly one cow width. The other car went off the road and into the ditch and up the bank, leveling a line of fence posts, shot down the bank and across the ditch and back onto the road and continued on its way. The truck went lumbering across the highway and into the ditch and up the bank, Hugo now stomping the brake pedal and hauling back on the wheel as though on a pair of reins, his eyes shut tight against the collision and/or the blowout he expected momentarily.

The truck rolled to a stop and Hugo opened his eyes to find himself and his family alive and unhurt. They had stopped on the crest of the roadbank, were tilting sharply toward the roadbed. The Mattoxes all climbed out and Hugo ran to inspect that spare tire. There it stood, plump and sound. So did the left rear. The right front was another matter. Hugo got to it in time to see a rubber bubble swelling from a break in the cords like a bubble of bubble gum. It burst. That corner of the truck settled. The rear spring shackles snapped one below the last with a sound like a handful of knuckles being cracked. A solitary, louder snap succeeded. "Stand back!" yelled Hugo, and a good thing he did, for that big snap was the rear axle breaking in half, and with that the truck keeled over, strewing three bales of unbaled cotton from one side of the highway across to the other.

Trixie, on the road in her customary outward-bound course, appeared to have escaped whole and unharmed. However, she laid down at regular intervals on the pavement a trail of drops of blood. Examination by her mistress, who caught her some minutes afterward, disclosed that Trixie had somehow lost the tuft of her tail in the encounter. This is a small part of a cow, but indispensable. Without it she cannot switch flies. They torment her to distraction and she goes off her feed. Her yield of milk dwindles. Maddened by irritation, she may even turn dangerous. Mrs. Shumlin was not exaggerating when she declared that Trixie was worth nothing to nobody now but the knackers.

The silence lasted only a moment, then the men beneath the pear tree heard the car roaring down the dirt road with undiminished speed and above the tops of the pines saw the dust rise in billows like smoke.

This car did not stop in the road below the house; it shot up the drive, plunging to a halt in front of the garage and disappearing momentarily in the swirl of dust drawn after it by the vacuum its passage had created. When the dust settled it was seen that one entire side of the car was corrugated, the top dented in, the hood sprung, the rear bumper twisted loose and flapping, the rear window a spider's web of cracks. Out of the car came a chorus of voices, the cries, the whimpers of children, above them a woman's voice wailing and sobbing brokenly. Out of the dust, without looking back, Lester Renshaw came striding. His brother Ballard rose from his place in the circle of men beneath the pear tree and crossed the lawn to greet him.

From the car now came a moan, a rising wail, ending in a loud sob, and then in a choking voice, above the crying of the children and the ministrant murmur of the neighbor women, the woman shrieked, "Oh, you don't know! You don't know! Nobody knows what I've been through!"

"All right, honey. All right. It's all over now. Get out of the car, Sybil, dear, and come in the house and lay down and rest. Come on now."

"I begged and I pleaded with him. I threatened to jump out of the car. He only went all the faster. Youall don't know. Nobody will ever know what he put me through."

"Ssh. There, there, honey baby. It's all over now. Here you are all safe and sound. All right. All right. It's all over now, hear?"

"I don't know how we came through it alive. I don't know how we did it. We like to have killed an old woman crossing the road to her mailbox and still he never slowed down. I begged him with tears in my eyes to let the children out at least, stop and leave them with somebody along the road. How was it going to help his mamma if he killed himself and his wife and own children, can anybody tell me? Oh, my babies! My poor innocent babies!"

"Don't work yourself up no more now, Sybil, dear. Come on now. Come in the house and lay down and rest yourself. Try to get a hold on yourself now. It's all over now, you hear? Ssh. Don't take on any more. You're upsetting the children. It's all over now, hear?"

"You couldn't even see the road go by, the telegraph poles. It was all just a blur. Three hundred and seventy miles we drove like that. I begged and I pleaded with him. I—"

"Run get the doctor, somebody. And somebody get the children out of there."

"And then we came to a turn in the road and there was a cow and a truck coming the other way and he never even oh I think I'm going to—"

"Hurry! And tell him to bring his little black bag!"

XI

The three sisters bore up well on meeting, so long as their circle remained incomplete. With the arrival of Amy, the last of them to get home, all three broke down. They had to leave the house, leave the porch, and withdraw to a corner of the yard. Reproaching themselves for not appreciating their mother until it was too late, each offered the others comfort while refusing all comfort herself.

"Ah, such a good woman!" This from Gladys, whose voice, coming over the seared lawn, reached the men down around the pear tree, causing them to shift their feet and clear their throats, reached the Negroes out in the side yard and, like a hand brushed across the strings of a guitar, drew from them an echoing chord, melodious and woeful. "Such a good woman! Such a good mother! Thinking always of her children, never a thought for herself. I took her for granted and now it's too late to ever make up. How can I ever forgive myself for all the heartache I brought on her?"

"Oh, you were good, Sister!" cried Lois. "You've been good. You were a joy to her. It's me. I'm the one. I was always the troublesome one. She worked and she slaved for me and all her reward was disappointment and tears."

"Oh, if only I could bring her back!" Hazel wailed. "Just for one hour! Just one more chance to show her how much she meant to me."

Then the drone of the neighbor women: "Honey. Don't take on so. She wouldn't want youall to take on this-away. She may yet recover. Where there's life there's hope. The Lord giveth and the Lord taketh away. She's going to her everlasting reward. She's had a good long life, a fine big loving family—all a woman could want. Don't take on so, sweetheart, you'll do yourself harm."

"I never answered her last letter!" cried Gladys. "Oh, she's gone from me forever and I never even took time to answer the last letter I'll ever get from her. I kept putting it off from day to day, never thinking she might be taken from me, and now it's too late. Too late!"

"None of us deserved her!" cried Lois.

"Now, baby. Now, baby. She understood youall were thinking of her all the while. Now now now. Don't youall carry on like this, hear?"

The three sisters wailed to one another, "How can we give her up? How can we do without her? Oh, what will become of us?"

"She was too good for this life!" Hazel cried. "Too good for it!"

"An angel from heaven, hon. Ne'er a finer woman drawed the breath of life. But stanch your tears now, love. She's going to a better world."

. . .

Needless to say, it would never have occurred to Amy Renshaw Parker to doubt the sincerity of her sisters' grief. Their lamentations were heartfelt. But Amy could not help contrasting her sisters' grief with her own. She could not utter a sound—not one monosyllable of woe. Her sisters might ask themselves how they could live without their mother, and for a while might find it all but impossible; but they had their children and their children's children to live for. Amy had no one. Of all the others only Clifford would be left as desolate and inconsolable as she.

Amy was not only childless, she was friendless as well. Her entire emotional life had been expended upon her family, and the approaching death of her mother, head and symbol of it, seemed to Amy to signal the family's break-up. To a lesser extent this was true of all the Renshaws, but for Amy outsiders had scarcely existed. Oh, she had Ira, to be sure—her husband; and she was fond of Ira. But he was only a husband, after all.

Excepting Hazel—who professed to have less than any —Amy was the only one of the girls with money of her own, being the only one who had made a career. A registered nurse, she had always earned good pay, had invested regularly in blue chip common stocks, and had seen their worth multiply into a very considerable sum. Early in marriage she and Ira had come to an arrangement. The costs of living were divided between them, she paying the grocery bills and car costs, he the mortgage and utility bills. She bought her clothes, he his. Whenever they dined out, as they often did, Amy's schedule leaving her little time for housework and she being an indifferent cook, they asked for separate checks. Thus it was none of Ira's business if her savings were always available as an emergency loan fund for her brothers and sisters and her favorite nephews and nieces, amongst whom she was flagrantly partial, those of her brothers and sisters whose children she scanted not daring to take exception, being too deeply in her debt for favors rendered them.

Edwina Renshaw had taught her sons to court ruination but had omitted to teach them how to avoid or endure it. Their idolatry of their mother kept them from ever going to her when they got into trouble. Instead they went, as to a second, less awesome, less exacting mother, to their eldest sister. Amy was always ready with sympathy and cash, patient with repeated lapses (a little too unsurprised by them, indeed), and confidential. Amy helped them because she loved them, but more because she believed it to be her main duty in life to intercept any worries and keep them from reaching Ma.

She had intervened at some crucial turn in the affairs of each and every one of them; yet though there was not one whom she herself had not preserved from disgrace as the result of some defect of character peculiar to him, or to the extravagance which, Clifford only excepted, was their common failing, Amy stoutly maintained, in between lapses, that her brothers were all perfect, each possessed of some one outstanding virtue (to which her husband Ira found his own faults frequently contrasted), all models of the greatest virtue of all: filial devotion, family loyalty. She was perhaps a trifle more allergic to shortcomings in her sisters; but she would permit none of them to criticize another in her hearing, would defend even Hazel, would smile and shake her head in mild admonishment and lay her finger on her lips whenever they launched into a comparison of her own generosity with Hazel's penuriousness. Tribute, even thanks, for her help, Amy steadfastly refused. She rather enjoyed suspecting them of ingratitude, or at least of very short-lived memories. To feel that they took her somewhat for granted only strengthened Amy's sense of dedication.

A show of contrition for having done a thing which, if she should know about it, would break Ma's poor heart: this was all Amy asked of them in return for her help. This of course they would have made without any prompting from Amy—though perhaps they would have let themselves off lighter than Amy let them off. Amy made them feel so miserable, it was a question whether Ma herself would have made them feel that bad if they had gone and confessed themselves directly to her. Indeed, some of the things which they agreed with Amy would have broken Ma's heart to know—well, Ma had a stronger heart than that. And more of a sense of humor. Some details of the scrapes they had gotten themselves into, and to which Amy listened so gravely, would probably have broken Ma up in laughter. But in the end it was no laughing matter—they would not have been there seeking help if it were; and by going to Amy with it, although they came away feeling criminal, they had the comfort of knowing that Ma had been spared pain and disappointment, and that was the main thing.

When they came to her for help and Amy had heard their confession, had shriven them and had written them a check and sent them away to sin no more until the next time, she shed tears. Their misdeeds and their indiscretions saddened Amy as a priest is saddened by what he hears in the confessional: not for any betrayal of him, but for the disappointment to their Holy Mother.

Amy's patriotism, her politics, her religion, all resembled her piety toward her mother and her allegiance to her clan. A fundamentalist, she believed in a hot hell, a chilly heaven. A royalist with a worship of authority, she voted always for the incumbent. George Washington's decision not to seek a third term as President, Calvin Coolidge's choice not to run again had always confounded her, as did Truman's in her own time. Had she been of voting age she would have voted for Hoover in 1932 because he was President, then would have voted for Roosevelt for a fifth, a sixth, a seventh term because he was. The only time she had ever sided against time-honored institutions was in the abdication of King Edward VIII (the British royal family came just after her own in Amy's affections); however, she was very young then. A tireless slacker-baiter—there was probably not another woman in greater Waxahachie who had accosted so many ablebodied-looking young men on streetcars and street-corners and demanded to know why they were not in uniform as Amy Renshaw Parker.

In Amy's pantheon even Franklin D. Roosevelt, Winston Churchill, Dwight D. Eisenhower and Queen Elizabeth II were mere idols in the side chapels leading up to her mother's high altar. The others, her brothers and sisters, all acknowledged Amy as the most devoted child of them all. Her reward for her devotion was to be the child her mother loved the least—the one whom she did not love at all.

Introspective and self-critical, Amy knew she rather craved a feeling of being insufficiently appreciated. But her mother more than gratified this craving. Amy tried to reason why. Her mother disliked feeling beholden to anybody for anything; could it be that, all Amy's covering up notwithstanding, she chafed at a sense of indebtedness for the help Amy had given her brothers and sisters? For it is one thing to dislike unpleasant duties, something else again to feel obligated to somebody for doing the unpleasant duties you have neglected. Perhaps Ma resented Amy's interference. Perhaps she would rather the children had come to her with their troubles. At times Amy almost felt that her mother hated her, positively hated her, for knowing all her other children's failings, those guilty secrets which only a mother has the right to know.

But Amy's love for her mother was like the camomile: the more it was stepped on the more it grew. She bore her lot patiently, penitentially, telling herself she deserved no better, never letting up in her attentions but persisting in hopes of someday winning her mother's trust and affection. Yet it pained and saddened her.

One particularly painful thing was her mother's dislike of being alone with her. Amy knew herself to be oversensitive, prone to exaggerate her wounds, even to invent them; but this she had seen too many times to be mistaken, and more and more just lately: her mother's uneasiness whenever they were alone together, her relief at the appearance of another person, at remembering something else that she ought to be doing.

Amy attributed this in part to her profession. Her mother had a terror of death, and a consequent dislike of doctors; and the next thing to a doctor was a nurse. She might enjoy being babied by others of her children, whose concern over her health she could dismiss as arising simply out of love; but Amy's concern frightened her, and because it frightened her it angered her. Probably she suspected that Amy had noticed, and knew how to interpret, what had passed unnoticed by the others: a certain bluish swelling around the bases of her finger-nails, which she herself knew to connect with her heart condition because the two had appeared at the same time, and that Amy might have caught and identified the odor of valerian and digitalis in her bedroom. When Amy was around she went to great lengths to keep her hands, with their tell-tale bluish swellings around the nails, hidden from sight.

Between the two there was also another barrier, and that was Amy's childlessness. Edwina, mother of ten, could not help pitying a barren woman, and Edwina's pity was what in another person might have seemed almost like contempt. Over Amy, Edwina had not the hold she had, through their children, over her other daughters.

Amy and her mother were divided on yet another matter, that of Amy's baby brother and his disaffection. Amy was the only one ever to dare speak of this to Ma. She could see it was painful to Ma, but she could not hold her tongue, her feelings were too strong for her. She did not understand, she did not ask, she did not want to know the cause of her brother's final quarrel with her mother. It was not to be understood, only condemned. And there, for Edwina, was the rub. This was something worse than being disagreed with; this was being agreed with when you did not want to be. For by day Edwina might be unforgiving and inflexible and proud of herself for it, but by night, across the years and the miles separating him from her, Edwina pleaded with her errant baby boy to come back home to her, abjectly promising to forgive him and take all the blame upon herself if only he would come home to her; and Edwina did not like to hear from another of her children expressions of the rigor she professed to feel, knew she had every right and duty to feel, and did feel for just half the time.

"A bolt from the blue," said Gladys. She was describing the effect upon her of Ballard's wire.

Amy started. She had the sensation that her thoughts were being read. For her this was no trite figure of speech; indeed, it was not a figure of speech at all. Among Amy's most vivid memories was having seen a bolt from the blue strike and kill a living creature.

She was seventeen. One sultry summer afternoon a storm had blown up, one of those sudden prairie storms from out of nowhere that within a minute can change day into night. By the time Amy got to a window it was already so dark that the windowpane mirrored her own face and she had to cup her hands to her eyes to see out. This she was doing when a flash, a flare like some elemental short-circuit illumined the lot beyond the fence, the bolt striking dead the horse pastured there. It all happened in a fraction of an instant, and yet quick as it was, there had been a sequence to the events. The horse had leapt into the air not on being struck but before. It was as if it had been given an instant's foreknowledge of its doom and had risen to encounter the bolt, rushing to its annihilation. Just such an instant had Amy experienced when, knowing its contents before opening it, indeed already seeing it in her mind, she was handed Ballard's wire. And just as the stricken horse, suspended in air with its nostrils flaring, its mouth agape, its mane streaming as though each separate strand were electrically charged, had seemed in an ecstasy of dying, so to Amy had come a moment when anguish passed a bound, became a feeling to which she could not give a name, but the memory of which filled her with consternation and with a sense of deepest shame. "Disgusting!" she thought of it now, though why "disgusting" she did not know.

The very air had been electrified, washed with ozone, and breathing had been almost dizzyingly deep during that instant when the horse hung Pegasuslike in the burst of light against the livid sky. Then as the thunder slammed down overhead, darkness returned, and the horse, rigid as bronze, was dropped lifeless to earth. This too had had its counterpart in Amy's experience that morning. The halo of light surrounding the pimply-faced Western Union boy, waiting for the tip he never got, burnt out, her mind darkened, her body stiffened: it had been a moment of death, and to recall it now was almost to endure it again.

"A bolt from the blue," said Gladys.

Observing Amy's silence, her sisters turned to her, deferential as always, now a little shamefaced, as the voluble always are before the mute.

"Poor Amy!" said Lois. "It's hard on us all, but *you*—!"

Again it was as if her mind had been read, and Amy shrank from her sisters' solicitous gaze. All day she had been haunted by words her mother had once said to her. Finding the courage to speak of what she could not bear to contemplate in the knowledge that it was even more unbearable, because more real, to Amy, her mother had said, "You will all be sorry when I am gone. But you, Amy, will be the sorriest of all." The words seemed now to contain some hidden and menacing meaning, like a letter found afterward inscribed, "To be opened when I am dead."

XII

She felt sorry for that little wife of his. She really did. Married to a man with no more grit in him than he showed. Them two little tykes of his, too, such a regular doormat for a daddy as they had, ready to just lay down and let anybody walk all over him. Ride all over him, rather.

All he was trying to do was just be perfectly fair and honest about it, Hugo said.

Him with his truck laying in the ditch with its wheels in the air and his cotton all strewed from one side of the highway to the other and he was just trying to be perfectly fair and honest about it. Well, said Mrs. Shumlin, she thought she had heard just about everything but—

All he meant to say was that if anybody was to ask him he would have to admit that he too had been on the wrong side of the road when—

Out of my way, Mrs. Shumlin said, cause here I come!

Off of the road, all you pee-ons. Shoo! Into the ditch if you don't want to get knocked down and run over. All you poor lone widow women's only cows, all you poor hard-working cotton farmers trying to get your crops in, out of the way, cause my name's Renshaw and I'm coming through.

—when that other car came into that turn. And if he was to be sworn to testify under oath which one of them it was that actually clipped her cow, well, he would have to say that the minute he saw that car coming toward him—

Going ninety miles an hour if it was going a one, Mrs. Shumlin said.

—he had winched his eyes and never opened them again until—

"Hugo?" said Mrs. Shumlin.

She had stopped. Had planted her feet wide apart and stood with her fists on her hips waiting for Hugo to hush.

He concluded by saying that all he meant to say was that while he couldn't honestly swear it wasn't him that had hit her cow, he couldn't honestly swear it was, either.

"Hugo?"

"Yes'm?"

"Hugo, can you afford to buy me another cow?"

"Ma'am?"

"Hugo, have you got a cow of your own?"

"What we do," said Hugo—

"I ought to have known better than to even ask," said Mrs. Shumlin.

"What we do, we've got a neighbor with a cow that gives more than they can use so we buy ours off of him," said Hugo.

Mrs. Shumlin said she just felt sorry for that little wife of his. She would be ashamed of herself if she was him, having to have a woman show him how to be a man. Now what?

Nothing. He had been just fixing to say maybe it would be better if they was to wait and come back again some other time because with all these cars here it looked to him like they were throwing a party or something.

Well they were fixing to have a couple of uninvited guests. Now then, he was to march right up to the front door, not go sneaking around to the back, she said, shaking the tuft of Trixie's tail at him, and call his man out—it was that Lester that he wanted—and have it out with him. Hear?

Yes'm, Hugo said.

Stand right up to him, Mrs. Shumlin said. Not back down an inch. Stick up for his rights. Hear?

Yes'm, Hugo said.

XIII

Member the time, Lester, Mrs. Edwina made you whup my little brother Mitchie?"

The other men attend, and Prentiss Partloe, with a reminiscent chuckle followed by a sorrowful sigh, clears his throat and says, "We was staying down the hill here on the old Kirby place at the time. My brother Mitchie, as most of you may know, was the last of us—about six years old at the time I'm telling about. Lester was then the youngest of the Renshaw boys, for that was before Ky— I mean, Lester was about the same age.

"Us older Partloe boys wouldn't have nothing to do with our little baby brother, of course, and the older Renshaw boys was always running off and leaving little Lester behind, so the two of them played with one another. It was always Lester that come down to our place, for Mitchie was scared to death of Mrs. Edwina, and with good reason. Them two little devils, they didn't neither of them have no other playmates, and yet all they ever did was to fight. They couldn't be together for five minutes without a scrap, and it was always Mitchie got the best of it, for he was a strapping youngster, big for his age, while Lester—you wouldn't think it now— couldn't hardly look into a standing rubber boot. Mitchie whupped poor little Lester so regular that Mrs. Edwina forbid him ever to come down to our place. That never stopped him for one minute, of course. Every day right after breakfast he would sneak off and come running down, and ten minutes later he would be running back home again, with a black eye or a bloody nose or a lip that looked like a bee had stung it. Halfway up the hill Mrs. Edwina would be waiting for him, and switch him all the rest of the way home.

"Well, on the day I'm telling about, Lester run off and come down, and sure enough, in less time than it takes to tell it, him and Mitchie was at it hammer and tongs. 'Fore long Lester had his tail tucked 'tween his legs and was going up the hill for home. There was Mrs. Edwina about halfway up just waiting for him, and that day it was no switch she had in her hand but Mr. Renshaw's old leather razorstrop. She grabs Lester by the ear and instead of whupping him home she marches him straight back down to our place.

"When Mitchie sees her coming with that strop swinging in her hand and not whupping Lester with it, he scampers into the house howling that Mrs. Renshaw was coming to kill him—as he felt he deserved. Then out of the house comes my mama, hissing like a gander. 'I hope you ain't aiming to take that strop to e'er child of mine, Edwina Renshaw,' she says. For although she was scared of Mrs. Edwina herself, Mitchie was Mama's favorite of us all—poor boy, dead at twenty-two and far from home in a foreign land, God rest his soul. 'My Mitchie never starts it,' Mama cries, and in that she was right. For although you got the worst of it, it was you that generally started it, if you remember, Lester. 'It ain't his fault if my boy always whups him,' cries Mama. 'If you don't like it then why don't you keep him at home where he belongs? We don't invite him to come down here and get his nose bloody.'

"Mrs. Edwina listens to all this, screwing up a little tighter on Lester's ear all the while, like winding a clock, so that he was bending with it, and standing on one foot, and practically turning a flip, but never letting out a whimper. 'You hear that?' she says to him. 'You hear it, sir? Now then ain't you ashamed of yourself?' And she tightens up another turn on that ear. 'Now then, Mrs. Partloe,' she says, 'you'll oblige me by bringing out that young world champion of yours. My little man here challenges him. And this time it's going to be different. This time he is going to pin your boy's ears back. Ain't you?' she says, looking down at Lester. 'Cause if you don't, Mister,' she says, giving her own leg a cut with that strop, 'then I am going to flay the hide right off of you.'

" 'Pin my Mitchie's ears back?' yelps Mama. 'That little sugartit?' And she slams into the house and yanks Mitchie out by his ear. 'Mrs. Renshaw here would like to see how you whup the snot out of her boy all the time,' she says. 'Show her.' And she gives his ear a twist, and Mrs. Renshaw comes back at her with another twist on Lester's ear, and the two of them stand there like two kids winding up their toys for a race.

"So them two little banty roosters were set on one another. Gentlemen, two boys with their daubers down you never seen the like! If they could just have called off that match they wouldn't ever have had another cross word between them. They circled one another like a pair of gears that won't mesh, and the one looked at his mama and the other looked at his, both pawing the ground and praying not to land a blow nor get one and bawling and whimpering, till at last Mrs. Edwina says, 'Enough of this Alphonsing and Gastoning. I'm here to see some fight,' and she gives Lester a cut across the calfs of his legs with that strop that raised a welt like a branding iron.

"Well, after that, Mitchie was no match for that boy. Bawling and crying, Lester was on to him like they was two Lesters.

" 'Sick him, Mitch! Sick him!' my mama yells. But poor Mitchie couldn't even find him.

"In short, Lester like to have killed that poor boy that day. It got to be a regular slaughter at the end, but every time Lester would try to let up and stop the fight Mrs. Edwina would cut him again with that razorstrop, until finally his legs was raw as butcher's meat. But though he could scarcely walk, you never seen such a little pouter pigeon as Lester Renshaw strutting back up that old hill for home. Mitchie come to be a great favorite of your Ma's after that, didn't he, Les? Nobody daren't say a word against Mrs. Edwina whenever Mitchie was around. Not that anybody ever did, you understand. That is just a manner of speaking."

Now the shadow of the pear tree lies on the far side of the lawn, tied to the base of the tree, like a balloon on a string. Overhead chimneysweeps and barn swallows and scissortailed swifts and one lone bullbat glide and swoop, squeaking like mice. The cows have come up the path, Belle in the lead, shaking her head, tossing the yoke she wears to keep her from jumping fences, and now the six of them stand in the barnlot, lowing softly.

One of the men—it is Odell Grissom—gets to his feet, then others like Odell with no sons left at home to do the evening chores, follow, leaving gaps in the circle, and soon is heard a grinding of starters and the catching of motors and the rattle of springs and truckbeds in both directions along the road.

Clifford gets to his feet—asleep both of them, numb—like a squatting idol come to life. Someone says, "Want me to do it for you? I can do it." Clifford stares at the man. "You want me to milk? I'll milk for you if you want me to."

It is his brother Lester. But to Clifford, his mind still half submerged, it is his father as he looked thirty and more years ago when one day down behind the schoolhouse privies he, Clifford, had fought in his father's defense the last fight of his childhood and the first one of his manhood, his faith in his father gone even as he fought to defend him against an accusation which the other boy did not even know he had made. He was twelve, the boy he fought two years older and a head taller; but before they could pry Clifford loose he had knocked out two of his adversary's teeth, and had they been much longer subduing him he would have realized his intention to gouge both the boy's eyes from their sockets. He had lost nonetheless, was losing all the time he was winning, knowing which was why he had fought so furiously. They held him—it took five to do it—while he gasped, "Take it back. Make him take it back or else I'll kill him."

"He's gone crazy!" the other boy screamed. Blood bubbled from his mouth and trickled down his chin. The teacher was there now and the boy screamed at him, "He's gone out of his mind! He's crazy as a bedbug! Keep him away from me!"

He was beaten like the grown man he had just become—or as near to one as this day was ever to let him become—by the teacher, who laid it on all the harder because of his stubborn refusal to divulge what the other boy had said to provoke him, using a belt as thick as a harness strap, the holes for the buckle tongue raising blisters on his flesh as if he had been peppered with shot, then sent home bearing a note saying he was expelled from school for the remainder of the term. But it was long past midnight and nearly twenty miles away before the search party found him and brought him home. By that time he knew not only that he had fought for a foredoomed cause but that he had been a fool. He was ashamed now of not having known what he had fought to prove untrue. He was a farmboy. He had seen the bull mount the cows, the dogs stuck together for days, and had long known the difference between himself and his sisters; but he had made no connections. By the time they caught him on the road that night he knew—he had known it even as he fought—that his father was guilty of doing as the other boy had unwittingly charged, and that he would never in his life forgive him for doing that to his mother. And when they got home and his father garaged the truck and he stood waiting, not to take the beating he knew was coming but to fight him now with the same heedless fury as he had fought for him when he was a child a lifetime and ten hours ago, and the beating never came, he took this for an admission of guilt. Afterward, for three months, until they dismissed him as unteachable, he would sit beside his father on the truck seat each morning and afternoon going the six miles to and from school in the neighboring settlement, pretending to be somewhere else, speaking if spoken to, in monosyllables. He knew all there was to know then, so he thought. He had not noticed what must have been evident to everyone else until his mother told him to expect a new little brother or sister. He had hated that child—Gladys it was—for years. Within two years he had proved to himself for the first of many times the bestiality of his own sex and the woman's lack of enjoyment in the act. When, years later, his mother gave birth to his youngest brother, he had not once taken his eyes off his father as they sat beneath the pear tree all the long while that she was in labor. It was a long and difficult delivery and through it all Clifford had not eaten, he had not stirred, he had not opened his mouth. When it was over and word came down from the house that Ma was out of danger Clifford said to his father, "If she had died I would have killed you. Now leave her alone. Don't ever go near her again. She's taken all of that off of you she should have to."

The presence in the kitchen now of the neighbor women disconcerted Clifford. Methodical as a clock in doing his few chores, he was thrown off by the least disarrangement in his narrow familiar world. Under their collective gaze he reddened and his tongue seemed to grow too big for his mouth. He found the milk pail and the wash pail but could not remember where he had last put the rag with which he washed the cows' udders. He filled the wash pail with hot water, then realized he had forgotten to put in the disinfectant powder. He got as far as the door, then remembered the funnel, went back for it, was almost to the door again when he had to turn back for the strainer.

In the barn the cows stood each at her stanchion, snuffling, licking their slimy muzzles, scraping up the crumbs of their morning's feed with tongues as rough as rasps. Milk dripped to the floor from their ripe expectant teats; the air was heavy with the chalky sweet smell of it. In the shafts of sunlight from the windows, dust motes filtered endlessly. When he had closed and locked the stanchions around their necks Clifford fed the cows. Each received first a scoop of crushed cottonseed hulls. On top of that a scoop each of bran. Then half a scoop each of cottonseed meal, dense, delicious-smelling, yellow as granulated gold.

From the steaming bucket Clifford took the rag and washed the first cow's udder. She, Daisy, had recently freshened, was swollen with milk. The touch of the hot water quickened the drip from her teats into the puddle on the floor beneath her. Drawing up the stool Clifford grasped her forward teats and commenced to knead. The first milk struck the bottom of the pail with a noise like a bullet. As the pail filled, the sound deepened, the twin streams, solid and uninterrupted, slicing through the foam, coming with such force as to open a hole to the bottom even when the pail was nearly full.

At the barn door Mrs. Shumlin stiffened her back and primed herself with wind, filling her lungs like a bellows, hoisted her battle ensign—the tuft of Trixie's tail—and stepped inside just in time to see Clifford Renshaw pause in his milking, slump on his stool and bury his forehead in the hollow of Daisy's flank. Daisy stopped munching and looked around and mooed inquiringly. "Ma is sick, Daisy," said Clifford. "Real sick." The foam on the milk in the pail made, in settling, a faint fizz. "What will become of poor me?" asked Clifford. Mrs. Shumlin hid Trixie's tail behind her and, still holding her breath, tiptoed backwards out of the barn.

When Mrs. Shumlin let go of her breath it went out of her as though she had been punctured, and left her deflated. She would get no compensation from the Renshaws for the loss of her cow. Today all roads, all lanes, belonged to them. The world would not only extenuate, it would applaud Lester Renshaw's endangering himself and everybody and everything else along the way in his haste to get home to the side of his dying mother. Trixie's owner would be expected to feel honored in having been chosen to contribute her cow for a sacrifice upon the altar of reckless Renshaw filial devotion. A longtime neighbor of the Renshaws, and a mother herself, Mrs. Shumlin would have felt that way about it too if the cow had been anybody else's. All she could do was congratulate herself on having been spared committing a breach of etiquette. Had Clifford Renshaw spoken a moment sooner she would have missed it, a moment later and she herself would have spoken.

A sly look spread over Mrs. Shumlin's face. She had thought of another way to get herself another cow: Hugo. This sly look lasted only a moment; it was overlaid, as with a second coat of paint, by a slyer look. Mrs. Shumlin had thought of a way to get herself much more than just another cow. All this took only an instant, yet in that instant Mrs. Shumlin's life changed, and she looked past her immediate surroundings like a person focusing upon a distant prospect. In that instant she had foreseen and solved all the many problems to arise from the change she was about to make in her life. Mrs. Shumlin faced about and strode to the barn as if she owned it.

Mrs. Shumlin peeked with one eye around the frame of a window. Clifford Renshaw sat as she had left him sitting, slumped on his milk stool with his forehead against the cow's flank. Mrs. Shumlin drew back, rested the back of her head against the wall, cupped one hand to her mouth and said in a voice not her own, "I am so worried about you, Son. I don't worry about the rest, only you. What will become of you when I am gone? Oh, Clifford, my poor boy, how will you manage all alone, with nobody to look after you?"

Mrs. Shumlin did not look in to see what effect she had produced. She ducked beneath the window ledge and scurried around the corner and along the wall and around the next corner to the window on the opposite side of the barn. There she crouched and peeked through a crack in the wall. Clifford Renshaw sat on his stool with his back to her looking in the direction from which she had spoken.

"I could go happy," said Mrs. Shumlin with a sigh, "if I knew I was leaving you with somebody to take care of you." That was all she had time to say, for Clifford spun on his stool to face her way. She saw his face darken with suspicion and his head toss and the aim of his eyes settle upon the spot where she was, and quitting that spot she scampered around to the far side of the barn. There she peeped through a crack and saw him leaning out the window where she had been and turning his head to look in both directions.

Mrs. Shumlin let go a long sigh of pain and regret that jerked him back inside and froze him with fear. "If only you had a wife. A good woman to look after you. One like that sweet little Mrs. Shumlin who lives down the road."

Clifford came tiptoeing to the middle of the aisle that ran between the stanchions. He was darting his eyes all about in confusion, fear and mistrust. His expression was divided between disbelief, fear of being made a fool of, and shame at his disbelief. Mrs. Shumlin shifted around to the opposite side of the barn.

Releasing another pained sigh upon the air, Mrs. Shumlin said, "I don't know if she would have you but it would be nothing lost by asking. Don't give up if she says no at first. Keep after her."

Again Clifford's brows knitted and his eyelids narrowed and he took steps her way, and again Mrs. Shumlin circled the barn.

This time when she spoke to his back he did not turn. Her voice had come to him from so many directions that now it seemed to be coming from all directions, from no direction at all, from out of the enveloping atmosphere. She said, "She is a pearl and if you could win her you would want to always let her have her own way in everything. Always take her side in any quarrel, even against your own brother. Let yourself be guided by her, for you know, Son, you haven't got much practical sense, and she has got a bushelful. I could go happy if I knew I was leaving you to her."

She could probably have concluded her message in safety from that same spot. She had him entranced. He had given up looking for the source of the voice. He believed. But lest any last minute doubts assail him, she moved one last time. She fetched up her most heart-rending sigh yet. "That," she said, "is your poor mother's last wish on this green earth of God's."

His back was to her but she did not need to see his face. In the stoop of his shoulders, in the inclination of his head, in the hang of his arms, she could read unquestioning belief, unresisting submission.

Despite her efforts to get away unseen, Mrs. Shumlin was seen by Hugo Mattox on her way back from the Renshaw barn. Hugo rose from his place in the circle of men squatting beneath the pear tree and excused himself for just a minute and ran after Mrs. Shumlin.

"It wasn't a party," said Hugo. "I guess you found that out, too. I'm sorry I said that. I wouldn't if I'd've known. Of course, I never said anything about my cotton and all that." Hugo looked past Mrs. Shumlin to where a cow would have been if she had been leading a cow, and said, "I see you never took one of their cows like you said you was going to, either."

Mrs. Shumlin tapped the tuft of Trixie's tail against the palm of her hand. "Hugo?" she said.

"Yes'm?"

"Hugo, I've been doing some thinking." She gave the tuft of the cow's tail a couple of taps against her palm. "About what you told me. You say that when you seen that other car coming to wards you you winched your eyes."

Hugo nodded, swallowed.

"And that when you opened them again you was clear across the road and everything was all over. Isn't that what you told me, Hugo?"

"Yes'm," said Hugo.

"In short, you never seen what took place. Did you?"

Hugo shook his head, and swallowed.

"And the last time you seen my cow before winching your eyes her hind end was to wards you. Is that right, Hugo?"

Hugo nodded. "Yes'm," he said.

The future Mrs. Renshaw gave the tuft of Hugo's cow's tail a final tap against her palm, then handed it to him. "I'll milk her for you this evening," she said.

"I'll have to ask you to let me work it off in installments," said Hugo.

"We'll work it out," said Mrs. Shumlin.

"Thank you, Ma'am," said Hugo. Then, "If it wouldn't be too much imposition I'd be much obliged to you if you would take in my wife and kids for the night, Mrs. Shumlin. Don't go to no trouble. Just make them down a pallet on the floor. Tell Audrey for me I'll see her and them just as soon as I can. I don't know just when to say I'll be able to get away. You see how it is. A man can't come and find folks setting up with their sick mother and not set with them, can he?" Hugo turned to look at the ring of men squatting beneath the pear tree. Permitting himself a shallow sigh, Hugo said, "Looks like this just ain't my day."

XIV

The place he had chosen for privacy was the least private place in the house. Three times already he had been interrupted by somebody rattling the door wanting in. The room was hot and airless and stank from its last user before him.

Doing to yourself what he was doing drove you crazy, he used to be told in his high-school Physical Education class. Maybe it did in the long run; in the short run what drove you crazy was not doing it. He had learned that. Scared by what he was told, he had quit, and had fought off the temptation until he nearly went out of his mind, until he got stone-ache and swelled up and turned blue and then got sick, real belly-griping sick, throw-up sick. That was what he had been headed for today. Now he learned that in the long run the gym instructor had been right: doing this to yourself as a grown man drove you crazy. Crazy with solitude and shame.

Crazy with frustration, too. He had thought that, considering the state he was in when he finally gave in to the urge, it would be over with quickly. The remorse could come afterward, at least the operation itself would soon be over. But this sorry substitute was not what he craved. This joyless friction, far from cooling desire, only rubbed it to a heat. The real thing was what he craved. And now even in fantasy she fled from him, tantalized him, tormented him. Those images of her that had goaded him into this state flickered and faded away now that he required them to help him attain relief. Parts of her anatomy—clefts—globes dusky and smooth as the skin of plums—moved in and out of focus upon the projection screen of his mind. Upon that screen shone more vividly the image of a boy, himself—shame-ridden then, how much more so now!—seeking self-solace upon this same seat, behind the same locked door. Super-imposed, like a double exposure, over this image: that of his dying mother lying unconscious now behind another door just down the hall.

He was growing more frantic by the moment. Curses and pleas, desire and disgust, self-pity and self-loathing, opposites that like the polar charges which combine to make electricity, sent through him a constant current of shock, setting his every nerve jangling, every nerve-end burning with shame. Adding to his distress was the sense that what he was doing resembled in some way the real thing as he had come to know it. Even when he was with her he wanted something more than that, too, though he had that in every form it came in. She seemed never to care what he did to her in bed, certainly she never objected to anything he did, so he did everything there was to do. And even at the peak of his pleasure he wondered whether the very indifference with which she endured such treatment from him meant that she would do the same, did the same, with some other man (and him black)? This constant craving for sex, what was it but a craving for something which sex alone had not been able to gratify? He called it sex: the itch for more and more of it and in all the forbidden ways, that made his mind, that made the mind of most men his age, into a non-stop stag film; but he sensed that his frenzy and his perversities signified a longing for something more. He wanted to do things with her that degraded them both and united them in secret guilt. He wanted her to have no privacy from him, no self apart from him. What seemed to be sexual frenzy was a frantic desire to possess her very soul. He might even almost have been able to endure the thought that he shared her body with another man if he could have been sure her soul was his. He assaulted her body as though it were a fortress that he might break through to her soul in its fastness. He knew that assaulting her body, though he were to do it ten thousand times, was not the way to conquer and capture her soul. Yet he would make that futile assault ten thousand thousand times before he would acknowledge that the only possible way to gain her soul was to ask for it, offering his in return. The desires of his flesh and his heart's desire might be one and the same, but to him they were as different as black and white. Better to be a lecher than a lover if to be a lover was to be a niggerlover.

He could not go on with what he was doing, neither could he stop doing it. He was on the edge of frenzy, breakdown, shaking all over, his breathing so labored, so deep-drawn that the swelling of his chest brought it in contact with the razor that dangled on the string from around his neck.

He looked down with hatred at himself; his glance took in the razor. In an instant, with one swift surgical stroke, he could sever that malignant growth from him and be free. Free of longing, free of guilt, free of her and all her kind. This was for him the one fitting punishment, atonement, and deliverance. Expiation for his sins as a son, a husband, a father, and a white man, and lifelong deliverance from his thralldom to that thing, that growth, which never had been anything but a running sore since it first rose on him, never any pleasure except the pleasure of momentary relief from its incurable ache.

He felt that it had been done, and he felt purged, cleansed and whole, complete unto himself, independent of women, of neither sex and thus superior to both. It would be a rebirth. He would be unique. He would be self-engendered, unreproducible, as unsusceptible to low lusts as a marble statue, as smooth and neuter, as innocent and un-troubled as a doll. He would be superhuman, made of flesh but beyond the temptations of the flesh.

He broke the string and swung open the blade and applied its edge to himself and instantly his courage deserted him, taking with it the last shred of his self-respect.

When the door rattled again he got up off the seat and flushed the bowl. He drew his drawers and his trousers up over the obstruction, and when the person outside had withdrawn to allow him to leave, slunk with his hands in his pockets down the hall and past the door behind which his mother lay dying.

XV

That's the last one," said Mrs. Murdoch, speaking not of the coconut custard pie she was removing from the oven of the great black baroque wood range, but of Ross Renshaw, whose arrival she had seen through the kitchen window.

"The last one that is going to come, anyway," said Mrs. Garrett in an undertone.

"Ssh!"

"Poor Edwina," said Mrs. Bywaters. "Poor woman. Poor soul. When my time comes to go I pray the Lord that I may have all my children and all my loved ones at my side. It is the one thing I ask."

"Amen," said a chorus of voices.

Then everybody's old Aunt Viola Mahaffey said, in that faint scratchy voice of hers like a worn-out phonograph record, "Amy." The other women all turned deferentially to attend her. She folded down her left thumb. "Clifford."

PROUD FLESH

Down went the index finger. "Clyde." Down went the
middle finger. "Hazel." And she crumpled the withered
digit which seemed to have been killed years ago, like a
banded twig, by the big, loose-fitting gold ring. "Lois." Her
closed brown fist looked mummified.

Lean women with lined faces, looking so much alike as
to be taken for relatives—which in fact many of them were
if the connection was traced out fine enough. Certainly all
of the same original stock, into which little outside blood
had been transfused for a century and a half. All with that
sinewy, dry, gallinaceous look of the prairie farmwoman, all
with those work-stiffened hands with swollen knuckles like
the joints on bamboo cane. With empty piepans, with folded
newspapers, with handkerchiefs they fanned their reddened
faces, *whish whish whish*, a sound like panting breath.
Around the range for a space of ten feet the air was un-
touchable. The smell of hot spices, of nutmeg and cinnamon
and cloves and vanilla extract, suffused the room.

"Ross," said Aunt Viola, starting in now on the thumb
of her right hand. "Gladys. Ballard. Lester." Her little
finger still stuck up, crooked, dry, withered. She bent it
down. "And—"

"Ssh!"

"Ssh!"

"Ssh!"

"Ten of them," said Mrs. Murdoch. "Like the fingers
of the hands."

"And her," said Mrs. Bywaters, "like a person with a
finger missing. Trying to keep it hidden from sight. And
from her own sight. Braving it out before the world. Trying
not to notice the itch. They say a missing limb itches. Not
the stump, the limb itself. You can feel it in its old place,
they say, itching. It's an itch that no scratching can ease."

1 1 3

"She was partial to that one. She could never hide it."

"She never tried to hide it."

"He come along after she thought she was past the age. Her Benjamin."

"The last boy is always the hardest child to bring up. He's forever running after his big brothers. Trying to measure up to them. Always trying to cut loose from his mamma's apron strings. So the bigger boys won't call him a mamma's boy."

"She brought it on herself. I say no more. It's a judgment on the way she brought him up. I feel for her. I do. She has suffered and now she must suffer more before she is released. But she brought it on herself. She has only herself to blame."

"She did spoil him. Spoiled rotten. Worse than any of the others."

"They all spoiled him. Like it is when one comes along after a family thinks it is all finished and made. When the child has brothers and sisters old enough to be its mamma and daddy. The last born in a big family gets spoiled worse than an only child. Especially if it be a boy."

"Mrs. Rainey, hon, would you mind just stepping outside there and telling one of them niggerboys to go chunk that turtledove away. I can't stand that sorrowful sound at a time like this. It goes through me like a knife."

"And then of course the others all married off, went to the war, and he was all she had left at home and so she clung to him all the tighter."

"It's hard on a family that's always been so close."

"And so stiff-necked proud!"

"Ssh!"

"Ssh!"

A sound outside the door caused a rolling of eyes, a

quickening of the swish of fans.

"Ah, here is Mrs. Herndon. Give Mrs. Herndon a glass of that ice-tea, somebody. Well, how is she?"

"No change. Ross come in."

"Poor Ross. He takes everthang so hard. That boy is all heart."

"Was it his heart he was off in Mineral Wells for?"

"Ssh!"

"Ssh!"

"Well, whatever it was it don't seem to have done him much good." Mrs. Herndon wrinkled her nose and fanned her face vigorously. "That was not mineral water," she said, "that I smelt on his breath."

"Sssssssssssh!"

"He was doing just fine until this," Avis, Ross's wife, told her sisters-in-law. "They don't fool around with you out there, you know. Or maybe you don't know but I can tell you. You don't taper off. You quit. Cold turkey. And this time around, Ross really did aim to quit. The AA man had given him a lot of support, so had Reverend Burnett. During the five weeks we were out there (he would have been sent home as cured just next Thursday), he never touched a drop. If you know Ross that's hard to believe, I grant, but it's true: not one drop—not so much as a glass of beer. Then Ballard's wire came and he just went to pieces. I said, 'Ross, hon, this is it. Five weeks now you have gone without. You've got it licked if you'll just be firm. Slip again and it's for good.' It was just too much for him to handle. I myself went out and bought him a fifth—that's the easiest town on earth to find a bootlegger in. So it was all for nothing and now what's to become of him, and me, the Lord only knows."

The meal that had begun in the early morning with Edwina's going down to the garden was ready at long last to be served. That day-long, murmurous beelike bustle out in the kitchen had produced a banquet. On the dining table rested a baked ham glazed with syrup, circled with brown pineapple rings, sprigged with sticks of clove. There was a roasted haunch of beef and a leg of mutton. There were potatoes of every variety: creamed, baked and buttered, boiled in their jackets, potatoes julienne, potatoes au gratin. There were black-eyed peas, English peas, field peas in pot liquor. On the buffet stood coconut pie, lemon meringue pie, apple pie, devil's food cake, angel food cake, baked apples stuffed with pecan meats. Each woman had fashioned her proudest dish. Now they looked forward with advance approval to seeing it go uneaten. Ranged in the kitchen doorway, with long faces and sorrowful eyes, they watched the family file to the table.

Big as the table was, four seatings were required to feed all the Renshaws that evening. First came the elderly aunts and toothless uncles and fragile great-aunts and delicate, decrepit cousins, helped to their places and served by the young women of the clan. Spoon-eaters, collar-bibbed, more than one of them belonging to that passing school of Southern country men whose way with their food was to stir together everything on their plates, then over the slop pour sorghum syrup, with the explanation that it all got mixed together anyway a little further down. Having buried many, and nearing the end themselves, they had license to gum their victuals with appetites unreserved in the presence of death.

Meanwhile out in the kitchen there was a great boiling of bottles and mixing of formulas and a din even more deafening than that caused by hardness of hearing around the dining table, as the infants and weanlings were fed.

The immediate family sat at the second table. Past the neighbor women they slunk in shame, each feeling himself personally to blame for the absence of the one now missing from their ranks. It devolved upon Clyde to say grace, as did so many social duties which ought by seniority to have fallen to the incompetent Clifford. Bowing his head and closing his eyes, Clyde mumbled, "Oh, Lord, we thank Thee for these and all Thy bless . . ." A catch in his voice, he broke off. No one lifted his head. From among the neighbor women in the doorway was heard a sniffle. Clearing his throat, Clyde said, "For these and all Thy . . ." Again he choked up, and raising his stricken face and pushing back his chair from the table, he got up and fled from the room, holding his napkin in front of him to hide the state he was in. Derwent left just behind him. From underneath their brows the family exchanged stricken looks. At Ross, whose turn it now was, they all tried not to look. Wreathed in alcoholic vapors, Ross sat blinking and swallowing down a recurrent hiccup, meanwhile nodding in self-agreement as he scored points in the argument in which, alone, against odds, he held the dissenting view.

Some moments passed in awkward silence. Then Ballard said through gritted teeth, "Oh, Lord, we—" At that moment Ross emerged from his stupor momentarily to utter a loud, "Amen!" whereupon the long-suppressed hiccup seized its chance and erupted. At this Ballard came towering up, groaning and gnashing his teeth, pushed back his chair and stalked out of the room. Shaking his head, Clifford next got up and lumbered out. Then Ross, thinking that everybody was leaving, and deducing from his empty plate (though it was still bottom side up, like everybody else's) that he had had his supper, got unsteadily to his feet, knocked over his chair, wove to the door, fell through it, and could be heard careening from wall to wall as he made his way down the corridor.

That left Lester. But Lester was already getting up to flee, and when he was gone there was another period of silence during which the sisters sat bowed in shame.

"Oh, Lord, we thank Thee for these and all Thy blessings, which we ask in Jesus' name. Amen," said Amy. And folding her napkin upon her plate, she rose and left the room, followed in turn by her three sisters.

From the neighbor women in the kitchen came a collective sigh of satisfaction.

XVI

Pallets had been made down on the floors of various rooms for the children, and throughout the house the lights blazed as they were put to bed. Then one by one the lights went out until all that was left burning was the hall light, visible through the fan window over the front door, and upstairs the traditional blue sick-light.

Out in the yard, beneath the pear tree, cigarette ends flickered like fireflies. Above the glow, as he drew on it, the smoker's face would materialize, gleam demonically, fade, then fall back into darkness. Conversation had died.

At just past ten o'clock a whisper, like rain sweeping over the roof, ran through the house, and the men in the yard saw the sick-light upstairs flare into sudden white. A moment later the lights came on downstairs, the front door flew open and a bolt of light flashed across the porch and over the lawn, throwing into skeletal shadows the craned and twisted faces of the squatting men. There was noise from the house now, the typewriterlike clatter of women's high heels on the stairs and words in urgent, loud women's whispers, and across the open doorway bent, skirted silhouettes, intent and harried, scurried like actresses hastening to take their places seen through a slit in the curtain. The wail of a wakened child started up, then in mid-cry broke off. Together the men of the family strode rapidly up the path of light, their shadows lengthening behind them. Bit by bit the door swung shut, closing down the beam like the segments of a fan being closed, and in the darkness, in silence, the neighbor men settled back on their haunches.

Inside the house people were running on tiptoes down hallways and up and down stairs from all directions toward the sickroom. Ross's girl Beth, half unbuttoned, her hair in curlers, shepherding her four children, the twin girls clasping hands, wide-eyed with curiosity and fright. Her sister Thelma, whose children, too young to understand and merely cross with sleepiness, dragged their feet and whined. Hazel's boy Arthur carrying their baby, his little wife Anita looking unhappy and lonely without kinfolks of her own. Old Aunt Lillian feeling her way along the wall with fluttering hand, clutching with the other one at all who passed her and croaking, "Tell Edwiner I'm coming. Tell her to hold on, I'm coming just as fast as I can come." Derwent wild with grief. Ballard grim, scowling. Lois vague, distraught. Ross reeling off the walls, his eyes blurred with drunken tears.

Inside the sickroom, with its stuffy smell, the in-laws flattened their backs against the walls and pressed their wives and husbands to the fore, around the bed.

Edwina lay propped up with pillows, her eyes closed. Her hair had been arranged, her face powdered, her lips painted, but the pallor of her skin was only heightened thereby. Against the whiteness of the bedsheet the bluish swellings around the roots of her nails stood out startlingly, making it look as though her fingertips had been subjected to torture, crushed and bruised. Dr. Metcalf hovered over her, haggard, apprehensive, studiously attentive to his duties. The family crowded close around, the children clinging to their mothers and fathers in fear, or rather, in fear of their parents' fear.

There was a long silence in which the breathing of many open mouths could be heard.

"Oh," whispered Lois, "is she not going to come to?"

"I hope and pray not!" hissed Gladys. She would rather her mother died without saying goodbye to the forty-seven descendants gathered around her deathbed than take leave of life with the thought of the forty-eighth who was not there.

"Oh, Ma, speak to us!" cried Hazel. "Can you hear me? Speak to us, Ma, darling."

Her old eyelids, crinkly and thin as the skin of a bat's wing, fluttered open. Her glance flickered over the faces ranged around her. Her eyes darkened with pain. She tried to concentrate her mind, the effort visible on her face. She tried to speak. No sound emerged. Again she searched their faces and again she tried to speak. It was only on her fourth attempt that the name she was trying to pronounce found utterance, and then in a plaintive whisper, but to her children it sounded as loud as a shout.

"Kyle?" she said, and shook her head, closed her eyes and fell back unconscious upon her pillow.

XVII

Yet she had rallied somewhat, and although she did not again regain consciousness, Dr. Metcalf felt that with Amy in attendance, the most devoted nurse a patient ever had, he could safely leave her and go home, with the promise to return early the next morning.

The neighbors all went home, taking with them as guests the most distant Renshaw kin.

"We can sleep four, Gladys, honey," said Mrs. McAdie.

"We can put up three," said Mrs. Murdoch.

"We can take five, if one of them don't mind the davenport," said Mrs. Dinwiddie.

"We thank you. You've all been so kind, so helpful. I don't know what we would do without such good neighbors. We hate to impose."

"Impose!"

"Awful good of you, Berenice. All right, youall take

Uncle Cameron and Aunt Beulah. Edna, if you would take—"

"No, we're going to stay right here, Cameron and me. Make us down a pallet on the floor."

"Hush, Aunt Beulah. You go with Berenice. If you stay here one of the boys will have to sit up, and you know they all need their rest."

"Nobody's going to have to give up their bed for us. Don't either of us ever sleep any more anyway. We'll sit up in a chair."

"Then you can just as well sit up over at the Edwardses'. Go on now. You can't be of any use here and you'll just wear yourself out for no good reason. We don't want you getting sick on us, on top of everything else."

"You call, Gladys, hon, if there should be any need, and Tom will run them right over in the car, no matter what time it might be."

"Thank you. Thank you all. Without such good neighbors I don't know what we would do. Won't you ladies take some of all that lovely food home with you? Well, we thank you, all of you, for everything. Now then, Ethel, if you will take Aunt Flo and Aunt—"

"Be glad to stay, Gladys, and sit up—"

"Thank you, Gertrude, but we can manage. Us girls will take turns, and we've got Amy."

XVIII

They put it off as long as they could. Theirs was the last light in the house to be put out. But there was no getting out of it. They were trapped. They could not excuse themselves and go home to sleep. Close as home was, it was too far away to be now, with Ma in her condition. At any moment throughout the night another call to her bedside could come. Summoned by telephone from home they might arrive just too late. They could not make a scene. Could not ask for separate bedrooms, even if there had been a bedroom to spare. Man and wife ask for separate bedrooms? Reveal to the entire family what the entire family knew? They could do nothing but what they had done: accept the nightclothes on loan—a pair of Clifford's pajamas for him, one of Ma's nightgowns for her—put out the light and change into them and then stretch out, he along one edge and she along the other. The first time in three years that Mr. and Mrs. Clyde Renshaw had lain down together in the same bed.

Three years, three months and a week, to be exact.
From the day it all began. For he was a man of principle,
and he had known from the start, had known even as it was
happening, that this thing he had done, and was going to do
again, regularly, this thing which he would not have confided
to his closest friend, if he had had a close friend, he was going to have to declare to his worst enemy. A worst enemy he
did have. He hoped she appreciated what he had done. Not
every man would have done it.

In his favor had been one factor: it happened over a
weekend. A Friday was when it all began, and that night he
had stayed out late. Not with Shug. He had gotten her back
to the farm by four-thirty that afternoon. But he had stayed
away from home, driving, until past midnight. He was pretty
sure Eunice was awake and had heard him coming in. She
slept like an underfed watchdog. Not that she was really
jealous of him. Not that she really cared a damn what he
did with himself. That was not the reason for her vigilance.
Just that things had come to such a pass between them. Dog
in the manger: that was what she slept like. He made enough
noise to be sure she had heard him, then went to sleep in
the boys' old room.

At breakfast Saturday morning he said he had come in
late, offering no explanation why but contriving to look as
though he was ready to lie to her if she insisted, and not
wanting to wake her, had gone to sleep by himself. Such
unexampled considerateness was enough in itself to arouse
her suspicions. That night at bedtime he said he had slept so
well the night before, not having to worry about keeping
her awake by his restlessness, he believed he would sleep
again in the boys' room.

He was skating on very thin ice. Hell hath no fury like
a woman scorned, and she was a woman just waiting to be.

All she needed to make her divorce him was grounds, and he himself was giving them to her. Fortunately it was a Saturday. The lawyers' offices were closed and she could do nothing until Monday. By then he was counting on a drop in the temperature.

Meanwhile he ran no risk of having her forgive him, of having her impute his openhandedness to any twinges of guilt or remorse or any sense of obligation toward her. She knew him better than that. Lying in bed by herself that night—a state she would find she really preferred but was conditioned to think she ought to resent—she would think, if he is telling me about it, it is because he wants me to divorce him so he can marry the other woman. Br'er Rabbit to the farmer: oh, please, throw me anywhere but in the briar patch. And she was just spiteful enough to do it even though it might be what he wanted her to do. Fortunately the following day was a Sunday.

That morning he moved his clothes into the boys' room.

She had all day to consider the implications of that move. It would take all day, all evening, much of the night, for the meaning of it to come clear to her. Lying alone that night he could almost feel the moment, like the day's low on the weather report, when the chill of comprehension would descend upon her. When custom, convention, taboo, her own pride, her knowledge of him, would all conspire to lead her to an overwhelming conclusion. That he would never have confessed it to her if it had been merely a common case of adultery; that he was quite capable of deceiving her for life if it had been no more than that. This was the freeze he was expecting, and after it would come no thaw. Monday would be clear and cold. He could skate safely.

There were acceptable ways for a woman to be wronged and unacceptable ways. One whose husband left her for another woman of her own color and class could count upon some sympathy from the world, but one whose husband left her for an inferior or to pursue some unnatural taste was herself disgraced along with him.

It had been a gamble, but honesty once again was the best policy. He felt better for it. She, his worst enemy, was now his accomplice. She would be as anxious as he was that his attachment not be known. Even more anxious than he was. So long as she alone knew it, she could live with it. Other women had and so could she. If she could count on his being discreet then he could count on her being accommodating. Thus their understanding was negotiated and sealed without a word being spoken. Which meant that she had heard nothing to have to deny to herself having heard. She could tell herself that nothing had happened if she wanted to. She could tell herself her husband had gone off to sleep alone so as not to wake her when he got up at night. And if he had her in his hands did she not have him in hers? That was turn and turnabout. What could be fairer than that? His shameful secret was in pawn to her, and though she could not foreclose on the pledge, neither could he redeem it.

He had abided by his part in the pact. He had been discreet. He had provided the wench with a husband and had provided the couple with a house, detached, and in full view of all the world, and he had never gone near that house—though often enough drawn to it!—had never gotten near enough even to look at it. It was the one spot on the place that he had put off-limits to himself. He had not done all this out of affection for her. The affection between them had not outlasted their wedding-present chinaware. He owed her nothing. It was not even personal. He, the child of his mother, would have done the same for any woman who happened to be the mother of his children. It was a matter of principle, of duty. Some men would have gone right on sleeping in her bed—especially as sleeping was all they ever did together there any more—but not he. His conscience would not let him. He just hoped she appreciated it.

In fact, it was not hard to live with. Not as hard as she had expected, certainly not as hard as he had expected. It had its compensations, one of them unlooked-for. Knowing that he would never again dare ask to use it, her body was restored to her ownership. It made her take a fresh look at herself. She felt a renewal of interest in herself. For a long time she had been neglectful of her appearance, going around any old way, in any old thing, as though she was old, finished, taking no care of her skin, her hair. She was not old. She was still young. She began buying clothes again, fixing herself up. Friends all said, "Eunice, you've had a second blossoming!"

Anybody would have thought she was the one having an affair. She was. An affair with herself.

Her vanity table became both an altar and an easel, she both artist and artifact, priestess and idol. Her duties were so many that even if she had not lingered lovingly over them they would have occupied most of her waking hours. Masked all morning while creams made from cucumbers, egg whites, oils from the glands of unaging turtles worked their wonders on her face, she attended to her hands. She laved them in lotions, filed, buffed and polished her nails, restrained with orangesticks the encroaching cuticles. After lunch came the ritual of the bath, after the bath, rubbing with oil, powdering, perfuming, depilating. Hair-grooming came next: washing, drying, brushing, combing, experimenting with new stylings. Then upon her pale unfeatured face she drew her likeness. Blackening the brows, shading the lids, drawing their outlines, darkening the lashes. An undercoat followed by coloring brought the skin alive, lipstick made the likeness speak. At night before bed it had all to be undone. Weather permitting, she went shopping every afternoon. She bought nothing but the best. Her reflection when she caught it in the mirrors of dressing rooms, in shop windows, told her that the best was what she deserved. On afternoons too hot to go out, after her bath, after making up, she stretched herself on her bed and, raising a leg and arching the foot, or raising her arms from the slender wrists of which the pale hands drooped like lilies, she thought that never had she seen such loveliness, and it was all her own. Sleeping Beauty with no fear of being wakened by the kiss of any Prince Charming.

So that, sitting in her parked car in the town's dark, deserted public square, she would be rigid with indignation enough for two. The indignation not just of a woman, a mother, one whose cooperation in order not to create a scene had been taken advantage of, but the indignation of an artist whose work had been vandalized, of a believer whose idol had been desecrated.

She would have been sitting there for some time already, not knowing what time it was, but she would know when 4 a.m. came because, seeing a car there at that hour, the town night watchman would come to investigate. This would be on the second of his three nightly tours through the square, the one that brought him in by the southwest corner where from its box on the wall of the bank he would take his clock key and put it in his clock, and then would see the car. To his question—Aaron Ashley's question—she had known him all her life—he had been the town night watchman for much of her life—what was wrong, she would say nothing was wrong, she was just waiting for the offices to open. That would be when he would look at his night watchman's clock that hung from his shoulder on a strap— it looked like the canteen carried by the marble Confederate soldier on his column in the center of the square—and ask if she had any idea what time it was? No, she would say, she had no idea. When he told her she would thank him.

She would be there when Aaron made his third and last tour of the night through the square and at that hour she would still be the only soul there. She would see, at dawn, the window-washer come with his pails and his long-handled sponge and squeegee and he would glance at her from time to time over his shoulder as he worked his way along the north side of the square washing the windows of those storekeepers there who subscribed to his services. She would be there when the first farmtrucks loaded with cotton came through on their way to the gin. She would see the first women come to the laundromat, and they would see her, and stare, and recognize, and gossip over their wash. The stores would begin to open—merchants with whom she traded. Then at exactly half-past seven, as he did every working day, the man she was waiting for would enter by the northwest corner and walk down the block to the middle of it and let himself in through the door on the frosted glass pane of which was lettered, FRANCIS J. FLEURNOY, ATT'Y AT LAW. She had chosen Judge Fleurnoy (the title was honorary; he was not a judge and never had been) because he better than any other would appreciate what she had endured. His dislike of Negroes went so far as to lead him once to hire a white housemaid. A white housemaid was an unheard-of thing, and all classes and both colors of the population were displeased, especially the women. The colored women felt that such work belonged by right to them, and looked down upon any white woman who would take it; the white women felt themselves implicated in this demeaning of a white woman—a girl from out of the deep piney woods with twins who between them had forty-eight fingers and toes but only one countable parent—and made life so miserable for her she had had to leave town.

"Are you a friend of my husband's?" she would begin by asking.

"Clyde? Why, I know Clyde," Judge Fleurnoy would say. "Known him all his life. Knew his old daddy before him. Old Dot-and—"

"Are you a friend of his?"

"Why, I've always managed to get along with Clyde. With all the Renshaw boys. Never had any—"

"I have to ask because I don't know who my husband's friends are."

After a moment then he would say, "Neither do I. Has he got any?"

"I want a divorce."

"Nothing easier."

"On grounds of—"

"Grounds? Sugar, where have you lived all your life? This is Texas. Does your husband snore in bed? Does he overcook the steak? I often wonder why people go to Mexico or Reno when here in Texas we have got the most liber—"

"I have got grounds. I have got grounds."

He would see then that he was dealing with an outraged woman, and he would say, "Adultery?"

"Is that what it's called when it's been going on for three years?" And she would not know where or when she

PROUD FLESH

had even heard the phrase but it would be there ready on demand and it would taste as sweet to her as its own venom in the mouth of a snake: "Alienation of affections."

"For that," he would say, tilting back his swivel chair, "you must be prepared to name a corespondent."

"Linda Carter," she would say. "Mrs. Linda Carter." She would let a moment pass, then would volunteer, "She's local."

"Is she?" he would say. "I don't believe I know her."

"You probably know her husband," she would say. Again she would let a moment pass. "Jug Carter?"

He would look blank for a while. He would be expecting a knock on the front door of his memory; it would take a while for him to realize that it was somebody at the back door. When he recognized who it was he would frown, but by the time he spoke he would be smiling. His smile would be fleeting and fatherly. He would compose his face as a father might to listen gravely to a child who was making a mountain out of a molehill.

"Eunice," he would say, trying to look grave but smiling with the corners of his mouth, parental, patient, wise, "Eunice, lawyers are not known for giving free advice, but let me give you a piece, will you?" He would look up at the clock on the wall. "The stores will be opening before long. Why don't you go and treat yourself at your husband's expense to a new fall outfit? Go get yourself a new permanent wave. Not that you need one, but just for the fun of it. It'll make you feel good. And let's both of us just forget that you were here this morning. Boys will be boys, Eunice, even when they get to be grown boys."

She had picked the wrong man. The Renshaws had this one buffaloed, as they did most men in town. "You don't want the case then?" she would say. "You're afraid of it."

"You haven't got a case," he would say.

Maybe not the wrong man, but she had picked the wrong lawyer. She would see then, and she herself would appreciate the irony, that this one, on whose sympathy and allegiance she had counted particularly, was too prejudiced against Negroes. He thought they were provided for just such sport as her husband was having, and further, that she lowered herself by conferring upon one the status of rival.

Then he would say, "Not a lawyer in this town would touch it. Not a judge would hear it."

White lawyers, that meant. The town had two colored ones. One was counsel for the plaintiff, the other for the defense, in disputes—nearly all settled out of court in the office of one or the other of them—among the colored people of the town. The revolutionary notion of going to one of them and becoming his first white client would then pass through her mind. Would pass rapidly through and out of her mind. If no white lawyer was going to risk making himself unpopular by pleading her case, no colored one was going to risk being run out of town.

"Now let's go back a bit," he would say. "If a divorce is what you're interested in, why, like I say, nothing is easier."

But she would not have worked herself up to brave the disgrace, the derision, the ostracism that she would face only now to take refuge in a charge of mental cruelty, incompatibility. A divorce was not all she was after now. She had been humiliated beyond bearing, she had been defiled by his mere touch, and the man must pay though it meant she pay along with him. She had already paid. For her it was enough that one person knew, and she had now told one. Had told one in whose face she could see how deeply she was disgraced. He could not conceal the disrespect he felt for a woman whose husband had left her for a colored woman.

No, she would say, a divorce was not all she wanted.
Then his look would be one not of disrespect but disgust.
Then she would see that his distaste was not for what her
husband had done to her but for what she was proposing to
do to him. Against a woman so demented by hatred and lust
for revenge he would stick by someone he disliked as much
as he did Clyde Renshaw. There was a code to govern a
woman's conduct in just her situation, and she had violated
the code. Convention decreed that she feign blindness to
what had been done to her. She was not up against the world
of lawyers but of men. When she came downstairs and out
into the sunny square she would feel that there was nothing
left for her to do but go home and kill herself. Then she
would feel that that was not left for her to do.

Thus on the following morning would end what would
begin in the night. When, desperate, he crossed the neutral
space of bed between them to his lawfully wedded wife and,
saying to himself, beggars can't be choosers, laid lover's
hands on her for the first time in four years. Saying, he provided her with a roof over her head and a car of her own,
three square meals a day and money to spend on clothes as
though there was no tomorrow, and for this what did he
get in return? He had his legal rights. She didn't have a
thing on him. He had admitted to nothing, had said nothing,
on that weekend three years ago. And, using the same words
he used to excuse himself with her opposite number, that
in the dark they all looked alike.

XIX

Cause it's mine. That's why. I'm going to need it for my old age, when I won't have nobody to take care of me."

He was responding to a question, or rather a taunt, from one or another of four people: Shug, Mr. Clyde, Ed Bing or Mr. Joe Bailey. The four people who boxed in his life like the walls of a cell, one of them always blocking him no matter which way he turned. The only people who ever spoke to him, they spoke only to taunt or to curse him. One or another of them, it did not matter which, had just said, "Jug, goddammit, what the hell do you need with that money anyway?" "It's mine. I earned it. I earn every nickel I get."

"Held out up to now," he said, replying to the question, "How much longer do you think your liver is going to hold out?" which had followed after, "Your old age? How much older do you think you're going to get?" "Held out up to now."

The year's crop of hay had been dug, peanut hay, dug with the nuts attached, from clay soil, dry now, so that there was dust in the air of the loft. God keep him from one of his sneezing fits. He could feel beginning to set in that stiffness of the joint where his skull and backbone met, which came, strangely enough, both when he was very drunk and when he was very dry, forerunner of a headache always, and which caused him such stabbing pain whenever he was seized by one of the sneezing fits he had been subject to for the past couple of years. He was up to nineteen sneezes, his record for a single bout, each one requiring that he blow his nose to keep from drowning, so that he was left dehydrated and limp from exhaustion. God keep him from one of those fits now. For it sounded when he got going like rapid-fire rifle practice, loud enough to be heard by everybody within three axle-greasings. God help him if anybody, meaning Mr. Clyde, should learn that he had spent the night here instead of at home where he was supposed, though he had never been told this, never needed to be told, to be chaperon to his wife, Clyde's woman.

The door of the barnloft had been taken off for ventilation so that in curing, the hay would not set itself on fire. It was hot in the loft from the heat of the curing hay. From his place in the hay he saw the last light go out in the big house. Instantly inside his head a neon light flashed on saying, OPEN ALL NIGHT! Steel balls bounced off the walls of his skull, dropped into holes, tapped out scores while colored lights popped. A warped record on a nickelodeon played at top volume a medley of comic drunkard's songs. Show me the way to go home I'm tired and I want to go to bed I had a little drink about an hour ago and it went right to my head how dry I am how dry I am nobody knows how dry I am yo ho ho you and me little brown jug how I love thee

hand me down my bottle of corn and I'll get drunk as sure
as you're born for all my sins are taken away taken
away . . .

A little drink was all he had had, and it was more than
an hour ago. What he had had to drink was just enough to
raise a thirst. All he had drunk was a pint of Bing's Tea,
as it was known among the colored population of the
county: a mixture of equal parts of caramel-flavored California sherry and sulphur-flavored water from Ed Bing the
bootlegger's artesian well. It was Jug's fate to be a drunkard
in a dry county. *Ed Bing:* that had ceased to be a man's
name and became a trademark, so that it was all right for
Jug to think of him that way, and even to call him that to
his face, omitting the "Mister." Mr. Joe Bailey had administered that pint of watered wine to him in homeopathic
doses, trying to prime the pump of his memory. It had worked
sometimes. Total amnesia would blanket his brain like dust,
obliterating all his recent footprints, but a sprinkling of Ed
Bing's adulterated sherry falling upon it would reveal them
and he could retrace his steps to the very spot where he had
hidden that money three, four or five days earlier. It had
not worked today, and Mr. Joe Bailey was running out of
patience, and credit. He had not been paid his bill in a
month.

"And suppose I was to? Then where would you be?
Who would you get to take my place?" he asked Mr. Clyde,
who had said, "Instead of hiding half of your money and
then not being able to find it again, why don't you drink it
all up and get it over with once and for all instead of this
slow drowning in the stuff?" "Nobody. That's who. If you
don't know it then let me tell you. Not another man would
put up with what I do. Is it any wonder if I take a little drink
from time to time?"

"I must have been. I must have been otherwise I wouldn't have," he said. This was in response to Mr. Clyde's saying, "You had been drinking for twenty-five years when you came here. You were drunk when you agreed to it." "I must have been," he said. Below him the cows snuffled and blew snorts and rattled the bars of their stanchions. He heard from time to time the plop of their dung on the barn floor.

"No, I can't. Not any more. And you know it. It was a time when I could have. But now I got too much money on this place to leave. Until I find it."

He had led Mr. Joe Bailey around today making a show of looking for the money in order to get that watered wine, and vaguely hoping, as he always did, to stumble upon the hiding place, or if not it, then one from some other of the many weeks when he had been unable to find it afterward. He had tried to shame Mr. Joe Bailey, saying this was no time to come dunning him when there was sickness on the place. But this, the third straight week that he had been unable to find his money, was the fourth straight week that his bill at Bailey's Gen'l Store had gone unpaid. Jug's one creditor (Ed Bing, whose second best customer Jug was, only Ross Renshaw being a better one, would not have let him have a drop on credit if he were in the throes of delirium tremens), Mr. Joe Bailey said of Jug, "He ain't a bad nigger. Drinks, yes, but knows his weakness and makes provision accordingly. He'll pay me what he owes me as soon as he finds where he's put his money." This did not keep Mr. Joe Bailey from cursing Jug to his face; it was how he explained to others his willingness to lend credit to somebody to whom nobody else would. Sometimes it might take Jug a little longer than at other times, but sooner or later he always did find or suddenly remember where he had hidden that half of his weekly pay from himself so that when he woke up thirsty he would not be able to go on drinking. "My daddy kept his in a saving account once. 1932. And I had a friend once that kept his in a bank that the president embezzled everything in it."

But with the passage of time Jug had used up a great many hiding places. It got harder and harder for him to outsmart himself. For also with the passage of time his thirst grew, making him more desperate, more determined, and thus more clever at finding his money when he came to, mouth parched, head splitting, stomach heaving, on Monday morning. Also he had to change his hiding place often to keep others from finding his money. Sometimes he did find it while drunk and then he was drunk all week long. This affected his memory. For these reasons now about every other week Jug was unable to find where he had hidden that seventeen dollars and fifty cents. Once or twice while looking for what he had hidden the Friday before, Jug found money he had hidden weeks, even months before. Generally, however, if not found the following week the money was never found.

"They after it, all right. Ain't I been up now all night for three nights chasing them off? All day long trying to find it my own self, then up all night trying to keep them cottonpicking thieves from finding it. Yeah, they looking for it."

Among the local Negroes and among the annual migrant workers estimates of the amount of Jug's money buried like a dog's meatbones around the Renshaw place ran into the thousands of dollars. It was universally held that as its original owner had had his chance and failed to find it, this money now belonged to whomsoever did. Time had reclaimed this wealth and made it into a natural deposit, the prize of him who was smart enough, and hard-working enough, to find it.

Show me the way to go home . . . He had been hoping without much hope that tonight she would take pity on him. She could when it suited her. Though she knew how to make being kind to him more bitter than when she was out to devil him. She could be as cruel as a cat and drive him out of the house and when he came home drunk he might wake to find that she had undressed him and put him to bed and bandaged a cut he had gotten somehow and that she had done him that kindness than which to a drunk there is none greater: left him a shot by the side of the bed for when he came to with the shakes. Then when he tried to thank her she would laugh a laugh that split his head and say she knew nothing about how he had gotten to bed, that in his drunkenness he had put himself to bed without knowing it. Before she would put him to bed he could sleep in the gutter for stray dogs to piss on him. If a car was to run over him there and kill him she would dance at his funeral.

It was not just for his drinking that Shug was punishing him when she drove him out of the house. It was not just for his part in their three-way arrangement. It was for knowing what he knew about her. Not his knowing about her carrying-on. That in his up-all-night out-all-day patrol of the property to find or to protect his hidden money he had seen things, things he alone had seen. She was not afraid of his telling Mr. Clyde what he knew. She knew he never would tell, but that was because he was afraid of Mr. Clyde; she would not have cared if he had. She was not afraid of that straight razor Mr. Clyde wore on a string around his neck, and which she must have seen every time he took his shirt off. She probably lusted to have him cut a man over her. There were women like that and she was one of them if ever there was one. No, what Shug could not forgive him for was knowing her secret, although she herself had revealed

it to him, had, in fact, forced it on him against his will. He
had troubles enough of his own. He wanted only a quiet
life and money enough to get soused on weekends, not
choosey even about his poison, grateful for the rawest rotgut.
He did not want to know anybody's secrets. Especially not a
woman's. Especially not anything involving a woman and
white folks. Especially when the white folks involved was
the man on whom he was dependent for that quiet life, that
weekly souse. Certainly he could not be of any help to her
with her problem. But nobody could be of any help to her,
and there he was, in the house, available, a man old enough
to be the father she did not have to turn to, legally, if only
legally, her husband. To whom else could she lay bare her
heart? To whom else try to explain what she could not explain to herself: that she loved the man who had raped her?
At least, rape was what it was called when it happened to a
white girl—what to call it in her case she did not know.
That she loved him because of what he had done to her. Not
just because he had forever in his keeping the trophy of her
maidenhead, but because in cutting her off from her family,
from her people, from the children she might have had, he
had left her with no one but him to love.

He was tired and he wanted to go to bed. Tonight he
had reached the point where he did not care if somebody else
found and stole his money and he was hoping she would
take pity on him, that is, ignore him. She could see by looking, anybody could, what state he was in. He was filthy, he
stank. Lack of sleep and the need of a drink made his eyes
smart and water continually and his hands to shake uncon-
trollably. He was hoping for a bath and a shave and a night's
sleep in bed. Or rather, on the living room couch which was
his bed. He had never needed to be told that the double bed
in the bedroom was as much off-limits to him as was the

downstairs at the picture-show even though the Colored sign had been taken down from over the door leading to the balcony. He had not even needed to tell Mr. Clyde that he understood this without being told. No provision of the understanding between them had had to be spoken.

Show me the way to go home. Home to that little bungalow, his wedding present, meant as a symbol to the world of Clyde Renshaw's respectability, and which she had so transformed that all it needed now was a red light over the door to look like a cathouse. Her destruction of that place had begun the first time she ever set foot in it. That was on her wedding night, when, uncarried over the threshold by her bridegroom—she all but carrying him, in fact—she had kicked in the new screen door. He had sobered and fled. Between that first night and this one, of the nights he could remember at all, he could not remember how many he had spent here in the hayloft. As many as at home, at least. Sweltering in the heat of summer nights and shivering in the cold of winter ones. He used to sleep under bridges, in storefronts and backalleys, when he was single; now that he was married and had a home of his own he slept in the barn loft. That wedding night the lights had blazed in the bungalow while the crash of objects against the walls and through the windowpanes went on into the small hours. The broken panes she stuffed with wads of newspaper. Within days the back door was in tatters, the gate of the prim white picket fence hanging loose from its upper hinge, the trim little yard littered with trash. He had tried to keep a step behind her destruction, knowing that he, old drunk and stumblebum that he had been, still was, would get the blame for its deterioration, but she wrecked it faster than he could repair it. The anger and defiance that she had no one to take out on she vented upon the unresisting house. "Get this place looking right yet!" she would say through gritted teeth as she committed her latest act of vandalism. "Get this place to looking like what it is!"

That was the home he had gone to because he was tired and wanted to go to bed. He might have known she would pick tonight to devil him. She had come in at once, as he was stretching himself out on the couch, having decided to forego the bath and shave; she was wearing nothing but a petticoat through which neither brassiere nor underpants was visible. Humming a little tuneless tune, rolling her eyes and leering at him, she began to dance, slow and suggestive, twining her arms as if they longed to be filled with a partner. He was already groping for his clothes.

"If you are bashful," she said, "then it's up to me to help you," and she began to wriggle out of her petticoat like a snake shedding its skin, peeling it down from the top. In his shirt now, he was struggling to draw his pants on. "Don't be scared," she whispered. "It's only little me. I won't hurt you. It's your little wife, your own little loving wife that you never have claimed yet."

He dared not call her to her face the name which he was shouting at her in his mind. He dared not let her know that he knew what she was. He dared not let anybody know that he knew that. Clyde Renshaw would kill the man whom he suspected of knowing what Jug knew about his, Jug's, wife. He could not talk back to her at all. The only thing he could do, perishing for sleep as he was, was to get into his clothes as quick as he could and not risk being found by Clyde Renshaw with his shirttails out alone in the house with her naked. For naked she was now, just about, and saying, sneering, "Hangs on you like an old sock, I bet, don't it? I bet it wouldn't rise and stand if you was to play 'The Star-Spangled Banner.' When was the last time you got it up?

Can you remember? Who was President?" And then standing before him bare and twenty in the pool of her petticoat while he struggled with his zipper, "Why, what is that I see? Can it be? Why, I do believe you is got some jizzum left in you, after all."

XX

The man's naked body lay on the bed where it had fallen with blood gushing from the cut and the severed windpipe wheezing. Hers too wheezed now and down over her slate-colored breasts and in the parting of her breasts her blood ran red. She could see it with her eyes shut. Next time she must keep them open until they shut by themselves. Now she could see it with them shut.

He had just left and as she stood looking down at herself, at her body, naked now as it would be on that other night, and listening to him hurry across the porch in the dark, she knew that what she had done was a mistake. Not that it mattered tonight. Tonight was not the night. But not again. Better to have him right here in the house at the time, which from now on meant all the time. Not just better but essential. The thing that had been missing up to now. The thing that at last had broken that piece of twine on which the razor hung from around Clyde Renshaw's neck. Then it was like at the picture-show being shown in the prevues of coming attractions what you would be seeing later on.

If he had been hesitating to snap that string so that what would be an instant when the time came had lengthened into weeks, it was not for lack of the will to do it. He was no coward. Her man was no coward. He was a hero. During the war, in Germany, when he was hardly more than a boy, he had killed men by the carload for no cause at all. It was not mercy that had stayed his hand on that razor up to now. Expect more mercy from a cottonmouth moccasin than from that man. It was his fear of the publicity that had had to be overcome, and an instant was all the time there was to do it in. She herself could not then say to him, "Go ahead. Remember Jug"—not even if in that instant he permitted her to say anything. How, in that split second when he was not going to be able to remember anything, not even that his name was Clyde Renshaw, to make him remember her husband? Until now the best idea she had been able to come up with had been to have a picture taken of Jug and put it near the bed somewhere so he would see it, take it in, in that instant while he was hesitating. But he was not going to be in a state to take in anything. He was going to be blind with rage. But if he himself on his way to the bedroom had just the instant before passed Jug lying on the couch dead to the world then he would not need to be reminded of him. Just one question remained—one quickly answered: would her husband's being there right in the room next to them scare away this whatshisname? Not if she saw to it that her husband was out cold, and nothing could be easier than that. She must change her ways, beginning tomorrow. Must make a happier home life for her husband and keep him in with her at night. Give him plenty of what he liked best. She would see Ed Bing tomorrow.

Meanwhile never mind. Tonight let him sleep in the barn. Clyde Renshaw had other things on his mind tonight— if Clyde Renshaw could get his mind on other things even tonight—and would have for some time to come. But once the old lady was dead and the funeral over and everybody gone home and only her own folks and Mr. Clifford were left on the place, then he would not have to care so much about appearances. Then he was going to get a lot bolder. Especially if between now and then she never let him set eyes on her. She knew her man. He was a man—man enough for two. She hoped his old mother was a long time dying— let him get his battery really charged. She hoped so anyway —long and painful. She was not dead yet. If she had died then all the lights would be on up there instead of just one.

How everything that happened now seemed to fit into its place! This sickness of the old lady's: she had not expected that, yet now it seemed as if she had known to count on it. There was no longer any backing out, if there ever had been. It was going forward on its own momentum now. The neatness with which the pieces fit together, the logic with which one step led to the next, made it inevitable, irreversible.

Meanwhile knowing that the last piece of the puzzle had been found she could wait for it to happen with all the patience it might take. If not tonight, another night. If not with this one tonight then with one of the others, if she had to take them on one at a time until she had worked her way through the whole cottonpicking crew. If not this fall then next spring, if not next spring then next fall. The seed had been sown; now time would ripen it. Not even she could prevent it now, not even if she had wanted to. Past the time when it might have been aborted, it must grow in her now until it came to term. If she had conceived a mon-

ster, who was the father of it? For the act of love he might
see to it that she took the pill, but against lovelessness there
was no contraceptive.

Now knowing that it was all perfected she felt detached from it all, and a sort of cool excitement, like what
she imagined must be the pleasure in playing chess, came to
her in deciding the lives of the people in her life. In knowing that it would be she who was moving them on the board
even after she was no longer here. It was a sense of power,
and that was new to her—the first time she had ever felt a
sense of power over the life of another person—the first time
since Clyde Renshaw came into it that she had felt a sense of
power over her own life.

Contrary to appearances, she was actually providing for
her husband. Actually securing his future. Once the trial
was over and Jug acquitted, Clyde Renshaw would have him
attached to him for life like a ball and chain. If only Jug
would have the sense to plead guilty. Never mind: his lawyer
would enter a plea of guilty. Ironical to think that the only
way for Jug to escape punishment for the crime which he
was the last man on earth with any motive to commit was
to stand up in court and declare that not only had he done it,
he would do it again. She would have liked to be there to see
that. What was more, Clyde was going to have Jug tied to
him for longer than he might otherwise have had, for although he would go on trial for his life, Jug's life expectancy
was actually going to be lengthened by his experience. Jug
was going to take the cure, thanks to her, going to get dried
out, whether he wanted to or not. Because it was going to
take a while to find twelve men who had not already decided the case in Jug's favor, who, black or white, would
not have done what Jug had done, or at least want the
world to think they would have, and because (amazing how

she could see it all, down to the last detail!) because in jail was where Jug was going to have to spend his time while waiting to come to trial, not out on bail. The only man who might have gone his bail, Clyde Renshaw, was not going to. He would not dare.

She knew this was not the night but just another night, yet she wished that fool would come on now and get it over with for tonight. It was getting late. In the big house the last light had gone out.

Would the moonlight shine on the bed like this that night? Shine on her body like this and on the unlucky field-hand's who had been drawn into this net, as they stiffened there in their blood through the night while the drunken man with the blood on his hands slept on the couch in the next room and outside the white man kept watch, waiting for morning to come, making sure no one entered the house before him and discovered the crime and raised the cry? Would he be drawn in to look at the bodies once more? And would he know then that he had condemned himself to live until he died? That no matter how terrible his need he could never do as she had done. That even thirty years later, even following public disgrace and the loss of all hope, or suffering from some incurable disease, he still could not do it. There would still be people to remember and say that this proved those old whispers about that dead colored girl and the man she was found with in that cottage there on his place all those years ago.

It was as if she were standing now over the bloody bed and looking down at the mangled bodies and she pitied them both and wished she might have done something to save them. It was too late. It had always been too late, right from the start.

. . .

There was a schoolbus, but there had been incidents aboard it and while waiting for it, some name-calling, some rock-throwing, threats from the white upperclassmen, big football-squad farmboys, of worse things to come, so, in the pickup, Archie drove her to school in town each morning and came to get her each afternoon. She was waiting for him that day sitting on the schoolhouse steps with a group of boys her own color when Mr. Clyde drove up in his car. He said Archie was busy doing something that had to be finished before nightfall. He would drive her home today.

She got into the car and put her hand out the window to wave goodbye to the boys, and suddenly she knew that something was fixing to happen—fixing to happen to her. She saw it in those boys' faces and in the way they did not wave back to her. She did not know yet what it was but she knew it was already on its way toward her—like when a bird flies toward the shot already fired which the hunter has timed to meet it at a certain point in its path of flight. Something was fixing to happen to her, had already begun to happen. She did not just think so later on because of what had happened that day. She had seen something in those boys' faces that told her so, that made her stop eating the apple she was eating, saved from her lunch. The instant before she had been going along living the same life she had always lived; in those boys' faces she saw something that changed everything, that scared her and filled her with a feeling of . . . Homesickness. That was the only thing she could think to call it: homesickness. Looking back at them standing on the schoolhouse steps not waving to her as the car pulled away she felt like she imagined a person must feel on leaving home and being taken to another country where the people were of a different race and spoke a different language and looking back at her own people for the last time. She knew what those boys knew: that they were seeing her for the last time. She knew she had just spent her last day in school. She knew what was fixing to happen to her.

It was as if she had been given second sight. She saw it so clearly it was as if it had already happened. She was already changed by it. Nothing had happened, nothing had even been said, yet already she was a changed person, a stranger to her friends, to her family, to her people, a stranger to herself. And yet although it was as if it had already happened and she was now looking back on it, at the same time her mind was racing ahead trying to find some way to keep it from happening. I'll fight, she thought. I'll kick. I'll bite. I'll scream for help. I'll call Archie. Help, Archie!

Then she saw Archie. Saw him in her mind as clearly as if he were standing before her. His head was bowed. He would not look at her. Wait a minute, he seemed to be saying, and she would know why. Then she heard Mr. Clyde telling him that he would pick her up at school today and bring her home. She heard Archie say thanks, but he had other things to do in town this afternoon anyway, he could get her. She heard Mr. Clyde say no, he would pick her up this afternoon. She saw Archie straighten, stiffen. She saw him lock looks with Mr. Clyde. She held her breath. It was not for herself that she was in suspense. She had been shown what was fixing to happen to her; it was as if it had already happened. It was her brother for whom she held her breath, though she had been shown already what had happened to him, too. As when two men join hands and each tries to force the other's hand down to the tabletop, when her brother's look was forced down she saw two things at once, for they were one and the same thing: that she had lost her brother and that her brother had lost himself. He would never be able to look her in the face again because he would never again be able to look himself in the face.

Next she saw her mother waiting now for her to come home. She saw the two of them meeting when she got home late from school today, Friday, for the first time ever. She saw her mother trying not to plead with her eyes to be told it was not so. Then it was Monday and she heard herself tell her mother that she was not going to school today and she heard her mother not ask why. Then it was Tuesday and again she told her mother she was not going to school today. She was never going back to school: the silence between them after that would be lifelong. And hearing herself say that, it was as though her mind were a blackboard and an eraser had just been drawn across it, and all those shorthand symbols she had worked to memorize were wiped away and her mind was a slate-colored blank.

Again she saw in her mind those boys not waving goodbye to her from the schoolhouse steps. They seemed forever caught in that pose. Already they looked like an old faded snapshot with people in it who had once meant something to you but whose names you can no longer recall. None of those boys would ever come near her again. They would know better than to. Around her would be a fence with signs saying to them, "Posted. No trespassing." She would never have a husband, a home of her own—things she had been too young to want until now that she was too old ever to have them. The boss had singled her out to be his. His mark would be on her like a brand for all to see, or as if she wore a collar with a tag saying, "If strayed notify Clyde Renshaw, Prop."

Neither of them had said anything. When he turned the car off the highway and down a side road and then down a dirt road and when he stopped the car and switched off the engine they still said nothing. They sat in the car staring out the windshield, not looking at each other, waiting for it to happen. There was a clock on the dashboard and the minute hand did not sweep smoothly like the hand on other clocks but jerked itself forward to the new minute with a little click each time. It was probably not noticeable ordinarily but now each click was as loud as a faucet dripping in the night, and with each one she made an uncontrollable little click in her throat. She could remember thinking that if she could just break the crystal and grab hold of that minute hand and hold it, then the time would never come for what was fixing to happen to happen. She knew how foolish a notion that was and yet she had felt the urge to do it.

Then she commenced to cry. She made no noise, just shed her tears silently. She was already somebody else, not herself any more, somebody she did not know and was afraid to be, and she was crying for the girl that in a minute she would never be again. She too was now like an old snapshot in an album. She was somebody she used to know.

And still they sat there just looking out the windshield at the low woods, the brown fields, the crows in the leafless trees. It was as if both knew it had to happen but neither knew how to get it started. She was waiting for him to do the first thing. Finally she sighed and dried her eyes and laid her half-eaten apple on the dashboard as if she meant to finish it afterward and blew her nose on the handkerchief he lent her. She was the one to get out of the car first.

It all happened in silence. He gave her no commands; there was no need for him to. She made no protest; it would have done no good. There was nothing to say. They might have been two deaf mutes. Or they might have been actors in a silent film. It was more like that. She could almost see it happening to two other people as she looked on, like watching a silent film on television. The only sound anywhere at all was the cawing of the crows as they flapped by overhead.

Did she now pretend that she had not also been flattered? He could have had any he wanted and he had chosen her. Her brother's boss, her mother's boss, the boss of that gang that came each year to work his land, an older man, married, rich, white, and he had chosen her, who had never been farther from home than Barry's Gap. She had not known that he had ever even noticed her.

When he got done she lay on the ground and could not get up. She wanted never to go home again. She wanted never to see her mother and Archie again. She wanted to beg him to send her away somewhere so she would never have to see them again. She could not bring herself to look down at herself. She had sensed before it happened that she was about to be taken from her family, her friends, her own people—now she learned that she had been taken from herself. She did not belong to herself any more. She was his. Until now she had been her own to give to some man of her own choosing one day.

At her wedding she wore her mother's gown. No private ceremony before a justice of the peace for her; a girl got married only once. She was a storybook bride—a sad story. Just seventeen and marrying a man nearly three times her age. Her husband had been a mystery man at first, although actually well known, a man about town. Of the people who got announcements none could place him. Until she took it, nobody knew he even had a last name.

So sad, said everybody, to see a young girl throwing herself away like that. She had a family—self-respecting people —how could they have let her do it? Their disapproval of the match and their unhappiness was plain for all to see. Why had they not set their foot down and forbidden it?

The bride was given away by her brother. When the preacher said, "Do you, Walter, take this woman—" the groom himself had not known for a moment who was meant. Until then nobody knew he had a first name, either.

If only he had touched her as she lay there unable to get up that day. Just touched her. Not kissed her. She never expected that. She knew better than that. Just touched her. Shown her that she was not ugly to him. Maybe then she would not have been so ugly to herself. If only he had not just pulled away and rolled off and stood up, as he still did every time, as if he never wanted to see her again. Like a man with the taste in his mouth of the cigarette he has just crushed out, one who would like to break the habit but lacks the will and despises himself for his weakness.

Lying there on her back while the crows flapped and cawed overhead she heard something hit the ground softly, like a ripe, a rotten-ripe fruit falling from a tree, and turned her head to look. At first she did not know what the thing was. It looked like a toy balloon with its air gone out of it. Not like a balloon that has never been blown up but wrinkled like one that has been and its air gone out. Then, though it was the first one she had ever seen, she knew what it was, and what the stuff was that came oozing out of it. Until then she had been a child herself and had not known that she might want children. There on the ground lay her children, like a gob of spit.

When the knock she was awaiting sounded softly on the back screen door she rose and went to answer it. She could see no one, nothing, in the shadows.

"Who is it?" she asked.

Her trick did not work. He said, "Who is it! What you mean, who is it? Who would it be?"

What was this one's name? Quick! Luther? Buck? Leroy? Henry? No matter. "Come in this house, tiger," she said, unhooking the latch.

XXI

All the windows and windowshades were raised, for the heat was stifling. When the last light in the house had been put out only the dim blue light of the sickroom was left to burn through the night like a pilot light for all the extinguished lights.

The blue sickroom light: an ordinary bulb wrapped around with the paper covering from a roll of absorbent cotton. Indigo blue. Soft on sensitive or sleeping eyes, inspiring silence, tiptoes, whispers. Traditional. It colored all Amy's childhood memories of sickness. Nowadays it was confined to farm families, or, among her patients, to families not long off the farm. Her childhood association of it with pain and fear had never left her. Yet that sickly blue light had been the beacon that drew her to her life's work. How many nights she had spent in near-darkness at the bedside of some sick or dying person! Sometimes when she left home on a case and moved in with a patient, the dim light of the sickroom was the only light she saw by for weeks, even months. She had learned to see like a cat in that half-light. It had become her habitat. Here in this indigo obscurity was where it had all begun.

What she was doing now was what Amy did all the time: private night nursing in patients' homes. It was the best paying kind of nursing because in all other ways it was the least rewarding kind, and most nurses refused to do it. It was lonely work, monotonous, generally depressing. Most of your patients were old people, many of them terminal cases, sent home to die from hospitals crowded for beds. But the main reason most nurses refused the work was that the hours made it impossible to have any family life. She and Ira rarely saw each other. Fortunately Ira was very self-sufficient.

Amy disliked her work for other reasons than the separation from her husband and being deprived of a family of her own. To sit all night long night after night in light too dim to read by, in silence and alone, without a radio or television set and unable to walk about for fear of disturbing the patient, with nothing to distract your mind and keep you alert and yet having to keep alert for any change in the patient's condition, required the self-discipline of a yogi, the serenity of a saint. People asked her how she stood it, why she did it. She did it because somebody had to do it, and because the appreciation she got from her patients and their families helped a little to make up for feeling unappreciated by her mother and taken for granted by her sisters and brothers. And because it was how she earned the money to help out her insufficiently grateful sisters and brothers and keep them from going to their mother whenever they needed help.

To sleep while the world went about its business and wake while the world slept turned everything topsy-turvy.

And the silence and the dimness and the isolation of those sickrooms made her waking hours into a kind of sleepwalking. She had forgotten how to speak above a sickroom whisper. Sometimes she felt that she hardly lived on the same planet as other people.

Today she had seen her shadow. For her that was a thing to notice. To most people their shadows were a part of themselves. She came out into the sunshine so seldom that seeing her shadow was about like the groundhog's seeing his. The sight of it today had prompted her again to wonder whether her contrary way of living had had its origin in a contrariness in her origin. Had her parents conceived her during the daytime? Was she, their first, when they were new to each other, young and ardent, the child of an urge that could not wait until nightfall, and had this had an influence upon her? By turning night into day was she seeking to right their turning day into night when they begot her? It was a silly notion, like astrology, like your horoscope, yet she wondered about it and would have liked to ask her mother about it. Strange to think that one's conception was a private matter between strangers, one's parents, and that one might not ask about it, must blush for being curious about it.

All those many long, lonely nights in other sickrooms had been in preparation for this night. It seemed to Amy now that this was the occasion for which she had become a nurse. She had saved, or helped save, many lives, all strangers to her; now had come the time to save the life that meant the most to her. The family was depending upon her. They slept, knowing that Amy was at her post.

All her professional life had been in preparation for this —and never had she felt so unprepared. It was as if all that she had been taught, all that she had learned through practice, had been erased from her mind, leaving it as blank and

gray as a clean blackboard. Like a nurse fresh out of intern-
ship and on her first case alone, she imagined every compli-
cation in the textbooks about to arise all at once and she tried
to think what she should do and all she could think to do
was cry for help. One of her untrained sisters or one of the
house servants could cope as well with any emergency that
might now arise as Amy felt herself able to do.

She was doing what she knew how to do, what she had
had years of experience in doing, and doing it for the person
whom she was most eager to do it for, most grateful to be
able to do it for: why, she wondered, was she so anxious, so
apprehensive—and then wondered why she had wondered.
Had she not reason enough to be anxious and apprehensive?
What greater calamity could befall her than to lose Ma? Yet
she felt a sense of foreboding not entirely to be accounted
for by her dread of her mother's death. Terrible as that was
to contemplate, she felt a foreboding that her mother's death
would be succeeded by something else, something equally
terrible, though she could not imagine what that might be
and was appalled to find that she could suppose anything
might be equally terrible. A feeling of great oppression
weighed upon her. She had difficulty drawing her breath.
Her heart was in constant tension. Moments of dizziness, of
faintness would come over her, moments when she did not
know where she was or who she was or why she was who
she was and not somebody else. Soul-sickening moments of
dislocation when she would have to reach out and grasp the
nearest thing to steady herself, to recover herself. This would
be followed by a feeling that she could only call "disgust,"
though why disgust, disgust at what, she could not explain.
But it was disgusting. She felt as if she had been turned inside out. As if her very soul had soured and risen like gorge
in her mouth. She kept feeling an urge to confess to some-

thing, so strong an urge that she would have confessed to anything, but she did not know what to confess to. She did not know what she meant by it, yet she said to herself, "I am ready. I have done all I can do. If that is not enough . . ." and along with this a panicky sense that she was not ready at all and that she had not done all she could do—but what was it she had not done?

They say it is essential to a patient's recovery that he have full confidence in his doctor and his nurse. Those who say that are not doctors and nurses and do not realize that that confidence is equally necessary to the doctor and the nurse. Let them feel the lack of it and their self-confidence diminishes, and with it some portion at least of their skill. Amy knew that Ma lacked confidence in her. She was in dread of Ma's waking and seeing in whose sole care she had been put.

It was in this very room, and when Amy was just starting out as a nurse, that her mother first refused her care. It was at the birth of her baby brother, Kyle.

That had been a worrisome delivery, a messy delivery, one necessitating an episiotomy, and still the baby could not get born, for it was a big one, and the mother, past the age for this and deathly afraid, was too tense in body and mind to cooperate with the doctor. Too late, he, Dr. Metcalf, saw that he ought to have been more firm in insisting that she go to the hospital—then newly built—and have a Caesarean despite her sentimental attachment to the room and the bed in which all her other children had been born, and never have risked such an incision as he had just made under conditions as primitive, potentially as septic, as these. His task was not lightened any by the corps of volunteer female assistants hovering about being helpful with advice and hot water. The two Negro women were worse than useless, the older one,

Rowena, because she refused to take seriously this increasingly serious situation, and who fancied she was cheering the patient on by pshawing at the whole business and boasting of how easily she had gotten through it; the younger one, Eulalie—because she was young and scared half to death by what she was seeing—almost required medical attention herself when that incision was made. And all this while right in the house there had been a graduate nurse. Once reminded, Dr. Metcalf remembered that she had recently finished her training. Let Amy be sent for at once. The moment was critical; to its mother's extreme discomfort, the baby was beginning at last to emerge.

Amy came without being sent for. Trained to know all the things that could go wrong, and sensing that this was taking far too long, she came just then on her own, meeting Eulalie at the door going to fetch her. Her entrance caused a most unexpected and shocking scene, a scandalous scene, painful for all present, for Amy devastating.

When she saw her eldest child at the foot of her bed Edwina Renshaw shot her such a hostile glare that all the women—Dr. Metcalf was too occupied just then to notice—snapped around to look. Gasping with pain and unable to speak, Edwina tried to rise, pushing back against the headboard, clutching for the bedclothes to cover herself with, pointing a finger at arm's length at Amy. She gave a growl, then in a voice that must surely have carried to her men down around the pear tree, she yelled, "You get out of here! Get her out of here! *Get her out of here!*"

Even Dr. Metcalf forgot his pressing duties for a moment to gape in astonishment. No one knew where to look for embarrassment. As for Amy, she was powerless to move. Stunned speechless and perishing of shame, she stood trembling like a puppy punished for it knows not what offense.

Then it was as if it had happened all over again as the full force of it struck her mind. She fended off a woman who advanced as though to steady her before she should faint and fall to the floor. She could feel a smile twitching upon her lips, and she heard herself, accompanied by her baby brother's first cry, whimper like a beaten and bewildered puppy. She shuddered, turned, and glided from the room on steps as trancelike as a sleepwalker's.

A nervous collapse that put her to bed struck Amy later that day, triggered when, returning home from a long solitary, rambling walk, she had come upon Rowena burying something wrapped in bloody newspaper in the manure pile at the foot of the garden, and realizing what it was, turned sick, then while making her way to the house to lie down, had seen the sodden mattress from her mother's bed lying on the grass where it had been brought to be scrubbed and aired, and, flapping on the clothesline, her bedsheet, which despite boiling in lye soap, still showed a large pinkish stain.

Not even the joyful news that the baby was a big bouncing boy, and that despite the hard delivery both mother and child were doing well, could dispel the hush that enveloped the house as it puzzled over Edwina's unprovoked and shocking outburst. To Amy it seemed to be a house silenced by second thoughts about her. Could something so shocking be unprovoked? That was the question she heard people asking one another, or asking themselves, in the silence that surrounded her. She shrank from being seen, even by the servants. What may have been intended as looks of sympathy seemed to her looks of wonder, of speculation— even of sudden awful enlightenment. And if she was wrong, and they were looks of sympathy, the question remained, sympathy for what? For being misunderstood and mistreated, or for having some hidden, some hushed-up affliction, some mental or moral deformity unknown to herself, exposed to view?

"Amy!" she could hear people saying. "Amy? If it had been any one of the other girls . . . But Amy?" Of course, such a scene was unthinkable between Ma and any of her daughters. But the distinction a person who might say that was trying to make was that it was most unthinkable of all for it to be Amy. Amy was devoted to Ma. Devoted to her. To have identified Amy to a recent acquaintance of the family who had asked which one she was, anybody would have said, "Amy is the one who is so devoted to her mother." And surely the person would have said, "Oh, yes. That one."

And, until now, might have added that that one was evidently her mother's favorite, too.

And to a recent acquaintance that might very well have seemed to be the case, although only to a recent acquaintance. Someone for whom Ma was putting on what she herself called her "parlor manners." Outside the parlor her feelings for Amy were perhaps not quite so warm and tender, as those who knew her better all knew. It was ironical: Ma demanded, and got, tireless devotion from all her children, but the one she got the most from . . . well, she seemed somehow to find Amy's tireless devotion tiresome. To be sure, Amy was perhaps excessively, maybe even annoyingly attentive. It was not that she wanted more than her share of Ma's love; it was just her share that she wanted, and Ma made her work harder for her share than she did the others. To be always told what a treasure she had in Amy must have seemed to Ma to imply a disparagement of her other eight— now nine—children, and perhaps she somewhat resented Amy for this. That was contrary of Ma. She was contrary; she admitted it—though there was perhaps a touch of self-complacency in the admission. Ma did expect to be forgiven

easily for her little faults. She did not expect to be judged
very severely for her contrariness. Indeed, she thought it was
rather lovable. Even rather adorable. And Amy did not stint
in her adoration.

Now this unexpected scene, this unprovoked and shocking, this humiliating scene. Amy felt herself disowned. Shut
up in her room alone, confined to her bed, ashamed to be
seen, the house whispering all around her, she felt herself to
be in a maze, a puzzle. But unlike a puzzle, in which one
starts at the edge and tries to find the path to the center,
Amy was at the center and found her way repeatedly
blocked as she tried to get out to the edge.

So Dr. Metcalf had a third patient to see when he came
on one of his postnatal visits to the mother and the new
child. Not on his first such visit, nor his second, nor even his
third, because Amy insisted there was nothing the matter
with her, that she was just resting, and forbade Eulalie to
speak to the doctor about her. But on the fourth day, when
she still had not left her room, Eulalie disobeyed her orders
and sent the doctor in to see her.

What could a doctor prescribe for a patient suffering
from rejection and public humiliation by the person she
loved most? It was her dread of seeing anybody that had kept
her shut up, especially of seeing anybody who had been a
witness to her mortification. The doctor's intrusion was un-
bearably embarrassing and she was infuriated with Eulalie.
Aware that she must look haggard—perfectly ghastly—she
protested that there was nothing the matter with her. She
felt naked. As if he were examining her with her clothes off.
She shrank from his quizzical gaze. He did not help her out
any. When she asked brightly after Ma his reproving silence
and his searching look crushed her. He conjured up an image
of the new mother with her baby guzzling at her breast un-

embarrassed by any self-reproaches for the way she had treated anybody in the world while she, Amy, was ashamed to hold up her head, and left her feeling crushed with neglect and self-pity. It all embarrassed her even in an impersonal way. How embarrassing for a stranger to have witnessed such a scene in a family that prided itself on its solidarity! And yet she was very glad to see the doctor. Really overjoyed. Grateful to Eulalie for sending him to her. She was eager to assure him that nothing was the matter with her and to excuse Ma's conduct.

She assured the doctor that Ma was now suffering the most awful pangs of remorse and she begged him to tell her the next time he saw her that she must not do that. That she, Amy, had forgotten all about it, and that she, Ma, must forget it too and think of nothing now but herself and the baby.

And what apology, what explanation for her behavior could she have given? It was something she could not explain to herself. It was something that needed no explanation. It was just one of those outbursts, momentary, impersonal—completely impersonal—unaccountable, attributable to nerves and—but who knows what makes us do some of the things we do? And at the same time there was a perfectly rational explanation for it. Or rather, not rational, not rational at all, just the reverse, but perfectly understandable and even admirable, or if not exactly admirable, certainly very excusable and even very endearing. Modesty. Plain, old-fashioned modesty—something the women of Ma's generation had so much more of than those of Amy's own emancipated, not to say abandoned, one did. To give it its right name: prudishness. True, Ma had never been typical of her generation in that particular before; on the contrary, she would have been called anything but prudish. But consider the circumstances. She had never been put in such an embarrassing, such an awkward and undignified and although at first it might sound paradoxical, such an unmotherly position before. Possibly even "modesty," even "prudishness," did not cover all the subtleties of this most unusual and delicate situation. Perhaps there was something here that could not be put into words. Something touching upon some old deep-seated superstition or taboo, something akin to Noah's shame at being seen naked in his tent by his son, Ham. Though to be sure, Noah was not in hard labor at the time but was drunk, and Ham was not a registered nurse.

She blamed herself. She ought to have heeded the inner voice that had warned her to stay away from her mother's room. She had had a premonition that something like this would happen. Something untoward and unpleasant. It was this, no doubt, that accounted for her having waited until the last minute before going. Of course she could not have foreseen what did happen, but she had definitely felt reluctant to go. Ma was right. Ma was always right. Her being there was improper.

What significance was there in the fact that while she searched for far-fetched and occult explanations of Ma's treatment of her there had been all along a simple and natural and very touching one? Ma had wanted to spare Amy, as she would any child of hers, the sight of her travail, and the self-reproach which the sight would entail. What child, seeing what Amy had seen, its mother's swollen, split, bleeding body, could ever forgive itself for having caused her that pain? What child, once it knows how babies are made and how born, can ever again feel that it was wanted, that it was sent for, not the byproduct of a moment's passion, the punishment for a moment's pleasure? The significance of the fact that Amy sought other, out-of-the-way explanations while that obvious and comforting one was there all along, was that she did not believe it. It was inadequate to the vehemence of that *"Get her out of here!"*

Throughout all the succeeding years, extending right up to the present moment here in the same room, there were times when her remembrance of that penetrating glare, that pointed finger, that piercing cry, "You get out of here!" and even worse, that appeal to the others present to *"Get her out of here!"* stripped all Amy's explanations from her and drove them before it like dry leaves in a winter wind, leaving her bare and huddling. In an unguarded moment her mother had revealed a distrust, a dislike—a hatred of her. No matter how she tried, nothing Amy could do could change that fact. Then with a patient sigh she would tell herself that this was her cross to bear through life. Every person had his. Hers was—and the very irony of it made it seem like something fated—to be, every minute of her life, in every cell of her being, a daughter, a daughter decreed and born, as some people are born fools; to be a daughter such as other mothers dreamed of having, and to have been given to the one mother whom nothing she did could please, one who welcomed, demanded, from all her other children the very idolatry that Amy was so eager to bestow upon her, but spurned hers as the Lord spurned Cain when he offered Him the fruits of the ground.

That scene in her mother's bedroom, and its aftermath, had had more to do than her horoscope with the shape that her career, then just beginning, had taken. Not that she had ever dreamed of being a Florence Nightingale or an Edith Cavell, but she had hoped to find in nursing a more varied life than her life in nursing had been, and surely Ma's exposure of her to all those people that day in her bedroom had confirmed in her a tendency toward loneness. She had

never been outgoing; after that it was harder still for her to
meet the world. In her case to meet the world would have
meant working on a hospital staff or in a doctor's office, and
now she shrank from that, preferring instead to work as a
private nurse in people's homes, alone and at night. Certainly
that bedroom scene and the ones that followed it, what she
saw in the garden, the blood-stained bedclothes, had given
her a distaste for obstetrics, work which she would have had
to do in a hospital—who knew? maybe it had contributed to
her lack of desire for children of her own. As her career was
her life, whatever shaped the first shaped the second, and
Amy had known from the start that choosing to be a night
nurse was to choose not to marry. It was one more inade-
quacy to feel before people, especially Ma, but she resigned
herself to life as a single woman. Luckily for them both, she
and Ira had found each other. They were meant for each
other. They fitted together like the two halves of a broken
dish. Like the two halves of a broken plate that had gotten dispersed and had miraculously been rejoined. Mended together, they made a presentable plate; they themselves knew
that the plate was for display only.

To Amy's distress, Dr. Metcalf that day had taken her
side, or what he thought was her side, against her mother. To
this day he still did that—or would have if Amy had let him.
She now declined to discuss Ma with him. She would tol-
erate no criticism of Ma, especially none made in her defense. She had made him promise that he would say nothing
about her to Ma and that whenever Ma asked about her he
was to say there was nothing the matter with her.

Why wait? said he.

Amy did not understand.

All right, he had said; when she asked him, that was
what he would tell her.

"Ah, you mean she hasn't asked about me," said Amy. "I was afraid you would say that. I was afraid you would say that. That shows how bad she's feeling. She's afraid to ask. You see, as I told you, she is full of—"

"Your mother," he said, "is full of—milk."

Disrespectful of her as it was, even she had laughed. Then suddenly the situation was exactly reversed. The same cast with their roles reversed. There was she in her sickroom with Dr. Metcalf attending her when the door opened and there, with her baby in her arms, stood Ma. Amy had shot her a glare, had pushed back against the headboard, had clutched at the bedclothes to hide herself. She had almost yelled, "You get out of here!"

Dr. Metcalf had risen at once to leave.

"Don't go!" she and her mother had cried as one. She would not have had it otherwise, but she could see that her mother had chosen a time when the doctor would be there so as not to be alone with her, that she had brought along the baby for added protection, though pretending that she had brought him to show Amy, and the bitterness of it she could almost taste. Ah, yes, she knew what bitterness was, though praised to her face so often for her sweetness. Hers, too, was a human heart, and in that poor soil grew more weeds than flowers. The weeds of resentment and jealousy, the weed—most noxious of them all—of self-righteous selflessness. She had tried simply to be a good gardener and root them out while they were still only seedlings.

It was the same situation only worse. To forestall what she dreaded most, that her mother apologize to her, or make a lame attempt to apologize to her, Amy had hurled herself at her feet. The memory of that moment even now was not to be borne. For instead of raising and embracing her, her mother had clutched her baby to her almost convulsively.

Totally bewildered, Amy had looked into her mother's pale, pained face and had seen that it took effort for her mother to face her. She forced herself to look into her mother's eyes, steeling herself to accept whatever reflection of herself she saw in them. She looked, and all the courage she had mustered was insufficient. What she saw was: nothing. What she saw was perplexity to equal her own. What she saw was a mirror image of her own distress. Her mother knew no more than Amy did what it was in her that she disliked, distrusted, feared. She could see that her mother—she for whom love of family came before love of God—was aghast that she should feel such unnatural feelings toward a child of hers, and to be unable to find any reason for it. For a moment Amy pitied her mother, and her pity deepened her fear. Her fear was fear for herself, but even more it was fear of herself. She felt herself to be under some congenital curse and powerless to lift it, even to know what it was, until she had committed whatever awful deed she had been predestined to do.

Then had come the worst moment of all. Recovering herself, her mother had smiled, a smile that was terrifying in its timorousness, and had offered the baby to Amy. As if to prove that she trusted her. As if she should feel the need to prove that. As if she were seeking to propitiate whatever dark spirit in Amy she had released by first revealing its existence to Amy herself in that moment when the baby was getting born.

You could almost date Ma's partiality for Kyle from that moment. For Amy did not want to hold him. Could not bring herself to take him. She could hardly bear to look at him. It was nothing against the nameless newborn child. It was instinctive and irrepressible. It was just that the child was associated with her humiliation and her pain.

She thought she knew herself, but did she? Did anybody? Ever? There were as many people inside a person as layers in an onion. At the core, who knew what lay dormant in her? Like those people who went berserk and killed everybody in the house and who in the newspaper accounts were described by their neighbors as quiet and orderly and devoted to the family. Had Ma had her examined by doctors when she was little and had they foretold that one day, maybe well along in life, but sooner or later, inescapably, she would exhibit peculiarities, irrational behavior, lapses—perhaps even criminal tendencies? One heard talk nowadays about a criminal chromosome; was that, like so many medical discoveries, merely the modern confirmation of immemorial folk wisdom? The criminal chromosome—what was that but another name for predestination, for what in the fairy tales had been the prophecy of the bad fairy at the christening: the parents of this child will come to rue the day it was born and the night it was conceived, for it will bring ruin and disgrace upon them.

Oh, when did one cease to be one's parents' child and become oneself? Did that come only after one had become a parent oneself? Was her childlessness the reason she remained, at an age past child-bearing, so much a child herself?

But had she really seen such awful things, or such awful nothings, that day as she thought she had seen? All that in a mere look? Perhaps it was all simply a misunderstanding that had been allowed to grow and get out of hand. One tiny germ, too small to be seen under a microscope, was, if neglected, enough to kill a big man. Sometimes Amy felt that she was like certain patients of hers whose very fear, when they first noticed the symptoms of some slight malfunction, that it might be diagnosed as cancer had kept them from having it examined, and a tumor that might easily have been removed while still benign became through neglect the very malignancy they feared, and ended by killing them. Treated early, might the difference between Ma and her not have been easily cured?

That there was another Amy whom she herself did not know and who was unlike the one she did know, Amy could not doubt, for she had it on the highest authority: Ma. And she had inner evidence that it was so. She had never accepted Amy Renshaw as herself. It was not that she carried in her mind, as in a locket, another image of herself which she wished she had been. It was just that the one people knew her by, the one she saw—reversed—whenever she looked into a mirror, was a mistake, a case of mistaken identity. It always surprised her whenever somebody whom she had not seen for a while recognized her.

Her years as a nurse had confirmed a truth she had first detected in herself: a person and his body were strangers to each other, strangers if not enemies. She had looked through the eyes of people as through the peephole of a cell door and seen that inside was a person of another generation, another race from his body—sometimes of another sex. Perhaps early in life body and soul fit, like a nut inside a shell, but as time went by the soul shriveled like the kernel of a nut.

Ma's rejection of something inside her had only strengthened the sense that she did not know herself. That she knew only a part of herself and perhaps not the essential part, merely the shell. That what she saw was what the mirror showed her, the reverse of what Ma saw when she looked at her. That what she saw in the mirror was flat, while Ma was able to walk all around her and see what she could never see.

If there was another being inside her, surely it was the same one who was inside everybody. Amy took care to keep him in the dungeon of her soul, behind bars, shackled and chained to the wall, but Ma might have gotten glimpses of him, and if so, then no wonder she drew back from what she saw. The Devil (it was currently the fashion to call him The Id, and how he must have enjoyed that, for he went always in disguise and under an assumed name, and his main effort was to persuade you that he did not exist) was in everybody. Of course he was just the opposite of her. Contrariness, perversity was his nature. He despised decency, was spiteful and cynical and sardonic, was always ready to find an ulterior motive and to smirk over any bit of cruelty and meanness anywhere in the world. She could hear his voice deep inside her often. For he was a chatterbox and thought he was clever and original and witty, but he was not, he was only wicked and contrary and irreverent. His wit just consisted in turning the truth topsy-turvy. But there were moments when she wondered, there alone in the dead of night and in that dimness, whether the Devil's main aim was not rather to convince you that he did exist, so that you could blame on him all the mean and selfish and cruel impulses that were really your own, that were the real you. The real you, that bitter core, not the sugar coating you had overlaid yourself with.

What if the truth about everything was just the reverse of what it seemed to be, of what we were taught was true? What a sickening thought that was! And yet what if it were true? Like our own faces. The one thing a human being never sees is his own face. When he looks in the mirror what he sees is exactly the reverse of what the world sees. Life was full of evidence that things were just the reverse of what they appeared to be. Our entire moral code, for instance. Take pride. A sin, so we were taught beginning in Sunday school, and what was more, it did not pay. Pride goeth before a fall. And yet the most contemptuous thing that could be said about a person was that he had no pride, while a proud man commanded everybody's respect. For instance, turn the other cheek. Anybody who did just got both jaws boxed. Turn the other cheek: that was held up as the ideal of conduct and yet anybody who did so was despised as a flunky, shunned as some sort of freak. The man who would sooner give a blow than get one, that was the kind of man people looked up to. For instance, jealousy. The green-eyed monster, yet people boasted of their jealousy and were admired for saying that if they ever caught their wife or their husband with another man or woman they would shoot him or her dead. Try to imagine a man with cause to be jealous of his wife who was not jealous of her. What kind of a man would that be? One with a place in heaven maybe but with no place here on earth. For instance, lechery. A sin. Yet what man would disavow a charge of being lecherous? Man not only flouted the laws he had created but boasted of his hypocrisy. Was everything just backwards? Was the truth just the opposite of what we were taught and did everybody know this or was she the only one to have suspected it? Alone in the middle of the night, in silence and in her half-light, Amy would sometimes feel that she alone of all the people who ever lived had stepped through the looking-glass and seen the other side of things. Then at other times she felt that not only was she not the only person to know this but that everybody who ever lived learned it sooner or later but that nobody told anybody else. Because if ever two people confided it to each other, then the illusion that human life was founded upon would end at that moment. The glass would shatter and there would be no more a division between what was and what seemed to be. People would not love their parents nor protect little children nor not steal and kill. The innocent and the guilty would be alike.

There was an unspoken conspiracy among humankind to keep this illusion up, for so fragile was it that a single word would shatter it forever.

Being the first born, the child Amy had been supplanted in her mother's affections by each child who came after her. In the line that formed to wait for Ma's attentions, Amy's place was at the foot, and the line grew longer all the time. Little Amy watched her little brothers and sisters being pampered and petted and was told she was too big to be babied any more and made to feel ashamed of herself that she should want to be. To keep from being jealous, Amy put herself in a different category, out of competition with the others. She identified herself with Ma. She made herself a junior mother to the rest. And, by dint of hard work, she brought home regularly the best report card of any of her class at school. She could not bear to be excelled by any of her classmates. Because when she was, and Ma consoled her by saying it didn't matter, not to fret over it, to her it didn't matter at all, then Amy was dismayed. Because if that didn't matter then neither did it matter when hers were the highest marks in class. Then all her work was for nothing.

And what work it was! Amy's schoolteachers were women of a now extinct breed: nuns of knowledge, missionaries to the dark continent of the child mind, whose choice of a career, in those days when teachers were forbidden by state law to marry, must have come to them like a call to take the veil—perhaps like some of those calls, following a disappointment in love, or the acknowledgment that love was not going to come. If the teachers of those days were forbidden by law to have any emotional life, the children of those days were presumed not to have any, or if they did, to leave it at home, not bring it to school with them. To school what they brought were their little minds, like pitchers to the well, and those old maid teachers filled them to overflowing. Reading and writing and 'rithmetic were their subjects, rote and repetition their methods. Each evening the children were sent home with an assignment for the following day which only a child could have done, no adult could have stood it. A hundred compound-complex sentences to parse and diagram. A poem to be learnt by heart. They were there yet, all the uplifting poems that had been carved in the tender bark of Amy's memory: Tell me not, in mournful numbers, Life is but an empty dream! If you can keep your head when all about you are losing theirs, Say not the struggle naught availeth . . . Fifty new words for the spelling bee, such useful additions to the vocabulary of a ten-year-old as onomatopoeia, rodomontade, exegesis, syzygy . . . And on one evening after which she was never again to be the same, to which she was even to give a title, like a chapter in a book, one mountainous problem in long division which she could not for the life of her solve.

One of ten it was, each higher and harder than the last —a whole Himalayan range. Atop the other nine one by one she succeeded in planting her flag, but the tenth turned her back time and again: an Everest of a problem. The porcelainized kitchen tabletop was covered with her figures: false trails leading nowhere. Her answer always came out the same, and different from *The Answer in the Back of the Book*. But Amy could not give up. To turn in a paper condemned from the start to a grade no higher than 90 was something she could not do. The curse of perfection was upon her.

She rested by doing her English assignment. That finished, she attempted the problem again. She merely retraced her former figures, like a lost person wandering in circles, retracing his own footsteps.

Joan Harvey, her closest rival in class, had probably solved that problem long ago and gone to bed, said Amy to herself. She erased all her figures from the tabletop and began afresh. She checked her calculations at every stage. The answer she got was the same as before. She heard her father climb the stairs and go to his bedroom. Alone in the kitchen in the stillness of the night her heart cried out for an end to her childhood.

At one in the morning her mother came down and told her she must give up and go to bed. It was silly to spend so much time over one problem. She went over her figures one last time, without hope, without avail. Before getting into bed she said her prayer:

Now I lay me down to sleep,
I pray the Lord my soul to keep;
If I should die before I wake,
I pray the Lord my soul to take.

But she knew the Lord would not take her soul with the sin upon it of that unsolved problem. If she should die before she woke, and she expected she would, she would go to hell, and there through eternity she would have to try to get her answer to that problem to agree with the answer in the back of the book.

She waited until she judged her mother was asleep and then got up and crept down to the kitchen again. Her eyes watered at the light. The clock on the wall said two.

Before beginning again she fortified herself with thoughts of all the hopes that she liked to imagine were invested in her.

Amy's parents were neither of them well educated. They were well enough off not to need to be, not to care—indeed, to be able to look down upon those who did. But in her longing for Ma's approval Amy had invented a role for herself in which her parents were not only uneducated, but lowly, and ashamed of their condition. The mother of this self-engendered Amy had sought to rise above her beginings, and those—still humbler—of her husband. She longed for gentility, and she believed that the path to it lay through the thicket of learning. In Amy, her eldest (sometimes in this daydream, her only) child, she placed all her hopes. In Amy she was determined to realize what in herself she had been denied. She could not bear for Amy to be anything but the best. —An exact description of the circumstances of Joan Harvey, Amy's closest competitor in school: that was what this was; Amy had swapped places with Joan in her imagination. With so much depending upon her, how could she let her mother down? Shouldering all these expectations, she again began to scale the slopes of that steep problem.

Again and yet again Amy's answer to that problem came out the same, and always the answer in the back of the book remained the same: obdurate and unattainable. The dead of night stretched around her; she felt herself alone in all the world. She was seized by a shivering she could not master. By 3 a.m. she could no longer see. She slunk upstairs and into bed and fell into a bottomless sleep.

Settled celibacy had given to Miss Allison Tate an awesome air of self-sufficiency. The severity of her disposition was reflected in her dress. This, which never varied, but was the same every day of the year, summer and winter, was as anachronistic as the habit of a nun: rusty black shot-silk, beginning in a high guipured collar, long sleeves cuffed in lace, the skirt terminating just above the tops of her fresh-polished, high-button shoes. She wore pince-nez glasses attached to a thin gold chain which, when the glasses were allowed to fall, coiled up on a spring inside a button pinned to her bosom, or where a bosom ought to have been. She sat at her desk as in a church pew; if one of her pupils slumped in his seat a glance over her glasses was enough to straighten him. When she passed down the aisles there came from her rustling skirts a faint dry fragrance as of a sachet of lavender long forgotten in a drawer.

Amy had lived for years in dread of the time when she would enter Miss Allison's class. In fact, she had liked her from the start. Perhaps "liked" was not the right word. One would no more presume to "like" Miss Allison than one would to like Mt. McKinley. But she was a fixed mark in the landscape, something to take one's bearings by. To Amy, Miss Allison's hard unsentimental character was a rock of stability in a world of uncertainty. Amy might be one of her two best pupils but Miss Allison treated her no differently, that is to say, no less strictly, than she did the worst dolt in the class. By giving Amy no more affection or encouragement than she got at home from her mother, Miss Allison spared her any pangs of disloyalty.

They used to turn in their assignments to Miss Allison on entering the classroom. The solutions were demonstrated to them in this manner: a pupil was called upon to go to the board. For this he was given back his paper, went to the blackboard and copied out his solution. He then turned in his paper again.

As she had known she would be, Amy Renshaw was called upon that day to go to the blackboard and do the one problem she had been unable to solve. Perhaps Miss Allison thought Amy was the only pupil able to have solved a problem so hard. Perhaps Amy's look of dread as Miss Allison ran her eye over the class had drawn her choice to fall upon her.

Amy went to the desk and got her paper. She did not say that that problem was the only one she had not been able to solve. With Miss Allison this was not done. One was not excused from going to the board merely because one had not solved a problem. One went just the same, and either copied out one's wrong answer or stood there facing the blank blackboard until Miss Allison took notice. It was then, generally, that either Amy Renshaw or Joan Harvey was called on to go to the board and show the class how it ought to be done.

Amy did not mechanically copy her wrong answer onto the board that day. Beginning at the beginning, she worked the problem one last time in front of the class. Her answer that time was the same as all the times before.

"That is not the answer in the back of the book," Miss Allison said.

Amy hung her head. "No, Ma'am," she said.

The class was hushed. It was the first time that Amy Renshaw had ever been humiliated at the blackboard.

"Who got that problem right?" Miss Allison asked the class. No hand was raised. Not even Joan Harvey's. But knowing that she was merely no worse than the rest gave Amy no comfort; on the contrary, by lowering her to the general level it deepened her shame.

"Do you want to try again, Amy?" Miss Allison asked. The offer was unprecedented, and made Amy feel more unworthy than ever.

Amy, choking back tears, shook her head. "No, Ma'am, thank you anyway, Miss Allison," she said. "It wouldn't be any use. It always comes out the same, though I did it a hundred times."

"Mmh, and always will, though you were to do it a thousand," said Miss Allison. "Your answer is correct, Amy. The one in the back of the book is wrong."

The class gave a gasp of amazement, then burst into gleeful laughter. The surprise was to find that schoolbooks could be wrong, that the world of teachers was not infallible. The laughter was triumph and self-delight. A world of their own had opened up to them and the pupils gazed at one another in a daze of self-discovery. The laughter swelled, passed out of control, became seditious. In it could be heard the rejoicing of a mob delivered from superstition and subjection.

But as for little Amy Renshaw, when the altars of discredited authority came crashing down she lacked agility, she could not jump aside in time, she was caught beneath, and crushed. Her answer was correct, her paper perfect. But Amy remembered her long lonely anxious hours in the night. She had trusted in the book, and her trust had been misplaced. If she could not believe in the answer in the back of the book, what was there for her to believe in?

"There is a lesson for you in this, Amy," Miss Allison said. "A lesson," she said to the class, "for all of you. The lesson is, it is not enough to be right; you must know that you are."

As one, the class nodded to show that they had learned this lesson. Amy dutifully nodded, too. But she felt as though she had been set adrift upon the ocean of life in a boat without any rudder.

Adrift now upon this deep dream of that childhood tragedy, she could see the shore where duty stood calling to her, but she was swept with the tide out to a sea of sleep.

XXII

L ong after the lights in the house had gone out, three sat on beneath the pear tree: Derwent, ghostly in the moonlight in his white sailor suit, Ballard and Lester. Twice Ballard's wife had come out in her nightgown to plead with him to come to bed. The second time he had not even answered her. None of the three had said anything. Yet in the air about them something almost crackled with imminence. Ballard himself seemed surrounded by a vacuum, as though he had sucked in all the air around him and was holding it in. So that on turning to leave, his wife had said, "Ballard? Ballard, don't youall do anything, hear? What are youall thinking of doing? Whatever it is don't do it. Hear?" Still she got no answer.

When she was gone, out of the darkness came Lester's voice:

"You don't suppose . . ."

"Forget it." That was Derwent.

"Hmm?" said Ballard.

"Forget it."

Silence fell. Then in a voice strained through clenched teeth, Ballard said, "Son of a—!

"Bast—!

"God damn the English language! Ain't there no way to cuss your brother without dragging your mother into it?"

▫▫▫ TWO ▫▫▫▫▫▫▫▫▫▫

I

Old Dr. Metcalf had brought into the world half the people in the county. He had nursed them and their children through the whooping cough and the measles and the mumps, and he was starting in now on their children's children. The men he had certified fit and sent off for duty in three wars. He had stitched them back together following disputes and set their broken bones following accidents. To Doc was owing the continued functioning of many a faulty organ, the continued pleasure in the company of many an aged parent, and to Doc was also owing, in many cases, his fee: he had carried half his patients on his books for years. Old as he was getting to be, Doc would still come out on call at any hour of the night and in all kinds of weather, though it meant getting over washed-out roads, getting mired in the mud and having to find and rouse from sleep some farmer with a tractor or a team to pull him out, often having to do the last mile or more on foot or on the back of the family mule behind the eldest boy sent down to meet him where the road gave out. All this to save the child of, or present with yet another, or, by the light of a coal-oil lamp, to remove the ruptured and gangrened appendix of some man who along next fall would come into the office and discharge his obligation with a mess of squirrels or a towsackful of hardshell pecans or maybe a pale, salty, undercured razorback ham. It was from just some such call that Doc had failed to return. He had disappeared, in circumstances suggesting foul play. It was a matter of concern and conjecture for the whole county.

The last person to see him was his wife. She reported that on Wednesday around five o'clock in the morning they had been awakened by the screech of car brakes in the street, followed instantly by a violent knocking on their door. Both had started downstairs, she in the effort to get there ahead of him, for she tried, without much success, to intercept these middle-of-the-night summonses—most of which, as it turned out, might just as well have kept until regular office hours— and especially ever since his last cardiogram some weeks earlier. As usual, however, he was quicker than she, and while the pounding on the door rose still louder and more peremptory, he went down to answer it, calling, "All right. All right! I hear you. I'm coming!" The murmur of voices had reached her, men's voices, though whether apart from her husband's there had been just one or more than one she could not say for certain. The doctor had then come back upstairs and dressed, saying that he had to go out into the country and for her to go back to sleep and not to wait up for him. To express her disapproval she had pointedly asked for no details, and sensing her disapproval he had volunteered none. She heard the front door slam, then heard a car shoot away and down the street and off into the night with a whine like a ricocheting bullet.

Mrs. Metcalf did not fret when at breakfast that morning her husband was still not back. He was often kept out all night, sometimes by a stubborn delivery, sometimes by an easy one when the anxious young husband had sent to fetch him at the very first sign of the wife's labor pains. Nor was she disturbed that no call had come; the nearest telephone was often miles away. She worried only about that recent cardiogram, and hoped he had found time during the night's vigil to snatch a wink of sleep.

At ten that morning the waiting room began to fill with patients and the telephone to ring. Mrs. Metcalf took the calls, made appointments, explained that Doctor was out on an emergency, that she expected him back any time now, promised to have him call as soon as possible. There came a call from the hospital, which was in the neighboring county, to say that one of Doc's cases appeared to be taking a turn for the worse. He had not made his customary morning rounds, nor had he put in any call there. The morning passed and the waiting patients all had to be sent home unattended. Mrs. Metcalf ate her lunch alone and afterward lay down for the nap she always took during the heat of the day, but that day she could not sleep. The afternoon passed with still no word. Patients began to come for the evening office hours and had to be turned away, some of them in pain. She knew the doctor would be provoked if she did anything foolish; but at half-past six, when a car which had seemed about to stop sped up and drove on past instead, she had picked up the phone and rung Sheriff Faye Benningfield.

Doc had not taken his car but had gone with his caller, or callers, in theirs. That they might have gotten lost was impossible. For even if the driver had been a passing stranger, Doc could have been set down blindfolded on any stretch of road or on any cowpath in the county and have found his way home again. Considering the speed at which, according to Mrs. Metcalf's account, the car was being driven, they might have had an accident. None had been reported, however; nor was any wreck ever found during the succeeding days. Theirs may have been the car which was going too fast to slow down for the pile of loose cotton lying strewn across the highway out near the Renshaws' that night, and which, plowing right through, set the cotton on fire by knocking over the kerosene flare put there to warn approaching drivers. But there was no way of knowing who had done that; for unfortunately the man who owned the cotton, Hugo Mattox, although he was lying in the field alongside, and although the skid marks left by the tires on the road measured fifty yards long, had slept right through the whole commotion, waking only hours later to find his cotton charred and smoldering.

It was certainly to be feared that Doc had met with foul play. Suspicion fell naturally upon the migrant workers with whom, it being ginning season, the countryside was filled just then. As yet there were no clues. But Doc was a much-loved figure, and feelings ran high, and busy as the season was, there was a kind of floating posse, men in town with cotton at the compress, always on hand in the square.

That Friday morning a plume of smoke seen rising deep inside North Woods drew a search party in there. They found a moonshiner's pot-still, or rather, found the smoking remains of one, the explosion of whose boiler had caused its owner to decamp in haste. There were stories of certain quart Mason jars of white-mule whiskey, but no evidence of the missing Dr. Metcalf or of his abductors. Meanwhile that day passed and so did the next one without bringing the ransom note expected by many. The finding on Saturday of a Panama hat caught in the overhanging alders at a point a mile downstream from the town started a movement for having the river dredged. For the time being nothing came of it. One minute Mrs. Metcalf would declare it was her husband's hat, the next minute deny that she ever saw it before. By then she was in no state to identify anything.

There were other doctors in the town, but Metcalf's practice was the biggest by far, and at once, in addition to the concern all felt for his safety, his patients and their families began to suffer great inconvenience and hardship through his continued absence. There were women about due to give birth, and who would have no one for it but Doc—as women are about the doctor who has delivered their previous children. There were those under his care for chronic illnesses and for injuries and for postoperative treatment (few of these, for a main source of Doc's popularity had been his slowness to draw the scalpel), and in the meantime somebody else came down daily with something new, people who had doctored with Metcalf for so long they hardly knew where else to turn, like Edwina Renshaw, for example, who, as luck would have it, had been stricken on the very eve of Doc's disappearance.

Days passed and not a trace was found, not a clue. Mrs. Metcalf had taken to bed and was being attended by young Dr. Weinberg. Sheriff Benningfield would race through the square and out of town in one direction or another carrying a carload of armed deputies, and sometimes a brace of bloodhounds in the bird-dog cage in the trunk. On coming in later he would shake his head and say to those on the corner of the square awaiting their turn at the suction pipe of the gin, "Nothing definite yet, boys. We're working on it." And the Sheriff would want to know from any who lived out the Renshaws' way the latest news of that other search for a missing man which all were also following by then.

For by then it was known to all—it was a scandal almost to make people forget the missing Dr. Metcalf—that the Renshaws had despatched two of their men to bring the missing Kyle home to his dying mother. Ballard and Lester. They had been seen and recognized—or rather, recognized though not seen, as they were driving at the usual Renshaw speed—on the road to Dallas. A mother lay on her death-bed, nine of her children at her side, but the tenth, her youngest and always her pet, him the family had not dared to trust to come if summoned by a wire but had had to send two of his brothers in person to fetch him home. It could happen in any family, and in any other would not have caused such a scandal; what made it such a scandal was the Renshaws' belief that it could happen in any family but theirs. Their mother was failing fast, according to reports, and whether Ballard and Lester would make it back with their renegade brother in time for a deathbed reunion was most doubtful. "If only old Doc was here," people sighed and said. "He'd keep her going."

As the days added toward a week and Doc Metcalf was given up for dead, disgust with the local officers of the law spread through the town and the surrounding countryside. News of Doc's disappearance now penetrated into the hinter-lands, into those roadless reaches where lived some of the men most beholden to him. Rough men these were, with rough notions of justice; their presence in the town was a cap to the fused and waiting charge, and a mood of lynch law hung palpably upon the sultry September atmosphere.

It was just the worst time of the year for such a thing to happen. During that week all but the big-scale farmers finished gathering their crops. Their cotton picked and ginned and their bales either sold or put in storage, they came downtown to swell the number of idlers on the side-walks of the square. It was the season when ordinarily the town was busiest, noisiest, gayest. Now, though crowded, the square was ominously quiet. The crowds were composed exclusively of narrow-eyed, tight-lipped men. Usually along with their last load of cotton they brought the family in to spend some of the money they had gotten either from the sale of it or borrowed against it from the bank while hopefully awaiting a rise in the market price; this year their wives and children had been left at home. The stores were empty, the merchants standing in their doorways with their hands in their pockets and the added seasonal salesclerks gazing out the show-windows. The abduction of Dr. Metcalf was hurting the town's entire economy. Only the barbershops and the marble-machines in the cafes and the bootleggers in the backalleys were doing any trade. Eggs, and also a beefsteak, were fried on the sidewalks in idle demonstrations of the heat. The air was seasoned with the odor of raw cotton, and along the curbs and against the store fronts cotton lint lay in dirty drifts like the last snow of spring.

As crops were gathered the migrant workers left. That Doc Metcalf's killer, or killers, might have been among those allowed to get away was a thought to make men gnash their teeth in helpless rage. Leaving town became a suspicious thing to do as the remaining number of workers dwindled and tempers meanwhile mounted, and the wise ones, the end of their jobs in sight, began to slip away unnoticed, some without even drawing their last day's pay.

Strange lawmen appeared in the town, reputed—the suspected crime being a federal offense: kidnaping—to be FBI men. The river was dredged, without result. One breathless evening a mob collected in Market Square outside the jailhouse, drawn by a rumor that a suspect in the case had been brought in for questioning. This proved unfounded and the crowd dispersed, but its size was such and its mood so unmistakably combustible that on the following day the local detachment of the National Guard sweated through a display drill on the public square. An event among the men observing these maneuvers aggravated the tension. Will Mahaffey dropped dead on the street. Will was near eighty and known to have been in poor health for years, but old Doc had kept him going, and the feeling was that Doc might have kept him going still if only he had been there to do it—another score to be settled with his kidnapers, or his killers, as the case should prove.

II

Just then occurred a new mystery.

Meeting his neighbor, Rex Bailey, on the square one morning just at sunup, Doak Westrup said, "Rex! You know my dog Speck. Well, somebody killed him last night!"

"Doak," Rex replied, "you took those words right out of my mouth. When I went outdoors this morning I found my dog Blue with his throat slit from ear to ear!"

Rex and Doak were joined by a neighbor of theirs, John Joliffe. John looked bad. He said, "Did you ever in your life hear such a howling of dogs as went on all last night? I never got a wink of sleep. As soon as one stopped another one took up. Somebody must have died. Edwina Renshaw, do you suppose?"

Rex and Doak were telling John their news when they were joined by Dean Watson. "What? Well now, what in the hell is going on around here?" said Dean. "When I stopped at the Renshaws' this morning to ask how Mrs. Edwina was, somebody had killed two of Clifford's coonhounds overnight."

The men exchanged grim looks. In a place where to harm a man's dog was a shooting matter, this new mystery, although it was a distraction from the affair of the missing Dr. Metcalf, instead of cooling passions further inflamed them.

"I have turned down offers of as high as a hundred and seventy-five dollars for that dog," said Rex. "You can believe that or not just as you choose, I'm ready to swear to it before a notary public."

"I believe you without that," said Frank Lovejoy. "I've shot over many a dog and some thoroughbreds among them, but never a better one than old Blue. I'd have given you a hundred and seventy-five dollars for him myself." For what it was worth, Frank, who lived in a different direction out of town from that of the men whose dogs had been killed, offered them each a pup from his bitch Jill's next litter, provided of course that Jill whelped that many.

Rex accepted Frank's offer with thanks, but his expression made plain that while other dogs might succeed, none could ever replace old Blue.

That night again, as soon as the sun went down, every dog in the district for a radius of ten miles set up a howl, the sound passing from one farm to the next and off into the night in an unending echo. Into this lugubrious chorus presently entered the baying of Tom and Jerry Partloe, Prentiss Partloe's pair of purebred Walkers, famed among foxhunters for the beauty of their voices when on trail: a clear ringing note like a crystal bowl when the rim is struck—but now just two more hellhounds making hideous the still, moonlit night. Twice Prentiss went out to quiet them; each time they

recommenced as soon as he was back inside the house. Toward midnight he had been on the verge of going out a
third time when they fell quiet on their own. In the morning
he had found them both dead, their throats cut.

And again that morning one of the Renshaw Negroes
had found another of Clifford's coondogs dead.

The third day it was Calvin Sykes's turn. "I thought I
seen somebody or something prowling around out by the
woodshed by the light of the moon," said Calvin. "Nehi
was carrying on, howling and howling, and I got up to look
out of the window. It was shining bright enough to read an
insurance policy, and I thought I caught sight of—"

"If it'd been me I'd've taken a shot at him," said Dean
Watson.

"Next time I will too," said Calvin.

"I get my hands on whoever done it I won't shoot him,"
said Rex Bailey. "I'll do the same to him as he done to old
Blue. See if I don't."

What were they waiting for? someone wondered aloud.
And like bees suddenly swarming after days of restless
gathering, that incipient posse began to stir.

But before the mystery grew half an hour older news of
a fresh development hit the square. Doc Metcalf had been
found and brought in.

III

He was found, alive, on the road at a spot ten miles from town, fleeing on foot from his captors, suffering from exposure and hunger and exhaustion, and reduced by fear and indignation to a state bordering on nervous collapse, so that nothing could be gotten out of him except a repeated threat to "put them so far behind bars it would take a dollar to get a postcard to them." Beyond this he was incoherent, the memory of what he had been put through making him sputter with uncontrollable resentment, and Dr. Weinberg, as soon as he had examined him, declared his condition critical, refused to let him be interrogated, and placed him under heavy sedation.

The farmer who found Doc and brought him in, Lee Fowler, had been on his way into town with his last load of cotton for the gin. It was just daybreak and Lee had the road to himself. As he rounded a bend he saw ahead of him an old white-haired man limping along with one shoe on and one foot bare, and carrying a small black bag no bigger than a woman's purse. Not until it was almost upon him did the old man hear the truck, much too late to escape being seen, yet he made a frantic, feeble attempt to hide himself among the bushes at the side of the road. Having seen that it was a white man, and thinking he might be a fugitive from the law, Lee stopped to render whatever aid and abetment he could. He got down from the cab and addressed into the leaves an offer of complicity. He was answered by a sob, and parting the branches, he found himself supporting the man, who fell into his arms. It was the missing Dr. Metcalf, but so altered that at first Lee did not know him. He was filthy and bearded and his face and hands scratched and his hair all matted and wild. He was covered with mud, the barefooted leg being caked to the waist, and his clothes in tatters. From his appearance Lee estimated that the old man had been in flight and in hiding for possibly as long as two or three days. But as to where he had been taken, by whom, and how he had managed to escape, at all this Lee could only guess, and for the time being, while they waited for Doc to regain consciousness, that was all the men on the square could do. Evidently he had been badly mistreated, according to Lee, and was in terror of recapture. As soon as he was questioned about his ordeal his head would commence to shake, his voice to choke, and his eyes to brim with hurt and angry tears. Then, the phrase having gotten lodged in his disordered mind, he would repeat his vow to "put them so far behind bars it would take a dollar to send a postcard to them." However, if only he did not die without having named them, his abductors would be lucky if they lived to see the inside of a jail.

While Doc slept, the town held its breath. The street he lived on was closed to traffic. Four sheriff's deputies

armed with shotguns guarded the house. Around the out-
lying blocks cars filled with aroused citizens cruised all day.
On orders from the Sheriff's office the hardware stores
suspended the sale of ammunition as meanwhile down on
the square Lee Fowler reproduced his affecting, his in-
cendiary portrait of Doc for those who had missed it. Dr.
Weinberg made several calls on his ranking patient, spent
half an hour indoors each time, emerged looking grave, refused to comment. Mrs. Metcalf also being under sedation,
the house remained dark all evening. The outside of the
house was spotlighted on all sides that night. To guard
against any attempt by his abductors upon Doc's life the
place was heavily patrolled. Chosen for duty from among
the many watchdogs volunteered by their owners were a
ferocious pit bull with a fixed snarl, an unapproachable
giant Airedale, and a Mexican chihuahua so jumpy it seemed
it would bark itself to death at the sight of its own minuscule
shadow.

IV

I did tell them! 'Od damn it, I did tell them! How
many times do I have to say it? I told them they
couldn't do it. What more was I expected to do?
Bar their way? One man against three and e'er one of them
ready to fight a circular saw? Nuh-uh. Not me. That ain't
what you pay me to do. I get paid to handle sides of meat
and saw and sell ice and chase away kids that pinch a bigger
chunk than a nickel's worth. I told them they couldn't do it
and they told me to open the door. You'd of stood up to
them if it of been you, out of doubt, but me, I opened the
door like they told me to."

The three men stood in the cold storage vault, their
breath visible, their sighs of exasperation drawn out whitely
in vapor on the air, their exclamations punctuated by bursts
of fog. It occurred to the Sheriff that you could almost see
what they were saying, as in the comic strip balloons. The
walls were solid with ice. Along one wall were stacked

crates of frozen shrimp. From hooks in the ceiling hung chines of pale gray veal.

Here in the deep-freeze was not where the Sheriff had expected to find himself at this hour today. The day the Sheriff was expecting had yet to begin. But even on the day when the Metcalf mystery was about to break, one way or another, such a call as the one from Mr. Gibbs, which got the Sheriff out of bed even earlier than he had meant to get up, had to be investigated. He realized while shaving, using hot water from the cold water tap, how much he was relying on Mr. Gibbs's ice house today. It was going to be a hot one—was a hot one already, and the sun was not even up yet. Not all the electric refrigerators in the town would be enough to supply the demand today for ice water—icewater: it was one word, and meant drinking water. By evening a cake of ice from Mr. Gibbs's ice house in your bathwater would be the only way to bring the temperature down to the tolerable, so close to the surface were the town's water mains laid, there being never any danger of frost.

Driving through the square the Sheriff had seen that already they were coming in, leaving their cars and trucks parked there and setting off on foot up West Main. He himself went out by Depot Street, past the gin and compress, meeting cars headed for the square with what looked like gunbarrels sticking up among the passengers. Country men these would be, idle now that their crops were in and always up earlier in the morning than town men, but especially on a day when it might be their civic duty to take the law into their own hands. He went past the vast cotton storage shed. That place was usually a headache to him at this season of the year. At this season of idleness and of money in circulation from the year's cash crop, the crap games that were played there among the maze of bales of cotton were usually good for at least two cuttings and an ice-picking per

Saturday. Not today. He crossed the tracks and went up the hill to the ice house. It was both better and worse than he feared. All Mr. Gibbs had managed to say over the phone was that there was a corpse in his cold storage vault. There was. And there seemed to be no way to get it out.

"They can't do it. Just can't do it, that's all."

"That's what I told them but they did it all the same."

The three men stood looking down at the pearl-gray metallicized coffin with the hip roof and the bright brass handles dewy with cold that rested on brass feet in the shape of griffon's paws.

"Christ almighty!" said Mr. Gibbs in an explosion of mist. "What's going to happen when all the folks that've got space rented in here get wind of this? Won't nobody in this town eat a shrimp for the next six months. Wait'll Bob Sewall hears about his veal! You know what veal is selling for in the stores? Christ almighty, looks like ever time I just take off for a minute you have to go and—"

"Me! I'd just like to of seen you tell them Renshaws anything. I'd just of liked to of been here to of seen you tell that damn Clifford Renshaw he couldn't put his ma in here on account of tainting a few boxes of shrimps. I'd of just liked to of been here to of seen you."

"When are them two expected to get back with that other one?"

"Kyle? How should I know? If you ast me they're going to have to find him first."

"What makes you say a thing like that?" This was spoken so low it was invisible.

"You ain't never noticed how they all hem and haw whenever you ast about him? 'Oh, Kyle, he's fine, just fine, yes, he's making out just fine, thank you.' Things like that. Nothing in particular. Nothing definite. And the way they look when you ast. Haven't you never noticed?"

"Oh, my Lord! Well, you get on the telephone and tell them to come and take her out of here and bury her. Tell them I don't mean no disrespect to their mother. But I've got a business to run. I'm responsible to a lot of people. They've got to realize when somebody is dead—"

"Clifford Renshaw is as mean a man as e'er God wattled a gut in. Nuh-uh. Not me. You can do your own calling. It's your ice house. Me, I just work here."

Wasn't there a law?

The Sheriff was blessed if he knew. Nothing like this had ever come up during his time in office.

By the time the Sheriff arrived on the scene it was evident that the town had taken a holiday to attend Doc Metcalf's awakening—or his failure to awaken. Evident, too, that the town would be unprepared to handle any emergency not connected with Doc that might arise. Half the fire department was there, at least, as was the total force the Sheriff himself could muster. The National Guard was there in force, out of uniform. The universality of Doc's popularity was attested to by the presence of black faces among the white, making this the first racially integrated lynch mob in the town's history.

The Sheriff's arrival was followed shortly by that of Dr. Weinberg. Another five minutes brought the stranger with the Northern accent who had been in and around the town for the past several days. He was passed inside the house by the Sheriff's deputy on guard at the door, thus confirming the suspicion that he was from the FBI, and arousing a new one: Doc was awake, awake and talking—or attempting to talk.

V

Cept Amy. I except her. I don't believe Amy was in on it. Not that she wouldn't have been if they had asked her. But they never had to ask her. I want to be fair. I except Amy—if she is still alive. But only her. The rest of them, the whole damned Renshaw tribe, I want to see them all so far behind bars . . ."

Thus began the tape recording of Doc Metcalf's deposition. What went before was missing because Mr. Murphy, the FBI agent, had switched off his machine.

Because as anybody could plainly see, anybody but the Sheriff—and he could see it, too; he just did not want to— the old man who lay staring at the ceiling. staring through the ceiling, was finished and done with this world. He seemed already to have shed its coloration and become a ghost. His head, still uncombed, with twigs and bits of leaves still tangled in his hair, was of the whiteness of the pillowcase beneath it, his chin was frosted with whiskers as

white as the sheet drawn up to it. A tourniquet of red rubber surgical tubing was wound and knotted around his
upper left arm like a phylactery, while in the sphygmomanometer the mercury which gauged his blood pressure stood
at the ebb. To the Sheriff's pleas that he tell how many of
them there had been, that he try to describe them or "just
one of them," he was deaf. He had the look of one past
caring for earthly redress of his wrongs and already laying
his grievance before the bar of eternity.

They had stood around the bed waiting for the Bible
to be brought. At her husband's request, his first words on
awaking and seemingly his last request, Mrs. Metcalf had
gone to the study to fetch it, sobbing all the way down the
hall. It was then that the FBI agent had quietly closed the
lid of his tape recorder. He was readier than Sheriff Benningfield to see the hopelessness of the case. His job did not
depend upon his solving this mystery. He was a stranger
here and would soon be leaving town. He would not have to
face that mob outside—quiet now, but wait until they heard
that Doc was dead!

"Ecclesiasticus," the fast-failing old man said, and the
sorrow in his tone and the awesomeness of the prophet's
name combined to wring from Mrs. Metcalf, just then returning with the big book held before her, a wail of despair.

"Not Ecclesiastes," he said. "Ecclesiasticus. Chapter 38,
verse 1."

Mrs. Metcalf was too distraught ever to have found the
passage had the book itself not come to her aid. Impatient
with her fumbling, it flung itself open with a flop to the
right page. All present gaped at this. It seemed to them that
the invisible finger of God had turned the pages of His
book. In fact, the book always opened there, at Doc's favorite passage of scripture.

In a tearful voice Mrs. Metcalf read aloud, "Honor a physician—"

There were tears in the old man's eyes. "Honor a physician," he said, his voice breaking. "That's the Bible, gentlemen. That's not *The Boy Scout Handbook*, you know. That's the Bible."

"Just give us a lead, Doc," the Sheriff begged. "We'll make them wish—"

Doc rose from his pillow; the mercury in the sphygmomanometer rose with him. "Honor a physician! Is that how to honor him, gentlemen: hunt him through the woods and the swamps like a wild animal? Is that how to honor an old man, and one not in the best of health himself? Is that how to honor the physician who brought them all into the world? Hold him prisoner and not let him even tell his poor wife he's alive? After all I have done for them? Who would believe it? I don't myself, and I'm the one it happened to. Well, I'll show them! I'll make them pay for it! I'll put them all so far behind— Except Amy."

He waved aside the hypodermic needle with which Dr. Weinberg was advancing upon him, and he ignored the doctor's disavowal of responsibility if he let himself go like this. A sedative was not what he needed now. He did not want to be calmed. He had been raging to himself for days, for a week, more, and now he wanted to make the world rage with him. He had the audience he had longed for: lawmen—his avengers.

He wanted to tell it all at once, could not choose where to begin, which of the wrongs done to him to place at the head of his bill of indictment. Long solitary brooding upon the outrage being done to him had robbed him of the capacity to distinguish the major injuries from the minor indignities; they were all the same size, all monstrous, all clamoring with equal voice for redress. His account of his ordeal was highly repetitious. Accustomed to universal respect, both for his profession and for his years, he could not believe what had happened to him and did not expect to be believed; thus he had to repeat everything to convince himself and his listeners that such enormities were true. He was somewhat evasive, too; for all the while he was pouring out his story he was struggling to keep back one part of it, a part which came out despite him. It mortified him for anyone to know the mistreatment he had endured and the unmanliness with which he had endured it. This came out unavoidably as time and again his tale forced him to show himself complying with his captors' demands without resistance, indeed with a cringing eagerness to anticipate their demands. To excuse himself he would remind his listeners and himself that he was an old man, and not in the best of health himself.

He refused the sedative but he did take the nitroglycerin pills that Dr. Weinberg gave him, which quickly stabilized his blood pressure, and while the FBI man got his tape machine going and after the Sheriff got done shaking his head and repeating, "So that's where you've been all this time!" Doc told how that first night, or rather morning, after a breakneck dash in the car with Ross's Elwood and that crazy sailor, that Derwent, at the wheel, through town at ninety miles an hour and across country at so much more he had not dared look at the speedometer ("That's the first thing I want them charged with: speeding and reckless driving"), into and right on through what appeared to be about half a dozen bales of loose cotton lying strewn at one point across the highway—for that was the only way a Renshaw knew how to drive a car, just as the only way they knew to stop one was to brake to a cliff-edge halt that automatically

ejected all passengers—they had arrived to find that they
were too late. And anybody who knew the Renshaws knew
what that meant. He cringed already from the accusing
looks he knew awaited him inside the house. He had been
wakened out of his sleep and rushed out there at risk to life
and limb every inch of the way, and he would get the blame
for getting there too late. Because halfway across the yard
they heard voices coming from the house and then—

Not for a moment could the overwrought old man be
coaxed into doing as the Sheriff urged: confine himself to
the main facts and fill in the details later on when he was
rested, stronger. Details were what his story was made up
of, what he had been marking down as a score to be reck-
oned up now and settled. Unless he went into details how
could they be made to feel what he had been through?

—Noises from the house. Wails, moans, shrieks: a
chorus of lamentations that seemed to be the voice of the
building itself, wrung from its very timbers. Doc's two
companions stopped, and between them passed a look not so
much of alarm as of utter consternation.

"Something's gone wrong," said one of them to the
other.

Which even at the time, ignorant as he was of the true
state of affairs, had struck Doc as an odd thing to say. Not
suspicious, not alarming—not then; but odd. Surely something *had* gone wrong to send them to fetch him at that
hour and rush him out there at that speed? What was he
doing there with those bottles of dextrose banging against
his legs unless something had gone wrong? He did not
know then that it was not a sudden turn for the worse in
their grandmother's condition but rather a sudden determination in their plans, plans which depended upon the very fact
that she was holding her own, that had caused them to come

and fetch him. He did not know that the two sent to bring back their missing brother were even then speeding toward Dallas. And how could he, how could anybody, possibly have imagined the part they had prepared for him in all this?

Brooding on it later—and he was later to have lots of time to brood—he had had to admit that actually they had not misled him. Not with words, at any rate. In his office it was not they but he himself who had said, "She's worse." They had not even answered him. Indeed, it was not even a question. In fact, they had not said anything. They had not even had to tell him to hurry. He himself, as he left them to go back upstairs and get dressed, had said, "I won't be a minute."

"You are saying then," said Mr. Murphy, "that they did not actually threaten you, force you, order you to accompany them."

"Eh? No. They didn't have to do anything like that. I had left their grandmother very sick only a few hours earlier. I was planning to go out there on my own the first thing that morning. Now there they were pounding on my office door at that hour. What else for? I knew at once, or thought I knew—"

"Excuse the interruption. Just keeping the record straight. Go on, Doctor, please."

Standing, stunned, midway across the yard, listening to the sounds of grieving inside the house, first one then the other of Doc's companions began to make a strange sound. It was a whimper deep in their throats, exactly, Doc thought, like a pair of stray wolves answering a howl of distress from the pack. He thought, what a hold that domineering old woman has—had—on all her offspring! And then he thought, no, it's not that, or not only that. It's the pack that is threatened when its leader is brought down, and it's as members of the pack that they are responding now.

And then they turned and shot Doc a glare that blazed even in that dim early light of dawn and shed another illumination upon the Renshaw mentality. It was a look hot with resentment, menacing, and Doc thought, they hate me at this moment. Not just because I'm alive and their grandmother is dead. Not just because I'm a doctor and I have not saved her with my skills. They hate me simply because I am not one of them. Their loss is not my loss.

They began to run toward the house, dragging Doc along between them, both whimpering, growling louder the nearer they approached the family's concerted wail. At the foot of the porch steps they stopped and stared. The door knocker was tied with a bow of black crepe. As they stood staring at this, a woman's black hand slowly drew the shade of one of the parlor windows, then the other one. Forgetting him, Doc's companions bounded up the steps and across the porch and inside, leaving the door ajar.

Doc went inside. In the parlor the Negro servant women were silently at work. In observance of custom the house was being darkened, the light of day shut out. They were rubbing soap on the mirrors and shrouding all other reflecting surfaces with bedsheets, for according to the old superstition, whoever sees himself in a house where death is will die before the year is out. A few electric lights left burning shed a murky light in the room and in this light the Negro women were like shadows without substance.

A woman in the living room screamed, "I killed her!"

Doc groaned to himself, weary already of all that Renshaw emotionalism, that Renshaw excess. That would be Amy. It could be any one of them, for the old woman had dressed all her children in homemade hair shirts, but the odds were it was Amy. The one with the least to reproach herself with, she would be the one to reproach herself the most. The sight of the guilt toward her that Edwina Renshaw had inspired in all her children (all except that one who got away), and especially Amy, sickened Doc, gave him the creeps. In fairness to Edwina it had to be said that Amy's fanatical devotion to her had given her the creeps, too. It was hard to be patient with Amy's breast-beating, with such wild expressions as the one she had just uttered. Doc had to remind himself that the feelings of very demonstrative persons were not necessarily insincere. Threadbare phrases often cloaked genuine and deep emotions.

"That's it! I killed her! I killed my mother! As surely as if I had taken a knife!"

It was not Amy. It was Lois. Well, as he had remarked to himself, it could be any one of them. On Lois's conscience lay that divorce of hers which had so displeased her mother that she had not dared show her face at home since it was granted three months earlier.

"Shut your mouth! Say that again and I'll kill you!"

That was Amy! That Amy? Amy who never raised her voice in anger, Amy of proverbial patience, gentleness, understanding? "Hear me? I'll kill you!" And there were sounds of a scuffle. There came another scream, this a scream of fright, and out of the room Lois came running, with Amy at her heels. Impossible as it was to believe, that was Amy, transformed into a fury, murderous. Right behind Amy came Clifford. He succeeded in grabbing Amy and holding her while Lois made her escape up the stairs. Next came Ross, weaving, drunk already—or still. He grabbed Doc's lapels and breathing fumes into his face said, "Make very sure. Hear?"

"I always do," said Doc.

"Make very sure. Cause if there was one thing she feared worse than death itself . . ."

"I always do, but I'll make very sure."

"Cause if there was one thing she feared—"

"You don't have to say it. I understand. I know. She spoke to me about it. I'll make very sure."

Often in the still of the night lying sleepless in the dark Edwina Renshaw had seen herself lying like that following one of her attacks. She had been in a coma, now she had regained consciousness. Had regained consciousness, but not the strength to move so much as an eyelid. Her pulse and her breathing were so faint they were undetectable. Her limbs were cold. Her children and grandchildren and all her relatives gathered at her bedside wept and wailed. She struggled desperately to speak, to make a sound, a movement, give some sign of life; she was powerless, paralyzed, incapable even of blinking when the sheet was drawn over her eyes. Next she saw herself lying on the cold slate slab of the worktable in the undertaker's parlor. She felt the prick of needles in her arms and legs, and not even this could rouse a response from her lifeless but living body. And so she lay stretched out listening as her blood was pumped from her veins and washed down the drain in the concrete floor.

On the only occasion that she could bring herself ever to speak to them about it, Edwina had secured from her children a solemn promise that when she died they would not have her embalmed.

Her second fantasy, which grew out of that promise, was even more terrifying than the first. In this she saw herself in her coffin, unembalmed, struggling to communicate that she was alive to the people who filed past for their last view of her or to bend and kiss her goodbye. Then the last one bade her goodbye forever and the lid of the coffin was closed, bolted. She was lowered into her grave. The dirt was shoveled in upon her. And thereupon her struggles suddenly availed: her strength, her voice were restored to her, and for half an hour, before she suffocated, she clawed at the lid and screamed.

"If anything will bring me back to haunt you," she had said, "that is it. So don't be in any hurry. Make sure I'm really gone before you put me away for good."

To her children, as to Doc, she had said it just once. That once to her children she had rather enjoyed. For if the thought of her death terrified her, at least it was gratifying to see that it terrified them even more, especially Amy.

The long upstairs hallway was packed now with the many survivors of the dead woman. In one corner lay a woman stretched out on the floor in a faint. A swarm of her women-kin keened over her. They were trying to revive her with a bottle of household ammonia held to her nose. That sharp odor pierced the stale air of a hot night and a hotter day just beginning and of the closeness of many bodies packed into a narrow space.

Himself often death's messenger, a doctor saw many bereaved families; Doc Metcalf, in the course of his long practice, had seen a very great many. Some—for families, like individuals, varied in their responses—bore their suffering privately, with little outward show, while others broke down in uncontrollable outpourings of grief. But in all his long experience Doc had never seen anything to equal that of the Renshaws. Like sufferers from some epidemic disease that deranged its victims with pain, so that they sought relief from worse torment in self-inflicted wounds, the women tore their hair and scratched their faces while the men punished their bodies for daring to feel and protest against pain when their mother's body no longer could, never again would, Clifford smashing his heavy fist against the wall, then staring contemptuously at his raw knuckles and smashing them again, scattering drops that glistened like bright red berries amid the printed foliage of the wallpaper, his brother Ross striking himself repeatedly on the chest with a noise like a drum, blow on blow, any one of which would have felled a man in his right mind, and not only did none of the others try to stop him, they watched in approval. Rending the air with their shrieks, they goaded themselves and their fellow-sufferers into an orgy of anguish.

Outside the dead matriarch's door the women of the clan were gathered as at the wailing wall, in sackcloth and ashes, that is to say, in their nightgowns and wrappers, their hair in hairnets or straggling loose, their unmade faces pale and puffy and streaked with tears. Clutching imploringly at him as he cleared his way through them, they thrust their twisted and ravaged faces into Doc's face and howled.

The children clung to their mothers, terrified by the un-bridled passion they were seeing. Instead of being quieted they were urged on in their screaming with shrieks that Ma was dead and they would never see her again until they saw her in heaven. The grown men, too, wept unashamedly, big, burly Derwent with his face to the wall and his head in his folded arms sobbing as loudly as any of the women.

At the end of the hall the fat sister, Gladys, had also fainted, fortunately in her case not without having given sufficient forewarning to be steered to a settee. Now she re-sumed consciousness and seeing Doc rose up disheveled and distraught and in loud dramatic tones cried as he entered the sickroom, "Doctor! Bring her back! Restore our precious mother to us, we beg and pray of you!" Hysteria, of course, if not pure histrionics, and not the first time Doc had ever been addressed that same supplication. But with this bunch you never knew. People were forever reading some news-paper account of somebody dead at ninety-three of heart failure complicated by lung cancer and with just a touch of Bright's disease being brought back to life—if that doctor out in Keokuk could do it what was the matter with you?

So if he had had any presence of mind he would have availed himself of his heaven-sent opportunity. Would have come back from the sickroom and said it was indeed out of all human hands now; however, with nothing to be lost by trying, he would see what he could do. And then have gone back inside, shutting the door behind him, and set to work on her, and when he had brought her around, returned to the hall looking as though he had just wrestled with the angel of death and thrown him for a fall, and wordlessly, letting them see that the struggle had all but cost him his own life, invited them in with a weak wave of his hand to see for themselves what he had wrought, what they owed him. But no. Better that he had done just what he did. Which was, turn down the bedsheet and take one look and, not even bothering to feel her pulse, dash to the door and fling it open and demand, "What is going on here? Stop your racket! Your mother is not dead. Whoever told you she was?" Because if he could do it once then he could do it again, had just better by God do it again, and if he had made them believe he had found her dead and had resurrected her then he would have been there still—what day was today? Saturday?—then he would be there still, working over a corpse now five days high in heat that hit a hundred and fifteen in the daytime and even at night fell not much below—

"Wait. Wait, Doc," said the Sheriff. "Just a minute. You've lost me. I don't—"

Not only was Edwina Renshaw not dead, she was, although unable to utter a sound and too weak, or too petrified with horror, to move a muscle, fully conscious, and as Doc could tell just by looking into her eyes, fully aware of all that was going on outside her door and what it all signified. No knowing how long she had lain there like that, in the very plight which Doc had just been reminded was her worst fear, with that sheet drawn over her face and she powerless to lift it, to call for help, to put a stop to those shrieks and wails and that battering of fists against the wall, so that whatever had been her condition on first coming to, by the time Doc got to her she was nearly dead from terror.

Now he was in a plight. His telling them that their mother was alive when they had given her up for dead was almost as if he had brought her back from the dead; to tell them now that with him in attendance she had died after all would be almost as if he had killed her. Out in the hallway now reigned a silence as loud as the commotion had been before, and in that silence Doc found himself praying to the ampule of adrenalin as to a vial of holy water attested to have wrought miraculous cures, and nicking its neck with the little serrated blade packaged with it and snapping it off, he filled the hypodermic syringe and administered the injection with all the awe and the fear and the hope of a priest administering a rite.

Looking about for a wastebasket in which to discard the empty ampule, he saw on the patient's nightstand the ampule of adrenalin that he had left the evening before for use in case of just such an emergency. Perhaps that should have put him on his guard right then. But what did he, a small-town doctor, a simple GP, know about such deep matters? He was no psychiatrist and certainly no detective. He was to have to become something of both in order to survive his ordeal, but he did not know then that his ordeal had begun.

VI

Only one person could have done it: the one who would most rather not have done it, the one predestined to do it, at whose birth the presiding fates had decreed that she would do something like this—Doc's next patient.

Anybody but Doc would have thought, seeing that unused ampule, that it could have been anybody in the house but one. Doc knew that that ampule had gone unused not by one of those who did not know how to use it but by the one who did know. Only Doc knew so much about the troubled, touching, contrary relationship between Amy and her mother. Knowing all that he knew, he felt a little to blame for what had happened. He ought to have foreseen something like this.

Amy would have sat at that bedside all through the night. If any of her sisters had offered to relieve her at her post she would have refused. Or if she had consented to rest for a while it would have been only for a while, and she would not have rested. It would have been on one of her watches that it had happened. It was Amy's fate to be the person in attendance at the time of her mother's death. It would be the fitting end, it would sum up their history. She had failed her mother in everything; now for the final failure. Now to fail her in what she was: as a nurse, professionally. We have all had that happen to us: the very fear of doing a thing makes us do it—who can say? maybe makes us do it in order to get rid of the fear. She had sat alone, the only person awake in the entire house, alone in that dim blue sicklight, conscious that the entire family was depending upon her to watch over their mother and bring her safely through the night. Doc could just see her sitting there in that halfdarkness with the fear growing upon her that during her watch her mother would die, until there came a moment when her dread brought to pass the thing she dreaded: she looked at her mother and she was dead. She would not even have verified her terrible surmise, as she would have done, she being a nurse with long experience, had her patient been anybody but who it was. She would have drawn that bedsheet up over her mother's face and in her eagerness to begin blaming herself would have set the servant women to draping the parlor in mourning and would—Doc could see her doing it—have gone herself out to tie that black crepe ribbon on the door knocker.

So it was as much for Amy's sake as for his own that he prayed as he sat there for the medicine he had given her to save Edwina Renshaw for the time being, at least, so that her death might not be attributable directly to the shock she had been put to. It was not for Edwina's sake. He had never liked Edwina Renshaw. How could you like anybody who liked herself so much? He had never liked Amy, either

—how could you like anybody who disliked herself so
much?—but he both pitied and admired Amy, and he had
always taken her side in the conflict between her mother
and her—although it was Edwina, not Amy, who made him
her confidant and tried to enlist his sympathy. Somebody
had to take Amy's side—she never took her own. Amy sided
with her mother against herself. It made your head spin, the
way Amy could twist things to her own disadvantage. It also
made your stomach turn. For her mother's mistreatment of
her Amy always had a hundred excuses, for herself never
one. To see it was touching, it was exasperating, and it was
. . . well, repellent. Though of course the minute you felt
that, you felt ashamed of yourself for it. For Amy was so
selfless, so patient, and so misused. Her mother herself knew
she misused Amy—and made Amy pay for the knowledge.
Her inability to supply a motive for her malice made her all
the more malicious. Doc was not surprised when he was
called upon next to attend Amy.

The parlor had undergone a restoration. The lowered
windowshades had been raised to their tops and the room
was aglare with sunlight. Under the direction of sister Lois
the servant women had washed the soap off the mirrors and
whisked away those bedsheets, and Lois's hissed commands
to them to hurry! hurry! bespoke the family's sense of the
unseemliness, the scandalousness, perhaps even the blasphemy
of their premature mourning. They were gathered in the
living room across the hall to recover from the double shock
they had come through when one of them looked out the
window and groaned. It was a repetition of yesterday.
There came Eulalie bent over pulling her toy wagon, in
which, her hands and feet hanging over the sides and trailing
in the dirt, lay Amy. Eulalie had found her down on her
knees in the cowlot with her blouse torn open smearing

manure on her breasts, poking it into her mouth out of which had come word of her mother's death and trying to force herself to swallow it.

Cowdung poisoning: in forty years' practice it was Doc's first case of that. He would have used a stomach pump on her if he had had one. As it was he pumped her full of antibiotics, gave her a tetanus shot, and one to knock her out. To himself he said, "If it's like this now just imagine what it's going to be when they lower the old woman into her grave!" And running through the calendar of his up-coming o.b. cases, he considered whether he ought not to reschedule his vacation so as to be sure to be out of town for that event.

So, bate them the first day. No criminal charges for that one. For it he would send them his statement. He would keep strictly to the letter of the law, and he had enough on them without padding the bill to put them all behind . . . Bate them the first day. Because they really had needed him then. They might not have known it when they came to get him, but events were already anticipating their precautions. He had gotten to Edwina Renshaw with not a moment to spare. Between her and Amy, and what with half a dozen of the other women showing sympathetic cardiac symptoms, not to mention a bit of emergency surgery he had been called upon to perform—never mind that—he could not have got-ten away from there much before evening even if they had been meaning to let him go.

She seems to get worse at night: start counting from there.

"She seems to get worse at night." This from the morose and menacing, the close-mouthed Clifford, was how, toward evening, his work finally done, his bag packed, hands washed, waiting to be driven back to town, he was informed that he would not be going home. Not asked if he would or could or thought he should stay. Told that he was spending the night there. Not even told that. Told, she seems to get worse at night.

It was infuriating, it was outrageous—it was pure Renshaw. Only they could have done it. He knew them. He had known them all all their lives. He knew what they were capable of. Knew they were capable of anything where their mother's health or happiness was concerned. He remembered her regaining consciousness to utter the name of that rebellious boy of hers, and he could guess the shame to the family's pride that one of them should be missing from their number now. So they were just going to keep him there in personal attendance upon their mother while they went to fetch that one home. The hell with the rest of his patients—who just happened to be their lifelong neighbors and fellow-townsmen. They must just make do the best they could so long as Ma required his exclusive attention.

But he figured, what, maybe twenty-four hours? The way they drove a car they ought to be able to get there and get home with him again in that time, no matter where he might be. Or if he had put himself beyond the range of a car, in these days of jet planes, hourly flights to anywhere in the world . . . Besides, Doc was not sure himself that she would survive removal to the hospital. That is to say, he was sure she would but afraid she might not. That if they consented, and she were transferred there on his recommendation and then she died . . . So he might fume to himself at their highhandedness (he could feel a sharp rise in his already high blood pressure) but the actual inconvenience to him, to his wife, to his practice—how great was it, after all? It would not be long before Edwina Renshaw resumed her place as just one of his patients instead of the only one. So although he already had enough in him to be dangerously explosive, he swallowed two more nitroglycerin tablets, and he put down the Renshaws' rudeness to their grief and anxiety, and agreed with himself to overlook it. At the back of his mind lurked the suspicion that to have protested would have done him no good, and he was afraid to protest lest his suspicion be confirmed. Had he even then been agreeing to stay in order to defer the moment when he might be told he was staying whether he agreed to or not? Anyhow, he stayed, and it was tacitly understood between them that he was not to go near the telephone.

And it was true, she did get worse at night. She did that night. Or maybe now he was getting hysterical about her. Right or wrong, he had thought it wise at one point to call them all to her bedside again—the whole clan packed inside the room and outside in the hall in hushed and tearful attendance. Hushed save once when her loud, labored breathing seemed to falter and they, thinking the end had come, dropped all restraint to sob and shriek and outdo one another in wild vows of penance if only she would not desert them. The whole clan save Ballard, of whose absence Doc was highly conscious. Lester's meant less to him. It was Ballard of them all who most intimidated Doc, and while he had no inkling at the time of just how far removed from the scene Ballard was, he found his absence comforting. All that was contained in the name Renshaw seemed to Doc to be concentrated in Ballard, the smallest of the lot but like the Oxo cube, with the whole bull in it. He was to learn later, as if he did not know it already, that the older brothers were every bit as Renshaw as Ballard—maybe, in order to take up any slack caused by Ballard's absence, a little more so.

"What, exactly, for the record, Doctor, did they

threaten you with if you should try to use the phone, let your wife know where you were, that you were alive, at least?"

"You are a stranger here, sir, and don't know these people like I do." A Yankee, he found himself thinking, with no understanding of how far family feeling can sometimes go. "They didn't have to draw me a picture. Think what they were doing. Carrying a man off and holding him against his will. Personal physician to their mother, if you please— like a queen. The hell with the health of the rest of my patients! Having gotten themselves in that deep, would they stop at making me regret any move I might make to get word to the outside? I thought about it. As the days went by I thought about it more and more. When I finally learned what I was in for—that they were going to keep me there until she died, however long that took, and that my duty was to see to it that she did not die—well, then the temptation to pick up the phone was sometimes almost more than I could resist. I knew what my poor Kate must be going through and I thought once that maybe even if I got caught at it they might let me get away with something like, 'Honey, I know you must have been worried to death about me, but don't worry, I'm all right, I'm just out here at the Renshaws' and can't leave because Mrs. Edwina is too sick.' I didn't, for one reason, because I didn't know what they might do to her to keep her from telling you, Faye."

"But they must have known," said Mr. Murphy, "that sooner or later they were going to have to release you. You don't go so far, do you, Doctor, as to believe they were meaning . . . not to release you? Eventually they would have to, and then it would all come out, and they—"

"It wouldn't matter to them then. That would be after their mother had been granted her dying wish to see her missing boy."

"Those boys and girls and their mother were always real close," the Sheriff commented. "That Renshaw blood is very thick blood."

He had had an assistant. Amy: rested, refreshed, scrubbed, powdered and perfumed, showing no aftereffects of her emotional debauch of the morning and with no wish to be reminded of it. Clear of eye, steady of hand, level of voice—hard to equate the neat, self-possessed, efficient-looking woman in the starched white nurse's uniform, white lisle stockings and sensible rubber-soled white oxfords, with the bare-breasted lunatic, face daubed with dung, whom Doc had seen, had treated, just hours earlier. To deflect any questions about herself, and to put him in his place, she was instantly all concern for him. He looked tired. He had had a long hard day. He was so conscientious, put so much of himself into his work. He should rest now. Her expression, bland and solicitous as it was, nevertheless had behind it some of her brothers' steely will, and it cautioned him not to question whether she was now fit for duty, whether she could safely be entrusted with the patient whose condition she had so disastrously misdiagnosed before. Her manner with him was professional. They were doctor and nurse together on a case. He was not to get the notion that her indisposition of the morning had made him *her* doctor, with leave to question or counsel or prescribe for her.

Perhaps after what had happened he ought not to have trusted her. He had trusted her because of what had happened. Its having happened once ensured that it could not happen again. And he was there—whether he would or no—in case of need. She was so eager to be helpful, to atone for her mistake. Her kinfolks would forgive her for plunging them into panic and unwarranted grief, but Amy could not forgive herself. Of course he had kept from her just how close she had come to bringing about the thing she feared.

But surely he did not need to tell her. She knew her mother's morbid, almost mad fear of death. She knew it better than anybody. Who but she, the one it would pain the most, was the one person to whom Edwina ever spoke of dying? The one thing that seemed to rob death of its sting for Edwina had been to sting Amy with it.

Edwina lived in terror of death and every death reminded her of her own. Those surrounding her saw to it that none was ever reported to her, whether that of a former acquaintance—she no longer had any close friends—or celebrities or heads of government. Time had stopped in her shuttered world, and she must have supposed that Roosevelt was still in the White House, George VI still on the throne. While for her part she would willingly have left it to the lower classes to do all the dying, whenever a person from among them presumed to die she was, before people learned never to tell her about it, quite put out, as though such individuals ought to know their place better than to make themselves an unpleasant topic of conversation. She had cut herself off from old friends, and her circle of acquaintances also contracted as those who formed it grew old and infirm. She found it too painful, seeing in the deepening lines of their faces and the stiffening of their joints, her own mortality mirrored. Religion offered her no solace. To go to church was to be reminded weekly that before one could attain to the life everlasting one had first to depart this one, so, although religious, or at least superstitious, Edwina Renshaw practiced her faith in a personal God and stayed home on Sundays, where she might receive Him more intimately as an equal. She refused ever to attend the local annual Graveyard Cleaning Day; indeed, she would detour twenty miles out of her way to avoid driving past the gates of a graveyard. It was fifteen years since she had visited her husband's

grave, almost as long since she had mentioned him. Not that
Edwina's memory of her husband was so very painful; what
was painful was that he was a memory, and that what of him
was mortal lay moldering in the ground, and that on the
other half of the stone above him where he lay was already
carved her name and the year of her birth, followed by a
dash and an expanse of waiting blank stone. Yet with all
this she would, when she was feeling very well and with no
thought of dying ever, taunt Amy with her death. Amy,
who but for the disrespect to her mother would have held
her hands over her ears and run screaming from the room.
Amy, who would have died for her, as Doc himself once
told her. It was the wrong thing to say. After thinking it
over for a minute, and realizing that while Amy might be
willing she was unable to do her that favor, Edwina had one
more grudge to hold against her.

So at last he had gotten around to his last patient of the
day: himself. He had indeed had a long, hard day. He had
been conscientious—he had been in terror of making some
misstep!—and now he was fuming inwardly—while looking
most agreeable—at his treatment by these people who owed
him such different treatment, so that he himself was ex-
periencing fibrillations. This had been brought on in part
by the nature of the case. He had detected a tendency in his
cardiac condition to act up whenever he was treating a
cardiac patient. No mystery in this. The sight of his patient's
suffering frightened him. His having to hide his fright
worsened his pain. So he had dosed himself well and gone to
bed in the room assigned to him adjoining the sickroom, and
he had slept soundly despite everything, worn out by the
day he had been through. What had wakened him? He had
come to suddenly with a sense of misgiving. He had tried to
dismiss it from his mind and go back to sleep, but it per-

sisted, grew, led him at last to get up and dress and go in to make sure everything was all right. It was two o'clock. Three hours past the time for the patient's medication, which lay on the nightstand where he had put it, while Amy sat in her armchair with an innocent smile on her lips, purring in her sleep like a cat.

VII

So there he was, the prisoner of that crew of motherlovers, trying to keep her from dying on his hands in order to escape being lynched until those two got back with that missing one, and with, for a nurse, a woman so distraught with worry and so worn out with overwork, and yet so determinedly helpful, he had to watch her every minute to keep her from killing his patient through negligence, absentmindedness.

It was one of those absolutely to be expected ironies of life: there lay Edwina Renshaw, the only thing keeping her alive, as one of her kinswomen had said to Doc, the hope of seeing that baby boy of hers one last time, and the family, not trusting to a wire, had had to send two of his brothers to fetch him home to his dying mother; meanwhile the child whom Edwina had never appreciated, never loved, never even liked, kept watch at her side hour after hour until she was ready to drop from exhaustion, her own breath hanging upon her mother's labored breathing, her nails dug into her palms to keep herself from nodding—ready, when her mother did die, to throw herself upon the funeral pyre. A life as singleminded in its dedication as that of a saint in the desert Amy Renshaw had devoted to her mother, and she had never wavered in that faith, though continually mocked and scorned and flouted by the very goddess she worshiped. If like Amy you take criticism well, then you will get a lot of it.

It was for this that Doc exempted Amy from the resentment he felt toward the rest of the Renshaw tribe for what they had done to him. This plus his certainty that Amy was not in on the plan to detain him. Oh, she would have been in on it if she had been asked, nurse though she was and aware of what it would mean to his practice. But they had known they did not need to implicate her. Amy undoubtedly believed that he was there working round-the-clock because he wanted to be, and that one or more of the town's other doctors was taking his practice for him in the meantime. She would not have been able to imagine that he could want to be anywhere else when her mother lay at death's door. Poor fool, ever ready to lick the hand that slapped her, while Kyle, his mother's favorite, had brought her nothing but heartache. Heartache indeed, thought Doc, remembering the times he himself had had to dash out there and treat her for fibrillations brought on by her latest row with that boy.

Every large family has one: an outsider, a defector, an escapee, or if the family's frontiers be sealed off against escape, an internal emigre. This in the Renshaw family was Kyle, and as might have been expected, where total allegiance had been demanded, total alienation had resulted. The rest of them did not like Hazel; but with all her faults, Hazel was one of them. But that one apple that had fallen far from the tree, Kyle, he was not one of them, and he lost no opportunity of letting them know it. It was Kyle who, at one of their reunions, over dessert, after listening to them all run down their neighbors, their co-workers, their acquaintances, everybody outside the pale, had commented, "I learned a new word the other day. Xenophobia. x–e–n–o–p–h–o–b–i–a. Xenophobia. It's a mental disease. The word is Greek, and means, 'a morbid dislike of strangers.' It's what you've all got. Our whole tribe has got it. All but me. Xenophobia."

"And do you know what mental disease you've got?" said Amy. "Just the opposite. Kin-o-phobia. k–i–n–o–p–h–o–b–i–a. That's what you've got."

And he: "Yes, I can get along well enough with most anybody as long as they're not kin to me."

And this was their darling. Not just his mother's: the darling of them all. The last born of ten, coming at a time when his mother had long thought she was past conceiving, a change-of-life child, the one whose childhood had been fatherless, with brothers old enough to be his father and four grown sisters all of them rather late to marry and get children of their own, he had been worse spoiled than an only child. The rub was, he was what they had made him, and against outsiders they were obliged to defend him because it was all their very own traits, especially all their most prized faults, which in him were pronounced and gave offense. He was the final print of which they were the trial proofs. Kyle, the last of the Renshaws, the grounds at the bottom of the cup, was more Renshaw than any of them. Contrariness ran in the family: Kyle was the contrariest of the lot. All were quarrelsome: his was the most quarrelsome disposition of all. The stubbornness on which they all prided themselves became downright mulishness in Kyle. Willful and headlong, Kyle rushed in where even other Renshaws feared to tread. If crossed in anything he would go quite glassy-eyed with rage, and he sulked past the time when even his brother Clifford would have given up out of sheer weariness.

His mother never tried to conceal her partiality for this Benoni of hers from the rest of her children. Nor did they resent it. Being so much older than he, some of them almost of a different generation, they were not in competition with him for her affection. As one by one her older children, despite all Amy's intercession, brought her the inevitable disappointments, Edwina turned more and more to Kyle—and Kyle was the greatest disappointment of them all. In her heart of hearts Edwina acknowledged that they got along so badly because they were so much alike. This made her love him all the more but it did not make it any easier to get along with him. And the irony was, when she and he had quarreled she was obliged to hide it from the others because she had openly favored him over them, to lie for him and put on a smile, sometimes with sass of his still ringing in her ears which his brothers, had they known of it, and had she not intervened to protect him, would have fought one another over which of them was to have the pleasure of thrashing him for.

"He's got no father to quarrel with, you see. Poor boy!" Edwina once explained to Doc.

Beginning over nothing, needing no cause, simply the clash of two identical wills, both powerful, both combative, quarrels between Edwina and Kyle never stopped short of verbal violence—sudden squalls blowing up into loud lashing gales. Headlong, heedless, soul-shattering recriminations which left them both white and trembling, left her in a condition requiring a visit from Doc—a fact which she kept from Kyle, and made Doc keep from them all. Nothing was ever left unsaid; they flayed each other raw, reopened every old wound, remembered all their unsettled disputes—and all their disputes went unsettled—in all their painful details. For old injuries from each other they both had total recall. Nor was any injury ever afterward repaired. Neither could bring himself to apologize, neither would give the other a chance to apologize. Over the lacerations they inflicted upon each other, tissue formed like proud flesh over festering wounds. Sullen, stubborn, unforgiving, most loyal to their mood when most in the wrong, they would let days go by without speaking to each other. Should another member of the family or one of the Negroes be so foolhardy as to try to make peace between them, both turned in fury on him.

Their last quarrel (another house call by Doc) had differed from all the others only in proving to be the last. Like all the rest, it had begun over some trifle. They had stormed and railed at each other, and when Kyle had had his say he had slammed out of the house and into his car and driven off. He had taken no belongings with him, intending no doubt to return home that night or the next day. But this time it must have come over him that he was a man, and the world was wide, and he had just kept going.

One summer day, out of school and idle, Kyle had swollen so with self-conceit over his marksmanship with his air rifle that he persuaded Lester, then a grown man already, but who trailed after his little brother like smoke behind a fire, to let him shoot a dime from between his fingers at twenty paces. They had practiced the trick out behind the toolshed where most of Kyle's errant schemes were hatched, and when he had grown sufficiently self-confident went, as he always did to show off his latest stunt, to find whichever of his brothers was about. They found Clyde and led him

back behind the toolhouse out of range of possible discovery
by Ma or any of the Negroes. Lester held out the dime with
fingers which trembled hardly at all, such was the trust Kyle
was able to inspire in him. Then Kyle, just about to raise
the rifle to his shoulder, had seen that his was not the role
that Clyde admired in the act. Lowering the gun, Kyle had
insisted that Lester change places with him. Now Lester had
been given no chance to practice the trick, and while he was
a better shot than Kyle, he lacked Kyle's boundless self-
confidence, or perhaps what Lester had that Kyle lacked
was the fear of hurting his brother. But neither protest nor
pleas availed. And so, shaking his head even as he was taking
aim, and even as he was squeezing the trigger already saying
to himself, "I told you so," Lester fired. The BB had taken
the thumbnail clean off. What Doc remembered was a pale-
faced boy with a jaw set like a steel trap who never uttered
a whimper.

Doc knew these Renshaws, as he knew most people, too
well. A doctor, an old doctor, physician to some families for
as long as forty years, got to know everybody too well. Because that too was part of his job: to act as confidant, confessor, go-between in those thirty-years' wars that marriages
turned into, in the endless wrangling between parents and
their children. And the thanklessness of the job! Not to be
stopped from pouring out their life's secrets, they then resented him for knowing them! And the futility of it! That
one lying there, Edwina Renshaw: she retained him, Doc
had sometimes thought, solely to grumble to him about this
daughter of hers now digging holes in her palms with her
nails to keep herself alert, this paragon of filial dutifulness,
the most loving daughter a mother ever had.

"She comes between me and the others," Edwina had
complained to him. "She keeps them from me. If they need
anything she makes them come to her for it. If they get into

any sort of difficulty she makes them keep it from me. She's the one they must turn to for any help. Oh, she says she does it to keep me from worrying, and possibly she believes that, who knows? Who knows what really goes on inside that head of hers? Oh, she doesn't try to turn them against me. She tells them to love me. She never stops telling them, so that now she thinks that if they love me it's because she tells them they must, that I owe it all to her. She's taken my place, that's what she's done. She's made her brothers and sisters—my children—into her children. They treat me as if I were their grandmother. If she wants children why doesn't she have some of her own? That's what a woman is for, and any woman who doesn't, there's something the matter with her. She's incomplete. In-com-plete, you understand?

"Well, I can see from your face, Doctor, whose side you're on. Everybody takes her side against me. They all say, isn't it a pity, that poor dear girl, she just lives for her mother and all that old witch can do is complain about her. You must be very tired of hearing me, so I'll hush. But does she never complain about me?"

"Not to me, she doesn't."

"It's so aggravating! That's her way of putting me always in the wrong. It's always been like that and I'm sick and tired of it, of being made to look like a monster of ingratitude. Does she never say anything to anybody? She's human, isn't she? Or is she? I sometimes wonder."

"All I can tell you is, to me she has never spoken one syllable against—"

"Then the more fool she! I've given her plenty to complain about, let me tell you. I'm human, if she isn't."

"Edwina, of all your children—"

"Amy loves me the best. Rrrrrrrr! If I hear that once more I'll scream."

"She worships you. She is always thinking of you."

"Well, I wish she would think about something else some of the time. I don't like knowing that anybody is thinking about me all the time. I would rather they never thought about me at all. How do you know what they're thinking about you? And don't tell me that if anybody made Amy what she is I'm the one. I know it. I admit I have done everything in my power to make my children all love me ahead of their wives and husbands and their children. I am a jealous woman—as jealous as Jehovah. My first commandment to my children was, thou shalt have none other before me. Ah, but I never said they were not to have any other after me. I wish Amy had had children. That would have given her something to think about without thinking about me all the time. That's what women are put here for, to have children, and when one doesn't she goes off on a tangent."

"Most people—"

"I am not most people."

No, she was not, Doc agreed, seeing in his mind Amy's face, grown frosty with that bleak pride in her self-sacrifice to her unappreciative mother which was all she had; unlike most people she had a daughter who would die for her—and regretted it as soon as it was out of his mouth.

"She is not my only child, you know. I have to remind people that Amy is not my only child. Have to remind her of it, too, now and again. The world may think she's my only one but she's not. I've got nine others. Nine, and they love their mother just as much as Amy does, though she may put on the biggest show. The others all love me just as much as Amy does, and would without her telling them to all the time. They don't need her prompting."

She herself did not know what made her treat Amy as she did. And for that reason, or lack of reason, there seemed to be nothing she could do about it. She tried. She really did.

The depth of her dislike for this one child of hers obviously dismayed her. It frightened her to feel such unnatural feelings and not to be able to account for them or overcome them. She forced herself to be affectionate, and the fact that it was forced was plain even to poor affection-starved Amy, and turned her away more hurt than ever.

Then there was the maddening contrast she had always before her of Amy and her favorite. She and Kyle could not be together for five minutes without him saying something to provoke her; Amy never gave her a cross word. Edwina would come fuming fresh from some clash with Kyle and find Amy all care and attention, and all her anger would pour out over Amy's bowed and patient head. Anybody else would have looked daggers but Amy would just look at her with eyes full of love, and not even injured love, not even reproachful. She would just bite her lip and wait for the storm to blow over. She had forgiven her mother already. Provoking as it must have been to be forgiven when she had not asked to be and when she knew she did not deserve to be, this was no excuse for Edwina's animosity. She could not forgive Amy for being the child that Kyle was not.

And even worse: when she no longer had before her the contrast between her first-born and her last. When Kyle left and time passed and he never returned. Then Amy's solicitude became pure poison to her mother. She fancied she found the bitter taste of spite in it, like a dose of medicine disguised with sugar. The implication that she needed medicine, and that it would be bitter, was not lost upon her. Anybody else in Amy's position would have gloated over how her favorite had repaid her; Edwina's mistake was in thinking that Amy was anybody else.

What most maddened Edwina was that nothing she could do could provoke Amy nor bate the love Amy bore her. That image—that ikon—that idol that Amy had fashioned of her was a reproach and a goad to her, and she could not get at it to smash it, to topple it from its pedestal. Amy had enshrined it in a sanctuary where no one, not even its model—especially not she—could get at it and desecrate it. There she kept it inviolate, and before it she kept her votive candle always burning.

Then Edwina got old, and sick, and scared, and then she tried to make up to Amy a little for all her mistreatment and sought to gain a little of that attention and affection which she had only had to ask for all along. Not even ask for. Just accept. Just not repulse. Edwina's way of gaining forgiveness was characteristic of her. Not by showing Amy any love but by allowing Amy to love her a little. But that was all Amy asked for, and she, poor fool, was happy. Or rather, not happy, not happy at all, for she was in a state of anxiety bordering upon panic for fear her mother was about to die, knowing as she did that only that, the fear of imminent death, could ever make her mother speak a kind word to her. The trouble was, poor Amy did not know how to love a little. If only she might have been a little less ardent! She was awfully intense, eager. And eagerness does somehow repel people. It is not a matter of suspecting its sincerity. Eagerness just does somehow repel people. Amy really was guilty of indecent exposure of the heart. Of course she was driven to excess by her mother's lifelong rejection of her. She pursued her mother with all the ardor of a rejected suitor, and with the same outcome. Amy could not locate in herself what it was that turned her mother from her. Her mother's unspecified suspicions of her made her suspicious of herself. She invented faults for herself. Better to confess to a known fault, however awful, than not to know what awful fault to confess to. It filled her with self-doubts, and sad to relate, that makes a person unattractive to others. Her mother could not tell her why she disliked her—it must be something too awful for words. Her mother seemed unable to tell herself why she disliked her—it must be something too awful for thought. And so poor Amy was filled not just with self-doubt but with self-hatred, and that, even sadder but even truer, makes a person still more unattractive. The world is ready to accept a person at his own self-estimation, especially if it be a low estimation.

Old and ill and expecting that she would be repaid as she knew she deserved to be for all her mistreatment of her, Edwina now did Amy the final injustice: she grew afraid of her. No doubt she expected Amy now to gloat over the signs of her failing strength and her dependency as she would have done if she had been Amy. With no reason whatever, or rather, with every reason in the world had it been anybody but who it was, she had grown afraid of Amy. And this too, the ultimate misunderstanding in a lifetime of misunderstanding, the ultimate injustice in a lifetime of injustice, Amy had borne with the patience of a saint.

Sitting there with her in that sickroom hour after hour, day after day, Doc knew he was in the presence of a saint. He knew because she brought out the Devil in him. He felt himself coming to understand and even to sympathize with Edwina, even to side with her, although to do so disgusted him with himself. Yet the selfless dedication of this paragon of daughters, so ill-rewarded and still so persevering, began to exasperate him, too. Imperfection is bearable, being the universal human condition; one glimpse of perfection makes it unbearable. To the ordinary selfish, sinful mortal, like Doc, there was something unnatural, something inhuman, something monstrous about a saint. There was also something very irksome. To live with a saint took the patience of a saint. No wonder the world rid itself of them by burning them at the stake, unraveling their live entrails and winding them on windlasses, boiling them in oil—driven to such atrocities in search of something for which their victim would be unable to forgive them.

If she were mine, if I were Edwina, I wouldn't be able to stand her either, Doc found himself thinking. All that meekness and goodness would make me contrary and mean to her, too. That foregone forgiveness for whatever I might do to her would only goad me into doing it. She would make me hate myself, knowing how far short I fell of her ideal of me, and that would make me hate her. It does make me hate myself, just imagining it. And for a moment Doc wondered whether that might not be Amy's unconscious motive for her obdurate love and forgiveness. Could it be that for some people, long-suffering, uncomplaining forbearance, returning good for evil, was a weapon, the most insidious, the most powerful of all, against which there was no defense? A kind of psychological jujitsu—the weapon of the weak—it employed your own force against you.

VIII

It was a question whether the Renshaws would not
have monopolized his services to the neglect of the
rest of his practice in any case that week, when
with so many of their kin, elderly and infantile, under their
roof, they were practically running a sanitarium out there.
He was continually being called upon to attend one or another of them. The longer they were away from their own
homes the more the elderly ones complained of ailments.
The young ones, too. Their mothers, too, all in a state of
nerves from sleeplessness, from protracted anxiety, suspended
grief. Small wonder that none of those who were not in on
the plot to keep him prisoner saw nothing remarkable in the
fact of his being nearly always there: there were enough
legitimate calls upon him almost to account for it. He ought
to have had, in Amy, a trained assistant; but Amy was worse
than useless to him, herself in need of his attention, a menace
to his main patient, because of worry and overwork.

And so, all alone, himself unwell, exhausted, afraid, afraid to sleep for fear Amy might fall asleep at her post, forced to keep a lid on his simmering rage, disgusted with himself for his truckling to his captors, sick with uncertainty over his wife, unable even to bear to think of what might be happening to some of his other patients, he went his rounds of the house, from the children's ward, where an epidemic of summer colds had broken out, to the bedrooms of the various aged and infirm, sufferers from kidney gravel and sciatica and arthritis and other ills real and imagined, all this in that stifling heat. He had kept a list of all those whom he had treated and he intended to render a bill for his services that would bankrupt them, that would reduce them to such straits they would not be able to retain a lawyer to defend them against the criminal charges he intended to bring against them.

What had they threatened him with? Everything! Nothing! That was the hell of it. That was what made it all the more unnerving, all the more maddening, all the more humiliating: their sinister silence. They left it to his imagination, they never bothered to put into words what he might expect to happen to him should he try to escape or smuggle out a note or show himself at the window to the neighbors who came to ask after their mother, and whom he could imagine passing on to the Renshaws—too engrossed in their own troubles to keep up with the news—the information that there was still no clue to the whereabouts of old Doc Metcalf. Just as—with another rise in his blood pressure—he imagined them sharing a sigh over him with the pharmacist when they took in to have filled one of his prescriptions which, without any prompting, and with no acknowledgment, and certainly with no thanks from them, he dated from before his "disappearance."

That was the part that rankled most: they had made a flunky out of him. Not only had they kept him prisoner, they had made him act a part, made him participate in the mockery that he was under no restraint to stay but was free to go whenever he pleased. That if he stayed it was out of choice, because of his concern for them. He had been forced to do their bidding without their having to bid him do it. He had been made not only to acquiesce but to collaborate in the wrong being done to him, and to do it cheerfully, as though there was nothing he would sooner be doing. He, their victim, had been obliged to relieve them of any necessity for threatening him. What was he to do—an old man, weak, not well himself—he was no match for any one of those bullies, male or female, much less for the whole bunch of them together? And what thanks did he get for the pains he took in order that they might be spared having to intimidate him openly? Plainly they despised him for his cowardly compliance. They just dared him to complain, even to look resentful. If he resented his enforced attendance upon their mother, then was he really attending her as he should? And if he was not—!

In the privacy of his room, there only did he rebel, and even there he fulminated in whispers, vowed vengeance in silence, savored secretly his coming retribution. Then on emerging to answer yet another peremptory summons to the sickroom, he flushed with fear lest these expressions of revolt which he had indulged himself in might have left telltale traces on his face like pilfered jam around a schoolboy's mouth.

His presence in the house—his detention—his captivity—was kept from all but the immediate family, and he was made to conspire in keeping it from them. By day, when not at the patient's bedside, he was confined to his room. Not that he was led back and forth under guard. It was simply understood that when he was off duty—he was never off call—he was to keep himself out of sight. To those house servants and the more distant kin who saw him only in the sickroom and only when they were summoned once more to be present at the end, it no doubt seemed that he had just dashed out from town in answer to the call. "Oh, Doctor, you are so good to give us so much of your time, to come so promptly when we need you," said one of the old aunts once; he smiled a disclamatory smile. Also tacitly understood was the prohibition, when in his own room, against going near the window, where he might have been seen by, might even have been suspected of trying to signal to, the neighbors who called to ask after their mother.

Much can be said though nothing be spoken. Doc understood the Renshaws' silence perfectly. He was constantly nagged, though, by anxiety over whether they understood that he had understood them. So he acted with such alacrity upon their unspoken commands that he often anticipated them, perhaps even exceeded them. Abject now, he did what he thought they wanted of him without their having to suggest it, much less order it, much less threaten him, much less use force. He gave them every out, every face-saving way. How could he know when he had done enough when he did not know what enough was and when he was terrified to think what might happen to him if what he had done was not enough? Take that matter of his window once again. Not content with never approaching it, almost cowering away from it into the farthest corner, he took to keeping the shade drawn so that it was night all day in his cell, and hot and close as the black hole of Calcutta.

The house had the atmosphere of a tomb and the few sounds outside the house were funereal: the plaint of the mourning dove, the shriek of a jay, the daylong dirge of the pickers at work in the distant cottonfields. Inside people walked on tiptoes, spoke when they met, if they spoke at all, in husky whispers.

Honor thy father and thy mother that thy days may be long upon the land which the Lord thy God giveth thee: though fifth in the list of the Ten Commandments, that one came first with the Renshaws. Even Doc, though he owed all his present trials to it, could not but give grudging admiration to the Renshaws' filial fanaticism. Each of them behaved as if his own life hung in the balance with their mother's. When they said that without Ma they would not be able to go on living, it was no mere expression. Who would love them in despite of all their imperfections when she was gone? What authority would overlook their offenses? Who—although she was actually stronger than any man, yet could plead a woman's defenselessness, a widow's self-dependence, a mother's fond love—would spread her wings for them to hide under and escape reprisal from those whom they had transgressed against?

Doc began to understand their truculence. The Renshaws were angry in advance at a world in which their mother would no longer be, and in which few but themselves would notice the difference her absence made. In their mother's passing they foresaw the passing of their way of life. They fought to preserve her in defiance of custom and propriety and good measure with the fanaticism of a last remnant of devotees to the cult of a dying god. Through the black scowls they wore to camouflage it could be seen red embarrassment, as though they were shamed by this mortal illness of their deity whose deathlessness they had maintained to a disbelieving world.

For days they had not rested but had kept themselves

within earshot, ever-ready to come running in response to the doctor's summons. They had kept themselves undistracted for fear of missing his call when it came. Each time—and Doc himself lost count of the number—they were summoned for the end they had worked themselves up to the pitch of anxiety and despair, and each time they were sent away carrying their feelings with them undischarged. The suspense was more than flesh, even flesh of Edwina Renshaw's flesh, could bear. Now the anguish of waiting made them long for the very thing they dreaded. When she did die their guilt over the relief they felt would drive them wild; meanwhile the mere suspicion of it drove them—and drove them to drive Doc—to greater and greater exertions to preserve her.

Such was the power of the old witch's spell that even Lois's twice-divorced husband, Leon, showed up to join the vigil over her. Doc was witness to the welcome he got from his double-ex, as Leon made his appearance during one of Lois's rare turns on watch with him in the sickroom.

"What are *you* doing here?" she demanded.

"Why, Lois, I just heard that Ma was sick and I thought—"

"*Ma!* What do you mean? She's not 'Ma' to you any more. What's it to you if she is sick? What business is it of yours?"

"Well, Lois, hon, I just—"

"*Hon!* Don't you 'hon' me!"

"I just meant to say—"

She shut the door in his face and resumed her seat with a *hmmph!* But Doc could see that she was not displeased at this testimony of her mother's far-reaching domination.

That would have been during one of the periods when Edwina was conscious, or semi-conscious. It was then and only then that Amy yielded her post. At the first flutter of her mother's eyelids poor Amy fled. And so her mother never knew of her constant care. It was always one of her other daughters whom she found watching over her. Did she notice this? Did she, who was to blame for Amy's never being there, and who would have been displeased if she had been, hold it against her? Edwina was capable of that.

The sisters, intending to share the duty of sitting with their mother among themselves and to exclude from it sisters-in-law and suchlike, had begun by dividing the day into four six-hour watches. But Amy, tireless, self-sacrificing Amy, could seldom be induced to relinquish the post. As she was a trained nurse and more useful there than they, and as she was accustomed in her work to long sick watches, and as they could never win any argument with her, her sisters let Amy have her way.

She had grown touchy. In a reversal of their customary roles, Amy now found herself being watched and worried over by her sisters, and Amy did not like being watched or worried over. "Look after yourselves," she told them. "I'm all right. I'm not special. You will all be just as sorry as I am." It sounded almost like a threat. Amy knew her sisters meant well, but when they worried that she was driving herself too hard in looking after Ma she reacted as though they meant to cast doubt upon her endurance, her professional competence.

Amy's monopolizing the bedside watching left her sisters idle. Those three seemed to be vying with one another in showing the most concern for their mother by showing the least concern for her own personal appearance. Hair uncombed (in Lois's case untinted and starting to streak with white), faces unmade (in Hazel's case unwashed), they neglected even to dress but instead slopped about the house all day in wrappers and carpet slippers. Doc's award for tackiness went to Hazel, hands down.

They did not remain idle for long. Very soon they were

immersed together in something, and Doc just hoped to God it was not he who had roused them. For roused they were: roused, wroth and resolute. With those three harpies out to get him, some poor devil was a gone gosling. Doc wondered why he had so readily assumed that the cause of their displeasure was a man, then wondered why he had wondered.

Doc, upon some enforced errand of mercy about the house, would happen upon them caucusing in some corner, their heads nodding together in grim agreement like three cobras to the same tune. They were always deep in papers, which they always gathered to them at his approach. He soon learned that they had thrown themselves into the chase after their brother Kyle. Some little delay was being encountered in tracking him down. He had moved about a lot, it would seem, and they were having to trace him through old addresses . . . Doc suspected the truth was, he had been found but was refusing, possibly under torture, to come back with them. If he could have seen the look on his sisters' faces he would have held out against whatever torture was being applied to him. In any case, his continued absence gave the three sisters something to do with themselves instead of just wringing their hands over Ma, or over Ma's will, in the case of Hazel, who wandered about the house looking for that nonexistent document without letting herself know that that was what she was doing. It lessened their feelings of uselessness and gave them a sense that they were doing something for their sick mother even though she might never know about it. It roused them from their state of shock. Unable to face it herself, Edwina Renshaw had done nothing to prepare her children for her death. They could not accept it; they rejected it angrily. Their anger sought an object; it found one ready-made in Kyle.

For this task of bringing their baby brother to bay

the three sisters were better suited than Amy. She was childless but they were mothers and could put themselves in Ma's
place and feel a dying mother's disappointment toward an
undutiful favorite child. Indeed, all three were just then
feeling rather piqued at their own children, with whom this
family crisis had rejoined them. Comparing notes, each found
that her sisters had also begun, coincident with Ma's coming
down sick, to detect in their children signs of the disobedi-
ence, the ingratitude, the independence, the disrespect for
age and authority and tradition so prevalent among the
younger generation. Each grew more incensed against her
own offspring from what she learned now about those of
the other two. With Gladys, hatred of youth had been a
cause ever since, at thirty-nine, she relinquished her own—
her ruling passion after her love of her family. The two
emotions were really heads and tails of the one coin, for
Gladys traced the waywardness of today's youth to the
decline of families with a strong, old-fashioned family sense,
like her own, and on this she put the blame for young men
on buses who let her stand while they sat, unmarried mothers,
boys with long hair, dropouts, campus agitators, dopefiends
—for the disappearance of decency, manners. She herself
had children not a great deal younger than Kyle. He must
be made an example of to them. Hers was the most implaca-
ble hatred of them all for Kyle, or quickly grew to be. For
if to Amy the family was a religion, to Gladys it was a
state; and if to Amy her brother's defection was apostasy,
punishable by excommunication, to Gladys it was treason,
punishable by—well, corporal punishment, at the very least.
So, with stout Gladys at their head, lean, hungry Hazel next
and long-grudging Lois bringing up the rear, the three sisters
set out in pursuit of their renegade brother, a sense of mission, along with a mounting discontentment and a consequent

severity toward their own children, growing upon them by
the hour. To their agents in the field, Ballard and Lester,
they dispatched on every outgoing mail suggestions and ex-
hortations, pursuing the unfilial one with all the fury of the
Eumenides. They saw themselves as avengers not just of
Ma, but of all mothers everywhere dishonored by their
children.

Their cause was Doc's cause. The sooner that boy was
trapped and brought home the sooner Doc would be allowed
to go home. Why then had Doc found himself half-hoping
that Kyle would elude them, or would resist their pleas, or
would defy their threats, and preserve his independence?

Meanwhile Doc's assistant, the assiduous Amy, was fast
becoming his major problem. Amy was headed full speed—
full Renshaw speed—for a nervous breakdown. He was no
psychiatrist, but you didn't need to be one to see that. He
once made the mistake of beginning a conversation with
her, meant to be soothing, with the words, "When this is all
over you ought to take a good—" and she nearly broke
down on the spot. Half-hysterical with concern for her
mother, half-dead with exhaustion, she nonetheless insisted
not only on being in almost round-the-clock attendance in
the sickroom, she insisted that he let her relieve him, that if
he was to do his job he must get some rest, he looked ready
to drop. So he was, and she was one of the prime reasons
for it. He was never more nervous about the patient upon
whose survival his own depended than when he was supposed to be resting while Amy spelled him beside the sick-
bed. Yet a second time, roused from sleep by sudden fear, he
had found her asleep at her post. He did not dare tell the
poor thing of it. Once, after refilling the bottle of dextrose
which fed the patient intravenously, she forgot to reopen the
pinch-clamp on the rubber tube. Once, in place of the

adrenalin he had asked for, she had handed him from out of his kit an ampule of morphine sulphate, which was not only counterindicated in the case, but would very likely have proved lethal. He had actually filled his syringe with it. He had caught the error in the nick of time. Out of kindness he had concealed it from her. It would have killed Amy to know what she had very nearly done. It had very nearly killed him. There he was, then, with all of them ready to lynch him should he let the old lady die before those two got back with their missing brother, and with, for a nurse, a woman so flustered, so distraught with anxiety and over-work, so conscious that her unconscious mother expected the worst of her, and yet so determined to do her best, he had to watch her every minute to see that she did not kill his patient accidentally.

The three sisters were in constant confabulation, drafting letters and telegrams, poring over what seemed to be a map which although he pointedly did not look at it they always folded away at Doc's approach. They had set up their headquarters in the kitchen, had chosen as their working hours the night, after the Negro women had finished their chores and gone off to their quarters. There, with the house asleep all about them, they spread themselves out upon the table, read and weighed the day's reports from the field and plotted their strategy for the morrow, fortifying themselves from out of the coffeepot on the range with a black bitter brew as thick as pitch. They were still there one night—or morning—anyhow at an hour when a poor old man himself not in the best of health ought to have been home in his own bed—when Doc, being careful to disturb nobody's rest and despising himself for his craven consideration of his captors, made his way downstairs to sterilize a hypodermic needle. Asleep on his feet, he had arrived at the kitchen door before he realized that the Weird Sisters were inside holding their midnight sabbat, then realized that by his stealth he had arrived there without their knowing it, either. Lois, in that thin little angry insect hum of hers, was reading aloud to the others.

" 'This is more of a job than you might imagine because the telephone directory here is a little bigger than ours back home. Five books, one for each borough, each about as thick as the Sears-Roebuck catalogue. We found a good many Renshaws. None named Kyle but might turn out to be, such as Renshaw's Bar and Grill, Renshaw & Whitcomb Pontiac-Olds, etc. Have now checked out about a quarter of these. So far no luck but will keep going down the list as many as we can get to each day. Meanwhile we have put a notice in the paper. Saw one in the "Personals" that said Angie please come home all is forgiven. Ours does not say all is forgiven. Please either. This a.m. went with an officer from the Missing Persons Bureau to the city morgue. I have always had a pretty strong stomach but what we saw today was nearly too much for me.' "

He could imagine what doing that must have cost them! To go to the police and admit that they had allowed one of their own to stray so completely out of their ken. To have the name Renshaw—even that of one unworthy of it—on the book of a precinct house, listed among the runaway husbands and amnesia victims and alimony fugitives!

"I don't know why," said Hazel, "they feel they have to do everything together. If they split up and one did one thing while the other one did something else they would cover twice the territory."

"The letter goes on: 'This is where every dead body that is found with no papers on it is brought and they keep them until somebody claims them or not. How long they keep them without anybody claiming them before they dispose of them I don't know but some we saw today had been there too long. Some of them have died of natural causes but many of them of very unnatural causes. I won't go into any details.

"'As you can see by the letterhead we have changed hotels. This one costs twice as much as the other one. Up here if you want segregation you have got to pay for it.'"

"Well," said Hazel, "they are never going to find him unless—"

"Boroughs?" Mr. Murphy asked Doc.

"Boroughs," said Doc. "Five boroughs. And then I heard her say they were never going to find him unless— It was all I could do to keep myself from screaming."

"Do you mean to tell me," said Mr. Murphy, whose accent grated upon Doc's ear like chalk dragged across a slate, "that they expected to find one person among nine million without—?"

"No, sir," said Doc. "They did not expect to 'find' him. It may come as a surprise to you, but us folks down here have heard of New York City. They never expected to find him. They were doing their duty. Their dying mother wished to see her missing son, and they were looking for him."

But that was not all. The only evidence they had that New York City was where Kyle was, was a story four years old that somebody from town, up there for the World's Fair, had seen in Times Square a man he thought was Kyle Renshaw and had hailed him. What convinced the man that it was Kyle was that he pretended not to have heard and disappeared into the crowd. That would be like Kyle, all right.

IX

Side Two of Mr. Murphy's tape—before it was erased—began, as did Side One, with talk of Amy Renshaw, but with a difference. With the other side of the tape came another side of Amy, one hitherto unexplored, unseen, like the dark side of the moon.

The tape had reached the end of Side One and must be rewound and turned over. A rest for Doc, a chance for the Sheriff to step outside and take the temperature of the crowd. Please God it had not kept up with the heat of the day! On coming out of the air-conditioned house the Sheriff popped out with sweat like a cold can of beer. The tarred street had come to a slow boil. Shoe soles, whenever a man shifted his stance after a while, pulled away with a sound from it. The Sheriff circulated among the men spreading assurance that Doc was going to be all right. He was telling everything and it was all being taken down. As to whether he had named names, all that the Sheriff could tell them for the time being was, the mystery was being cleared up.

Then the Sheriff heard—he had grown supersensitive to it—had developed an allergic reaction to it—the name he had been hearing all morning long—the one he was keeping to himself right that moment. It was not what he feared. They did not know what he knew. The crowd had been joined only a short while before by the contingent from out the Renshaws' way. A thing of interest and concern to equal the vigil for Doc Metcalf had detained them. Stopping by, as they did every morning, to ask after Mrs. Edwina, they had witnessed the latest misfortune to befall that troubled family. Overnight Edwina Renshaw had died and Amy had had the nervous breakdown Doc had feared. She had locked herself in the storm cellar declaring that she had "killed" her mother, and vowing never again to see the light of day. The Renshaws' neighbors, even the earliest ones upon the scene, had found the house deserted, the door ajar, the family, still in their nightclothes, weeping and wailing around the cellar like a tribe of Indians around their ancestral burial mound.

With so many of their relatives so long in the house even the Renshaws' big kitchen garden had been stripped bare, and Eulalie, pulling her coaster wagon, had gone out to the storm cellar in hopes of finding on its shelves some jars of something left over from last year's canning. She found herself unable to lift the heavy cellar door. She brought her boy Archie down to lift it for her. Archie could not lift it either. He was trying to when Eulalie stopped him. Then Archie heard it, too. Somebody was in there. The door was bolted on the inside and somebody was in there. Not the drunken Jug, as was their first thought, but a woman, and making sounds as though she were unconscious and groaning in pain.

The storm cellar—in fall and winter, after harvest and the canning season, the root cellar—was located fifty yards behind the house—about the limit for safety, as tornadoes, or "twisters," often sprang up with scant forewarning. The Renshaws' was big for a storm cellar, having been dug for a big family: a mound twenty feet in diameter and rising to a height of twelve feet, shaped like an igloo. The mound was solid earth; the cellar itself lay entirely underground. At the base of the side nearest the house, slanted so slightly as to lie nearly level, was the door to the steps by which the cellar was reached. It was of thick hand-hewn oak petrified by sun and wind, and hung on heavy hand-forged hinges. With that door lowered and bolted behind them, and covered by that mound of earth, the Renshaws were safe from the fiercest cyclone's wrath. A three-foot-wide culvert pipe of corrugated sheet-iron rising from the center of the mound supplied air.

To talk to Amy in the cellar it was necessary to climb the mound and speak down the pipe, on the knees, as the pipe rose only a foot and a half. Ira had gone first.

"Amy? Are you listening? It's me. Ira. Your husband." Ira had spoken low but inside the pipe his voice boomed. But in the vault below it was instantly muffled. He might have spoken into his pillow.

"What does she say, Ira?" Gladys called up to him. "What does our poor dear sister say?"

Ira shook his head. He seemed unable or unwilling to believe that his wife was there in the ground beneath him. Sticking his head inside the pipe (the wire screen that covered it to keep out animals had been removed) he said, "Amy? Amy? Amy? Can you hear me? It's me. Ira. Speak to me, Amy."

From the depths below had arisen a long-drawn hollow groan which drew from the women an echoing chorus of wails. Ira jerked his head out of the hole and gripped the pipe. Her voice, though unnaturally deep, was clear, and while it came out fairly loud, all sensed that she had actually spoken low. Indeed, that she had barely spoken aloud, that she had spoken not to Ira but to herself. It was the effect of that close and all but sealed-up subterranean vault: as if her inner thoughts were audible in that silence, amplified by those narrow walls and channeled up the pipe on that still air. Putting down a visible urge to rise and run, Ira again stuck his head inside the pipe. "Amy," he pleaded. "Amy, don't torment yourself this way. Your mother wouldn't want you to carry on like this. Be sensible, Amy. This is not going to help anything."

Gladys had been for forcing the door, breaking it in if necessary, and carrying their sister out. "I don't know what we're waiting for," she declared. "She's had a breakdown, a nervous breakdown. Gone out of her mind with exhaustion and grief. This had been too much for her. We've got to get her out of there. Get her to a doctor. To a hospital. Nurse her back to her right mind."

Hazel had disagreed. Amy had not gone crazy. They all knew how she felt about Ma. They might have expected something like this. Leave her alone and after a while she would calm down and come up on her own. For the time being she was where she wanted to be and until she worked off some of her feelings that was the best place for her.

Lois had sided with Hazel, though for reasons of her own. She feared Amy might do something desperate if they tried force. None of them knew but what she might have something with her down there, a gun or a rope or a bottle of poison. While they were trying to batter down that thick door . . .

"I know just how you feel, Amy, hon," said Lois in a tearful voice, and at the groan that arose from the pipe she nodded her head. "I know. I know. Without Ma life just doesn't seem worth living. I know. But at a time like this we ought to be all together. Come on out now, Amy, dear, and let us all be together."

Stout Gladys, when with the aid of a boost from her sisters she had gained the top of the mound and lowered herself to her knees, tried a different tack, saying, "You know how we all depend on you, Sister. You've been a second mother to us all. We need you more than ever now."

Hollow groans, strangled cries, hoarse guttural growls as though she were gagging on self-disgust, whimpers and grunts as of a wounded animal in its lair biting itself to allay a greater pain: these were all they could get out of her. Every effort they made to soothe her seemed only to worsen her self-torment. So they redoubled their efforts. Worn out by all they had been through, and now distraught at this latest turn of events, the Renshaw women wailed and shrieked around the mound, wept on one another's bosoms and tore their hair, while the Renshaw men stood around helpless and sullen, embarrassed at having this latest misfortune to befall them witnessed by the neighbors.

Frightened by Lois's fears, the Renshaws had decided not to force the cellar door. For the time being Archie and Jug were posted on the mound, instructed to keep both ears to the pipe and at the least suspicious sound below to ring the cowbell left with them along with axes and a crowbar for use in case of dire emergency.

It was when this had been reported to him that Doc produced the image of that other Amy. It was a reverse image, but perhaps it was the one from which the first had come—as in photography the print comes from the negative. It was an Amy the opposite of that one he himself had depicted on the other side of the same tape as a model—al-

most a monster—of daughterly devotion. Well, he had said
he was no psychiatrist and no detective; but this Amy was
different from the one the whole world knew. She had
fooled everybody, beginning with herself. Everybody but
one. The one the world had thought was so cruelly mistaken
about her all along.

The rest of them she had fooled so completely that now
when she wanted to unfool them they themselves would not
believe her. Poor Amy! There really was a curse upon that
woman. A worse one than this would be hard to imagine. It
was as bad as being falsely accused and finding nobody to
believe in your innocence. She might be able to convince
them that she was guilty of some other crime—any other
crime—but that. Never. She could say it till her tongue
lolled out and they would think it meant the same as when
one of them said it. "Killed my mother"—why, they all
said that. It was their way of saying how much they had
loved her. Their way of saying that, much as it was, they had
not loved her nearly enough. Amy had done her work too
well. Talk about chickens coming home to roost! A lifetime Amy had spent trying to prove her love to her doubt-
ing and distrustful mother, and all the world had felt for her.
Now her mother had proved right and shown Amy's real
self to her at last. And now she was the only one who could
see her real self while the rest held up to her gaze the mock-
ing image of that old false self of hers. Photography? More
like an X-ray. "See? Here are my insides, and here is the
diseased part. See?" "But here is your photograph and you
look just the same as ever." What a fate! To be falsely accused of a crime and unjustly punished must be one of the
bitterest things in life, but to be falsely forgiven, to want to
confess and to find no one among those you have wronged
who will listen, that must be a torment even worse. "I

killed our mother." "Yes, dear, we know." If she wasn't crazy when she went into that storm cellar, much more of that and she would be!

Was he saying then—?

Accidentally? One of those near-accidents of hers that he had been telling them about? One of her oversights—a moment's dereliction of duty—which he had managed up to then to catch in the nick of time and prevent—one of those had finally slipped by him and had caused—hastened—her mother's death?

Nothing had slipped by him. He was there right through it all. When, at the kitchen door that night, he had learned that things were not as he thought but even worse, from that time on he had not left Edwina Renshaw's side while Amy was there. Nothing had slipped by him. However, you might put it that way: "hastened." If she had been murdered then that would certainly have hastened her death.

Oh, it was not a case for the Sheriff. He was a witness—the only one. He had seen it all—all that there was to see. In the time his back was turned you could not have counted to three. And when he turned back Amy had not moved from her spot. She had not blinked an eye. She was paralyzed. Paralyzed by—whatever was passing through her mind at that moment. Besides, she was unarmed. No, the Sheriff would not have to swear out a warrant, go arrest her, gather evidence. There was no evidence to gather. No jury would convict her, no grand jury would indict her. An autopsy on the dead woman would show no violence. If this was murder it was an unusual case—without precedence —unique: one without a weapon. They had heard the expression "if looks could kill." He had always wondered at that. The most killing thing in the world sometimes was a look. Hearts could be broken forever, lives could be wrecked by a look. Some he had gotten in his time had made him just wish he was dead! *If* looks could kill? They could— deadlier than bullets, more painful than poison. He had seen one do it.

But—not to dispute his word—but if Edwina Renshaw had died just last night, and he had been asleep since—

"Last night? Who says she died last night?" Doc demanded. He grew alarmingly agitated. "That's a lie! Listen, I know when somebody has died—though you didn't need to be a doctor to know that she was dead, even to see that she was dying. The look on her face would have told anybody that. But in Edwina's case I ought to know! You can be sure I wanted to make absolutely certain. I examined her thoroughly. I examined her when all I needed was my nose to tell me. And even after that I examined her again. Then I really examined her! But that was only because I was beginning to be as crazy as a Renshaw myself. I hadn't really seen anything to make me doubt my judgment. I only imagined I had. She was dead. I defy anybody to say otherwise. When a Renshaw dies she's dead, the same as you and me. Last night! Last night? Wait! You mean to tell me—? Wait. What day did you say this was? Saturday? And do you mean to tell me they still haven't buried her? When she's been dead now—and in this heat!—for five days!"

X

From that moment on, late that night or early that morning when he had eavesdropped on the three sisters in the kitchen, Doc had not let Edwina Renshaw out of his sight. If he had been conscientious before, if he had been constant, careful, if he had been terrified of making a mistake before, what was he after that!

He had said that after what he had just overheard it was all he could do to keep from screaming. To himself he *was* screaming as, holding his breath, he stole away from that kitchen door. He not only dared not protest against what he had just learned, he dared not let it be known that he knew it. He realized that they had suspected him of knowing it right along. This explained how it was that no amount of diligence on his part could ever allay the mistrust he saw in their eyes—perhaps even deepened their mistrust. They had known from the outset what he knew only now: that he was to be detained not to keep their mother alive for as long as

the search for Kyle continued, but rather that the search—
that futile, that impossible search—would continue for as
long as he kept her alive. They supposed that he had guessed
as much himself—and knowing that bunch as he did, he
ought to have. In other words, they suspected him of knowing that by prolonging their mother's life he was prolonging
his own captivity. From there to the next step would be
natural for the Renshaws: to suspect him of trying to shorten
his captivity by shortening her life.

What happened, of course, was that he began to suspect
himself of that. And, in consequence, to be more diligent,
more conscientious, more scrupulous, and more scared, than
ever. Not just scared of them but scared now of himself.
What a hell of a position to put a doctor in! To make the
death of a patient in his care of benefit to him! To make a
doctor suspect himself of secretly desiring the death of one
of his own patients! The result was to make him his own
jailer. Thus once again without any embarrassment to themselves they got the most out of him. He must watch himself
night and day for any . . . Carelessness? Inattentiveness?
Oh, Lord, help him! Amy! Watchful as he had been before,
henceforth he would have to be more watchful than ever
over her.

So when the end came he was there. He was always
there. He went without sleep, without food, he drank enough
coffee to have floated a battleship, took enough nitroglycerin
to have sunk one. Exhausted as he was, half-hysterical himself now, he lived in that sickroom, he was there all the time,
especially any time Amy was there.

Tuesday afternoon—repeat: Tuesday afternoon—it was
hot as hell. Stifling. Hard enough for a healthy person, a
young person, to get his breath. Hers, Edwina's, was coming
short—a further strain on her already weak heart. To ease

her they propped her up with pillows—Doc remembered the phrase "dead weight" passing ominously through his mind—and prepared her for a shot, he going to his bag—that was the moment he had spoken of before, when his back was turned—while Amy sterilized a spot on her arm with cotton and alcohol.

It was, as he had said, only an instant that his back was turned, but it had been like coming in halfway through a movie when he turned back, for in that instant much had happened. That is to say, nothing had "happened." Neither woman had moved, neither had spoken nor even tried to speak. A look had passed between them. Or rather, in that short time already, a sequence of looks. From those on their faces at the moment he came in, Doc could reconstruct those that had gone before.

Edwina had wakened suddenly to find, for the first time since coming down sick, Amy bending over her. As always at the sight of Amy, she frowned. Being in pain, frightened, disoriented, no doubt she frowned all the deeper. This was just what poor despised Amy dreaded: her mother's waking and finding her there, and she was frightened and flustered. As always, her mother's frown brought to Amy's face that cowed and hangdog look she had, and set her lips to twitching with that uncertain, sickly smile. Doc had not known which of the two exasperated him the more: Edwina for her incorrigible misprizing of Amy, or Amy for her incorrigible endurance of it. To anyone else poor Amy's expression would have been pitiable; to her mother it was guilty. Guilty as she had always suspected, without herself suspecting until now the depth of that guilt. At that same moment Edwina's wakened body reported to her from all parts how mortally sick she was. A last illumination lit up her eyes, growing more incandescent momentarily, as a bulb flares up just before burning out. The look on her face declared more loudly than words, "You have murdered me."

He could have murdered her himself at that moment. The care that this daughter had lavished upon her, the super-human care, and this was her reward! He turned to comfort, to support, to sympathize with that poor misbegotten soul and saw—

Only his practice as a doctor could supply a compari-son. More than once in his long career he had seen people who had lost their faces. Had them burnt off, cut away, shot away—once saw a woman who had been thrown by a trusted saddlehorse head-foremost onto a gravel riding path and had her face simply scraped off. And after surgery, when the bandages were removed, had seen the stiff new man-made substitute and had watched as the patient was handed a mirror and hesitated, afraid to look, and then the shock, the shake of the head, the rejection. Such was Amy's face now as she looked into the mirror her mother held up to her. Raw, tender, sensitive to exposure as though freshly un-bandaged—and hideously ugly. The eyes in it begged him not to look, and not to look away.

He looked away—he couldn't help it; but not without first looking long—he couldn't help it. Her face was a map of dismay and despair. At what? At being seen for what she had been shown to be? Or at his misjudging her now as her mother had misjudged her? Before looking away he saw her face harden, and he exulted to see it. There was a bottom at last to even her bottomless patience, and Edwina had touched it. Then his exultation changed to alarm, from alarm to fear, from fear to horror. He looked away barely in time to keep from being turned to stone by that face. The last thing she saw, it did just that to Edwina Renshaw.

They, the living, stood for some moments as rigid as the

dead woman. Then with a low cry Amy threw herself upon the corpse. To Doc her intention seemed to be to mutilate it. Instead she pried open its jaws and put her mouth to its mouth. She was trying to resuscitate it, to breathe life into it, to breathe her own life into it. Doc succeeded at last in pulling her away. She gave a last groan—or a last growl: impossible to say which, as it was to say whether her last look at her mother's remains was one of reproach or remorse.

The corpse slumped against the headboard staring with eyes like bulletholes and howling with wide-open mouth. The reason he did not hear it was, it seemed to Doc, because he had been deafened by it. He·closed the jaw and held it closed until—it was not long—it set.

XI

There was one thing," said Clifford, "that Ma always feared worse than death itself."

"What?" said Doc, meaning, not what was it she had feared, but what had he said?

He had not been listening. His nerves were shattered by all he had been through. He was further agitated—elated —by the prospect of his imminent release—at seeing his poor Kate again—if she was still alive. His bag was packed. He was busy in his mind laying plans for avenging himself upon this family of outlaws. And now he was distracted by a thought just forming in his mind about this one here, Clifford. This thought was, that Clifford might be classifiable as criminally insane, and thus not responsible for what he had done to him, and that this might hold good for them all, and that they might escape his vengeance and go free. Criminally insane. Wouldn't any judge say so? Wouldn't he have to? Applying the legal test, M'Naghten's Rule: whether the accused knew at the time that what he was doing was morally wrong. Morally wrong? Of course Clifford Renshaw had not known that. For Clifford Renshaw it was not only not wrong to have kidnaped the family doctor and held him prisoner in personal attendance upon his dying mother, it would have been criminal of him not to have done it. Oh, Lord! He had said he was no psychiatrist, but had it all been psychotherapy all along? A family that would do what they had done to him. That mad search for their missing brother. One of them forcing herself to eat cowdung. Another one—

Ah. Would she—Mrs. Metcalf—mind just stepping out for a minute and bringing him a glass of ice water?

—Another one of them trying to mutilate himself! He had spoken—remember—of a piece of emergency surgery he had had to perform that first day? Self-mutilation—also his first case of that. There had been times when Doc had thought that somebody else had done it to him. There were some with cause. At least, there were stories. But would somebody else have stopped with the job only just begun? It had been self-inflicted. He had been going to lay *that* as his offering on his mother's funeral pyre! Shaving accident! Nobody shaved with one of those antiques any more. Not even the oldest man Doc knew. They went out with bustles. Their only use nowadays was as a weapon for drunken Negroes to carve one another up with in barroom brawls on Saturday nights. He ought to know: he had stitched many a one back together. Clyde Renshaw did not even shave with a safety razor. He ought to know. He himself had cured him of a chronic facial rash by switching him onto an electric years ago. Oh, Lord! Very well, instead of put in jail he would have them all committed to the insane asylum. One way or another he would put them all behind bars. All but

Amy. She was the only sane one of the lot, and she had just been cured after a lifetime of self-delusion.

"There was one thing Ma feared worse than death itself."

"What? Oh. Oh, yes. Yes, I know all about that. I know what you mean. Listen, set your mind at rest. Your mother is—" He broke off. The man could not endure to hear it said. He looked ready to pounce upon and throttle anybody who said it, as though to say it would make it so, as though the word were the thing itself. Did he suspect Doc of pretending that his mother was dead when she was really still alive so that he could go home? It was possible. With these people anything was possible. They were crazy. They were enough to make you think you were crazy.

"I could be mistaken, of course," Doc found himself stammering. "Such things have happened. If it would make you feel any better I could make one last—"

"I think," said Clifford, "it would be better if we moved you in here with her. Then at the least little sign . . . I'll be right out here in the hall."

"You were wondering," said Doc to the Sheriff, "what became of those three days between the time Edwina Renshaw died and the time I was found and picked up . . .

If any additional evidence was needed that that one, Clifford, was mad: that was the night the dogs commenced to howl.

It began with one of the ones on the place there, one

of Clifford's own coondogs, and just as it was popularly supposed to, at sundown. The most distressful, the most godforsaken, most spine-chilling sound this side of hell or Hollywood. Something to raise the hair on a dead man's scalp and wring tears from tombstones—almost human, like the grieving of an idiot. You didn't have to be shut up in a room with a corpse—though that helped. No wonder people had always associated that dismal sound with death!

"There!" he said—to himself—to his jailer on guard over him out in the hall. "Maybe that will convince you, you—!"

And had to break off. To take it back. To wonder whether that maniac might not be right. To— Well, he could tell it on himself now, but if anybody had walked into the room he would have denied to their face that what he was doing holding that cadaver's cold and rigid wrist was feeling it for a pulse beat. What had happened was that the dog had suddenly stopped its howling. Not just stopped. Stopped in a way so blood-curdling it made you long for the howling. A sickening sound, as though, having learned what a dreadful mistake it had made, the dog had bitten off its tongue in remorse. It had made him leap out of his chair and— Just remember, please, she had been thought dead once before, and by a trained nurse, when she was not. Or had she been? There was a possibility that had not occurred to him before. Did Edwina Renshaw possess the power of bringing herself back from death?

Well, not for a second time, at any rate. No more pulse in that stiff wrist than in the bedpost which his other hand held onto to steady himself. Confirmation of his diagnosis came from another dog off in the distance.

After howling for fully half an hour that dog, too, reconsidered and feel silent. Then before Doc had time to sigh in relief, the one, or another of the ones, there on the place started up again.

Just when Doc thought he could not stand another minute of it, it stopped as it had the first time with a hideous whimper that made him leap out of his chair and across the floor, only this time he went not to the deathbed but to the window to see if he could see what on earth was going on out there.

Edwina's room, at the front of the house, was a corner room with a window on the side. It was from that direction that that ghastly_sound had come, and pulling back the windowshade Doc peeked out. Clifford Renshaw came stalking across the yard to the house, to the faucet outside the kitchen door, where he knelt to wash his dirty hands and whatever the thing was that he carried. Before washing his hands he stared at them. Doc stared, too, and sucked in his breath. He let it out with, "You—!" Then changed his curse to, "You poor crazy fool!" For Clifford loved those hounds of his; apart from his mother they were the only creatures he did love, and now his hands, and the long kitchen knife, were red with their blood. And doubtless his sorrow over killing his own had goaded him, and by his reasoning gave him the right, to kill those of others.

On tiptoe Doc returned to his chair, and he switched on the lamp the better to watch that dead body just in case, as he had been told to do. A character determined enough to dispute death with dumb animals was one to be obeyed.

XII

Dead, anybody was to be pitied. Especially anybody who had died believing that she had been murdered by her own child, and perhaps all the more if she were mistaken. Even Edwina Renshaw, who had brought it upon herself. She was no less to be pitied for the way she seemed even in death to cling to the misjudgment which had proved fatal to her. The way Doc himself had set her corpse's jaw gave to it an expression of grim self-conviction as though at last she had proved to a doubtful and disapproving world how right she had been in her suspicions of that hypocrite of a daughter of hers. Pitiful triumph!

And yet . . .

You cannot win an argument with a corpse. The dead are always right. No argument as unanswerable as silence, no silence as deep as death. Try living for two days alone with a corpse in a little room and see if you don't find yourself being swayed by its air of unknown knowledge and apologizing to it for its accusing silence. Of course, he was not to be trusted. There under duress, set a mad and maddening task, to watch that lifeless body for signs of life—this after all he had already been through: his mind was beginning to be affected. He was ready now to believe anything. He was becoming as mad as a Renshaw himself. But looking at that face—and he had been told to watch it for the least little sign—now as fixed as marble in its expression of knowing what it knew, Doc began to wonder about what he knew.

He was there. He had seen it all. He had seen all there was to see. He had never seen so much in an exchange of looks as that between Amy and her dying mother. But what was it he had seen? He still was not sure. Not even after thinking about it for two days when he had nothing else to think about and had a desperate need to think about something to keep from thinking about what was happening to him and go completely out of his mind.

He had said that Amy's face as she looked at her mother for the last time had been the face of a murderess. He had thought that that murderousness had been born in that moment, born of resentment at long last against being so misunderstood, so unjustly judged. He wondered now whether it had been there all along beneath the cosmetic covering with which Amy made her own face each morning.

"Even now, looking back on it all from start to finish, I still have to ask myself, what was the truth, and what was my position throughout? There was I, working to keep Edwina Renshaw alive, with all her kin ready to blame me for it if she should die. Was one of them—though just as ready as the rest of them to turn on me when she did die—trying unconsciously all along to kill her? Gentlemen, I am no psychiatrist, and certainly no detective. But all those 'accidents' . . . Deciding her mother was dead and pulling that bedsheet over her face when she knew, she better than anybody, how her mother dreaded death, and even more, dreaded being thought dead when she was not. The times she had fallen asleep when she was supposed to be watching, and failing to give the patient her injection. Handing me the wrong medicine out of my bag. Forgetting to reopen the drip-feed tube. I had put down her mistakes and her oversights to inattention brought on by anxiety and overwork and the very fear of making a mistake. I had covered them up so she would not see them and blame herself for them. I didn't want to distress the poor soul more than she was already. Certainly not to point out to her that two or three of her mistakes might well have proved fatal if I had not caught them in the nick of time. I tried to let her think she was being helpful. I tried not to let her see that she was actually making my job all the harder for me. Had I unconsciously been Amy's accomplice in what she was unconsciously trying to do? Had I had as my assistant all along someone who was trying to kill my patient—or trying to make me do it—a murderer of the most dangerous kind: one who did not know it herself? Was all her care and concern a covering for the unspeakable thing she deeply desired?"

There was a curse on Amy, a congenital curse. Born as though in a caul with a curse upon her head. Whether she really did have a murderous hatred for her mother that only her mother could see, and then only as she was dying, or whether her mother's thinking so was a sickness of her own mind, it made no difference as far as Amy was concerned. The two things came to the same. Either way it was a curse on her.

Could a person teach another to murder her? Wish it upon her? He was ready to believe anything. Suspect a person long enough and that person will become what she is suspected of being. He was ready now to believe that by suspecting Amy of harboring the wish to kill her, her mother had taught her the wish. He was just as ready to believe the reverse of that. Which was, that Edwina had never had to teach Amy anything. That Amy was born hating her mother and had spent a lifetime hiding that horrifying sentiment from herself, her would-be victim, and the world. That Edwina had known to shun and fear the most adoring of all her children because she and she only saw that beneath that growth of mother Amy was all vinegar. That her anxiety to still her mother's fears of her was proof of her guilt. That the more anxious she was, the more Edwina had cause to fear her. After what had happened to him—and what was yet to come!—he was ready to believe anything. Including that Amy was as innocent as he had always believed she was and that even from beyond the grave her mother's motiveless animosity still pursued her, and had now driven her into a living grave of her own. He was ready to absolve all parties of blame and to say that the cause remained unknown: heredity? environment? psychological predisposition? some as-yet-undiscovered virus?—but the symptoms were unmistakable. As in that most dread disease of the body, an organ enlarged itself through gross reproduction of its own cells and became malignant. This was what had happened to Amy's love for her mother: through overenlargement of itself that vital organ had become malignant.

Then he would look again at that dead face with its injured and self-righteous set.

"I had always thought of Amy's love for her mother as a jewel. A diamond. Clear, flawless, indestructible. Proof even against her mother's attempts to smash it. Was it instead a pearl, spun in her entrails around an abrasive grain of hatred? I know this: Edwina Renshaw died believing that Amy

had killed her, and Amy knew it. Was that the final misunderstanding of a lifetime of misunderstanding? Or was that
—finally—after a lifetime—understanding? Had the worm
turned? Or had the worm been shown to have been a snake
in disguise? I don't know. I saw a mother and her child look
at each other in mortal terror and mortal hatred, and I shall
carry the sight with me to my grave. And maybe there I'll
understand what it meant."

By the afternoon of the second day decomposition had
set in. The bluishness around Edwina's nails, caused by poor
circulation to the extremities, had disappeared with the disappearance of all circulation. The waxiness characteristic of
death had made the skin translucent and now a certain puffi-
ness, the first stage of corruption, had tightened the skin and
smoothed the facial wrinkles out. Rigor mortis had stiffened
the corpse. But try telling that to the fanatic guarding his
door. Just try telling him his mother was commencing to
stink. Bring him in to sniff the air himself and he would not
have smelled it.

Under those circumstances he defied anybody to say he
would not have done the same as he did. Spend two days
locked in a room alone with a corpse watching it for life and
you too will want reassurance now and again that it really is
dead. He felt like a fool each time he did it, but that did not
keep him more than once from feeling that now unbending
wrist to make sure there was no beat of a pulse.

By then he was ready to believe anything—the more
unlikely it seemed to be, the more likely it was. If Amy Renshaw, the best daughter a mother ever had, was in reality a
secret matricide, anything was likely. If he could be kidnaped
and held incommunicado to watch over one of his patients,
and be still watching over her two days after she was dead,
this while they searched for one member of the family

among the nine-million-odd inhabitants of New York City without a clue to his whereabouts nor anything but the wildest of rumors now four years old that they were even close to his zip code, anything could happen.

His own reason was beginning to totter. The spell cast by that old witch was taking hold of him. Surrounded as she was by that band of believers in her divinity, she herself had sometimes seemed to wonder whether she might not have been chosen to be the one exemption from the common fate. Virgin birth was rare, too; but there was a case on record. Shut up alone in the room with that corpse and told to watch it in case it should come back to life, he began to do it! What was more, after he had watched it long enough the opposite happened to him of what had happened to Amy: it did!

XIII

That was when he made his break for freedom. Not when he finally found the courage to do so. When he had been scared by a fear greater than the fear that had kept him there. When he saw that corpse come to life. He had said they were crazy enough to make you think you were crazy. They were crazier than that. They could drive you crazy.

Perhaps, in fact surely, he would have been released in another day, perhaps even before that day was over. How much did it take to convince that maniac that his mother was mortal? But he could not wait another minute.

He had opened the door a crack and peered into the hall and found it empty, his jailer off duty. Off killing more dogs, probably, just in case they might want to howl that night. Carrying his bag, he sneaked down the hall and down the stairs encountering no one, hearing nothing. Was the house abandoned? Had he sat alone in it with the dead woman these past two days?

When he stepped outdoors it had seemed almost as if he were leaving his own home. He had been there so long and been so immersed in the life of that house that to leave it and come out into the light of day gave him a feeling of dislocation like leaving a picture-show in the middle of the afternoon. The mad intensity inside made the quiet reality outside seem unreal. He had skulked out of that madhouse feeling that he was betraying his Hippocratic oath, when what he was running out on was a two-day-old corpse already stinking—that was the extent to which he had been brainwashed by that band of believers!

He heard the chant of the cottonpickers in the field. An airplane flew its regular route overhead. The world went on. It made him wonder if it had all really happened. And that made him wonder—yes, even then—wonder whether Edwina Renshaw really had died. He had actually felt a prompting to go back and make sure, check her just one last time and make absolutely sure. What if he were leaving a sick person who needed his help? It was as much to keep himself from this act of insanity as it was to escape being seen escaping that he began running for the woods.

He would have a little more than an hour before his flight was discovered and chase given. Not much of a start for a man his age, in his condition. In about an hour there would come knocking on the door, bringing his lunch tray, you-know-who. He had shut that door behind him, he was sure of that. Quite sure. He was sure he had. He had, hadn't he? He was not sure whether he had or not. On the back of his neck he could feel the hot breath of pursuit. He broke into a lope. His heart at once reined him in to a walk.

He would have to get out to the highway but he would have to avoid the road out to it. That was too apt to have a Renshaw on it, and apt not to have anybody else, for it was practically their private road. So he took his bearings and charted his course, then turned about and headed in the opposite direction. He did that so as to throw Clifford Renshaw, a woodsman and a hunter, off his trail.

He knew to shun open spaces. The fear of them felt by all fugitives, by all hunted creatures, he found that in himself —an instinct. He lurked along inside the edges of the woods. Once when he heard voices he fled from them. As with all fugitives, all men were his enemies. When he was out of range—out of breath—and stopped, he wondered at himself. The only men his enemies were ones named Renshaw; the rest, to a man, were his friends, and ready to defend him against his enemies. But that was what the Renshaws had done to him: robbed him of his confidence in himself, his trust in others.

At sunset a dog off in the distance began to howl. He had just admitted to himself that he was lost, so now that dismal sound was a welcome one. As welcome as a foghorn— which it sounded like—to a ship floundering about in a fog. A dog meant people, and people meant help.

But that is a very hard sound to trace to its source—try it sometime—as hard as a horn in a fog—being so disembodied and unearthly. Even harder to judge how far off it was. Especially when other dogs joined the first one. They all sounded like creatures calling from another world. His— the one he was following—would howl itself out and he would have to wait, listening for it to come again. Finally it would. Or was that the one? Before it had seemed to be coming from that direction; now . . .

Darkness came on and he was still not out of the woods. And now behind him he heard his pursuer crashing through the undergrowth. He fumbled in his bag and found two pills which he hoped were nitroglycerin and took them dry and plunged on toward the sound of that baying dog.

He was getting near and this decided him to spend his last strength. Through it all hanging on to his bag, he thrashed through the brush, and it was then, crossing a slough, that he sank in mud, and pulling himself out, lost his shoe. It was sucked off his foot and in the mud and in the dark and in his haste he could not find it. Let it go: he was almost there.

He risked crossing an open field, though the moon shone on it like a searchbeam, knowing that he was that close now to sanctuary. Through a final thicket and then out into the clearing, ready to fall into the arms of his deliverer and pour out his tale, and there was the house and with his last breath he gasped, then choked, could have cried only there was no time to cry, no time for anything but to turn and run, begin all over again at the beginning. He was back on square one, at the Renshaws'.

So for the rest of the night—

No. To answer the gentleman's question: no, he had managed to keep far enough in the lead never to see his pursuer at any time. He had heard him—it had been that close —more than once—but no, thank God, he had not seen him, and when daybreak finally came, when he finally got out to the highway and ventured out onto it and that truck came along and . . .

It was Mr. Murphy who broke the long, embarrassed silence. "Ah . . . Doctor," he said, "I . . . ah . . . I've been listening to all you've told us, and, ah . . ."

He knew what was coming. He had been listening to himself, too. A distance had developed between him and what he was narrating. It sounded now as though he were listening to a playback of that recording tape. He knew he had come to the end of his story. He did not need this stranger or anybody else to tell him. He would a lot rather nobody said anything at all. Just quietly pack up and go. Erase everything from his magnetic tape so it could be used over again, and go. Leave him alone.

They were going to get away with it all. They could not be touched. There was no case against them. A man kidnaped, a physician dishonored, an old, sick man mistreated, the victim, the plaything of a pack of bullies male and female, who owed him their safe entry into the world and all reasonable care of their ailing mother for years, callously indifferent to their neighbors' health, their very lives, to his wife's anxiety—and there was no case against them. Not a charge could be preferred. Not by word or deed had he been forced to go with them. Not by word or deed had he been forbidden to leave whenever he felt like going. He had not been refused permission to communicate with his wife. He had never asked for permission. There was not a particle of evidence that when he did escape he had been pursued. No force, no threat, no coercion, no intimidation—none that would stand up in a court of law—had been used upon him. None had been needed. They had known their man. That was the worst of it: they had known him, and knew they could count on him. Through his own cowardly cooperation he had spared them having to incriminate themselves. He had complied. Complied? You had to be ordered to do something before you could comply. He had not complied, he had anticipated their wishes.

"A civil suit, maybe. Damage to your practice . . ."

Umh. Get up on the witness stand in court and tell it all over again. Entertain the whole county—even without the prompting of their attorney—with the tale of what a fool and what a coward he had been. They were going to get away with it all.

"A bill for your services, of course."

Some house call! There was just one weapon left him. One way to shame them. Not send them a bill. Treat them as charity patients.

Some house call.

□□□ **THREE** □□□□□□□

The mistake he had made was in not chasing the very first ones off of the place, with a shotgun if necessary, then it would never have come to this. And this was nothing to what it was going to be after this. After this they would have to build a Holiday Inn—a Hilton hotel—across the road. Not of course the very first ones. They were friends and neighbors who had come to condole with them over this latest calamity to befall them. Had come out of the same thing the later ones came out of: morbid curiosity; but being friends and neighbors they could pretend to themselves and to you that they had come to condole and there was nothing you could do but pretend along with them and let them have their look. But the next batch—strangers, total strangers—he ought to have run the first one that showed his nose off of the place with a gun.

Either that or else charge admission. There was a fortune going unmade out there. Parking fees—they already had the parking lot. Put Jug in a billed cap and one of those carpenter's nail aprons for him to make change out of. Put up a barbecue stand and let Shug sling sandwiches? Sell picture postcards? Souvenir plates? A china whatnot of the cellar mound? That ought to go over big. Put dayglo stickers on the bumpers like *See Carlsbad Caverns*? Yesterday he had seen a car out there with a Nebraska license plate. Nebraska! And all that had been just through word of mouth. After today they would come like those hordes in Italy swarming to see a statue of the blessed Virgin shed tears.

This when he was aching for privacy. When that wound had healed, leaving an itch—an itch on top of an itch. When the migrant workers, already here a month later than they had ever been before even in the rainiest picking season, ought, surely, to be done before much longer and move on, leaving their cabins vacant. A little privacy . . . if he didn't get it pretty soon he could no longer be held responsible for what might happen. Not strict privacy—privacy for two. Privacy! My God, he had a revival meeting on the grounds! And this was nothing to what it would be after today! There was no place where they could get together even if he had known where to find her, that whore. He could hardly remember any more what she looked like. Twice, just twice in all this time, he had caught glimpses of her—just the sight of her was enough to make him fairly slobber—and then he had been unable to get her eye, to draw her aside for a word. He had always kept strictly away from that house of hers and vowed he always would, but a little more of this . . .

"What would happen," he asked offhandedly, "to a person who swallowed gunpowder?"

"Who what?" asked Mr. Bulloch, the pharmacist, as he wrapped his bottle of milk of magnesia, his underarm deo-

dorant and his mouthwash. "Swallowed what? Gunpowder?"

"Accidentally. You reckon it would do them any
harm?"

"I don't reckon it would do them any good."

"What would you say to do?"

"Call a doctor."

"It's made out of saltpeter, sulphur and charcoal. Charcoal won't hurt you. Sulphur's good for you. It's in lots of
tonics. Saltpeter—well, you know what they say that does
to you. Any truth in that?"

"What?"

"They used to put it in our chow in the Army. At least,
so everybody complained. Why, I don't know. If they did
put it in it never had much effect as far as I could see. But
maybe they just weren't using enough for a bunch of young
goats like us, eh?"

"Nobody has, have they?"

"What?"

"Swallowed gunpowder."

"Oh. No. No, I was just curious. In case it should ever
happen. You know how kids are: put anything they find in
their mouths."

"Don't leave any laying around where they might get
hold of it."

End of a conversation he need not initiate because any
fool could see beforehand how it would go.

Wasn't there something about using it to rot stumps?
You bored a hole in a stump and filled it with saltpeter and
when you came back six months later you found the stump
all rotted out hollow? If it would do that to say a hickory
stump it ought to be able to take care of his problem—
though it might take six months to do it. You could buy some

saying that was what you meant to do with it. Only how would you know how much to take? If it would do that to a stump . . . Suppose you took an overdose? You might never again be able to . . .

Aspirin? It might help. Seriously. Headache, as the announcer was saying, was caused by too much blood swelling the arteries of the brain. Aspirin constricted the blood vessels and slowed down the flow of blood. It was blood swelling the arteries that caused the swelling he had. He had read that somewhere. Hah! Joke! Poor Ma was dead from hardening of the arteries and he was dying of arteries of the hardening. Oh, funny!

And now on Lone Star Television, Channel 6, following the mouthwash and antiperspirant and laxative and painkiller commercials: a News Special. On the screen appeared the old pear tree he knew so well and which he had only to turn his head and look out the window to see, and then the camera came up the path and drew near and there on television was the house in which he sat looking at the television. It reminded him of the box of salt with the girl on it who carried under her arm a box of salt with a picture on it of herself carrying a box of salt with— Then, the kitchen door—it was as though the camera had zoomed right through the house, or as though he had been drawn through the set and come out the back—and there was Eulalie bent over pulling that toy wagon of hers with—there it was, close-up, for all the world to see—the empty slopjar, along with the supper. With silver and a linen napkin in a napkin ring. That was keeping up the fine old plantation traditions under trying circumstances. A napkin ring, for Christ's sake.

Shot of the cellar mound with the steps cut into the three sides leading up to the culvert pipe. Like something Indian, Aztec. He had watched them slither and slide trying

to climb it just hoping and praying one of them would fall
and break a leg. Mmh, and then get some shyster to go
shares on it and sue him for liability because it happened on his
property and even if the insurance company paid off when
your policy came up for renewal your premium was tripled
if you were lucky and they didn't outright cancel your cov-
erage because after thirty years without ever putting in a
claim you were suddenly a bad risk. They had had to tell
Amy what they were doing so she would not think they
were trying to dig down to her and bring her out, and to
worry all the while whether or not she believed them. The
steps were already rounded with wear and that was nothing
to what they would soon be after today. He would have to
hire a mason and pour cement, lay flagstones.

Shot of the parking lot and of the parking lot attendants,
Archie and Jug.

"You want me to get shut of them for you?"

Mrs. Shumlin speaking. ("Call me Wanda.") "I'll get
shut of them for you. You just say the word." It was not the
pilgrim horde she meant. It was Archie and Jug. It was not
the first time she had made the offer. Not the first time she
had surprised him with a remark that showed she had been
studying him without his knowing it and reading his
thoughts in his face. He feared he was in for friction from
this new sister-in-law of his, this new broom so ready to
sweep clean. Already he disliked that smug smirk of hers
which seemed to say, apropos of niggers, mmm, but you
don't despise them as much as *I* do.

Clifford had kept a promise he had made to Ma, and
Mrs. Shumlin had yielded to his proposal. It had not yet been
made public, but in the family it was understood that as soon
as the period of mourning was over Clifford and Mrs. Shumlin were to be married. Lois's case was different. Hers, after

all, was not an occasion for rejoicing, and therefore need not be postponed. She was doing it as a public penance. It was the one atonement she could make to Ma. If poor Amy could bury herself alive in the storm cellar, then she could do this. Leon, of course, had not been consulted in the matter. Tipsy, as on the two former occasions, he married the same woman for the third time. The only difference was that this time instead of "I do" he had said, "I reckon." He still limped from the kick his bride had given him. Ross had taken a final pledge to give up drinking once and for all. How that would have pleased Ma! Poor Ross! His shame over his inability to keep his pledge was making him drink harder than ever.

In the beginning they used to leave their cars and trucks along the road at a respectful distance from the house and trudge the rest of the way on foot. But they were such a woebegone, forlorn-looking lot—the ones who began to come after the first wave of ghouls—old and infirm, misshapen, demented, crippled, careworn, cowed, that Eulalie, seeing them straining past, and in that heat, took pity on them and had Archie mark out a parking lot for them in the pasture nearer the shrine which was their destination. They touched Eulalie also because they were so considerate of the family's privacy, so anxious to avoid giving offense. For these, although they too were curious, were anything but rowdy. They had come to see a rarity, all right; but to see a saint, not a sideshow. They were not on a holiday, they were on a pilgrimage.

Just from hearsay as to what they were about to see, the people approached in a hushed and reverential manner. There was no jostling for seats around the mound. There were no seats. The seating arrangement being circular, and no one section inferior to the rest, it was hard for the colored people to know where their place was. Lacking directions, they disposed themselves throughout the audience; and as everyone, black and white alike, took his seat as softly as though coming late to church, their manner was not noticeably more self-apologetic than the others'. Remarkably, no one challenged them, despite the fact that among the whites were many from the class ordinarily the most sensitive to the nearness of a Negro. Perhaps it was the lack of seats for all equally that made the difference. Under a roof, at a table or a counter or in a pew, or on a public conveyance, a man might feel he had to be more particular about whom he let sit beside him than beneath the sky and on the ground. It was not the time or the place to raise a fuss. There was a feeling that the sorrowing woman underground had no race or color; she belonged equally to all.

By then it was already too late for him to do anything about it. It had already gotten out of hand. It was no longer a family affair. The woman in the storm cellar had ceased to be his sister and become a public figure. A sacred figure, in fact, and anybody, even her own kin, who tried now to take her from them, that mob of zanies out there would probably have torn limb from limb.

Their fear lest she heed the family's pleas to her to come out (they still made them, daily, it had become a part of the ritual, though she had told them in her farewell speech to leave her alone, that they were wasting their breath) was visible on their faces. When the preacher came and tried to coax her out, when the psychiatrist was brought in from Dallas, you could see them holding their thumbs in suspense for fear one of them might succeed in winning her over. The preacher's text was from Ecclesiasticus—"Let tears fall down over the dead . . . but just for a day or two . . . and then comfort thyself for thy heaviness. For of heaviness cometh

death, and the heaviness of the heart breaketh strength"—
the psychiatrist's from Freud; both fell on deaf ears. Having
failed with her, both men ended by sermonizing the crowd.
The preacher told them it was God's will that Amy's mother
be taken from her, and that she was being sinful not to submit to His will. To everything there was a season, he said: a
time to mourn and a time to stop mourning. And, saying that
they themselves were abetting her in it, he warned of another
peril to Amy's soul. There was a limit set, he said, beyond
which we were forbidden to love another human being,
even our own mother. God was a jealous God, and would
have none other before Him, and by adoring her dead
mother—and that was what she was doing—Amy was skirt-
ing very near the deadly sin of idolatry. The psychiatrist
told them that Amy was sinning against reason. She had not
killed her mother, she only thought she had. It was all in her
mind. So some said, agreed the farmer whom the psychiatrist chose to concentrate his reasoning upon. It was so. It
was all in her mind. Yes, said the farmer to the psychiatrist,
maybe so, but then, so much is, isn't it, if you know what I
mean?

　　There are people sick in body who change doctors continually in search of one who will cure them—they invaria-
bly wind up in the hands of a quack; there are people sick
of soul who change faiths the same way. These were such
seekers. Religious addicts. The comparison was apt. In their
hollow eyes burned the same unappeasable craving as of
someone addicted to drugs and ever in need of stronger ones.
In the pasture there was neither shelter nor shade. Beneath
the sun that beat upon their heads like a hammer or streaming with rain, patient as plants, they stood or squatted or sat
gazing at the cellar mound with the rapt attentiveness of the
already converted waiting for a new religion to be born. The

observable events of the day numbered two: the coming of one or another of the family to climb the mound and plead vainly with her to come out, and the appearance of Eulalie with her wagon bringing a bottle of drinking water, the meal she always sent back untouched, and a change of slopjars, but there they were ready and waiting—some of them since before sunup—waiting to participate with their mouths agape like a congregation of Campbellites at communion awaiting their half-shot of grape juice. Grandparents, parents, children: all sat gaping at that mean low mound of earth as though at a holy shrine, as though by staring at it long and fixedly enough they might see through it to where the sybil sat self-immured, doing penance and prayer for them all, in her dark, dank cell, waiting for the spirit to move her and she would speak.

She did speak, but not until these, the credulous, who had followed the curious, were themselves followed by the criminal.

Each day she stayed down there drew a bigger crowd. As word spread outward they came from farther and farther away, in cars bearing license plates from out of the county, from out of the state, from two, three, four states. And some who came farthest came on foot, burdened by nothing but their consciences, which it was impossible not to imagine looking like the motheaten, threadbare, tattered overcoats— often two, one over the other—which they wore in spite of the sweltering heat.

Eulalie now laying on for the TV reporter's benefit the mushmouthed old faithful family darky act: Wellsuh, for this evening I fixed her a breaded veal cutlet with mash potatoes and limas but if I know her— Yessuh, I fix her something hot but she— Yessuh, well, I try my best to think up things to tempt her appetite but— Nawsuh, just send it all back up. Nawsuh, never nothing but just them three-four slices of lightbread and a glass of water. She mortifying herself.

Shot of Eulalie climbing the steps with her rope and her pail. Letting the pail down the pipe on her rope and hauling up—

Cut, so as not to offend the users of the sponsors' laxative while the full slopjar was brought up out of the hole. Faces in the crowd as the camera roved. Jesus, who ever saw such a collection? Where were the police, the men with the straightjackets? What were these people doing outside of the penitentiary, the insane asylum? It looked like the faces on the wall alongside the rental boxes in the post office. No it didn't. Those were fugitives from the laws of society, wanted for ·mentionable crimes, like mail fraud, bank robbery; these had transgressed the very laws of nature. There, look at that one! Just look at that face! Child-molester was written in every line of that face. A face like that was enough to make you turn in your membership card in the human race. That one there! What uninvented atrocities did that degenerate have on his conscience that made him shirk away as the camera's eye sought him out? What was it for which the police in eleven states had orders to shoot that monster on sight?

A close-up now of the offerings at the cellar door. No matter how he stormed and railed at them to clear that junk away and burn it on the trash pile, Archie and Eulalie just drew that extra lid over their eyes which seemed to shut out hearing as well as sight. They were scared to touch any of those things. So now there was a heap there that looked like what was left unsold at the end of a flea market. For instance a glass breast pump with a rotted red rubber bulb. What in hell could that possibly symbolize to the nitwit who had left it there? The illegitimate child she had abandoned on the orphanage steps, and the milk left to curdle in her afterward? A pint, half empty, of Four Roses whiskey. A .380 caliber Colt automatic pistol, red with rust now from the seasonal dews but blue with oil when it was left there in its worn leather shoulder holster. A pair of aluminum crutches. A hypodermic syringe and needle. Bouquets and floral wreaths, fresh, faded, and plastic. And one—not shown—the biggest—so far—testimonial to the renunciatory spirit of the place: a 1961 Oldsmobile left down in the road by some penitent pilgrim who had been moved to journey along his straight new path in life on foot.

And now, following another break for a commercial for the laxative doctors recommend most, was Lois making her television debut. Well, he could sneer, but somebody had had to do it. In fact, Lois had had to do it. Who else? Ira had refused to go before the cameras. Clifford? Ross? He could never have gotten up the steps on his knees. Himself? People might think he was climbing up there to confess to something. Hazel? Not even if she had been willing. Show Hazel to the whole curious world? As for Gladys—well, she had won the disqualifying contest. All three of the sisters always went noisily to pieces in any crisis. It was Amy who had always kept her composure, her efficiency under stress. And so she had had to do, as her sisters were prostrated by the slightest mishap, totally incompetent, professed themselves so, prided themselves upon it. Helplessness in the face of calamity was their gauge of depth of feeling, and as they confessed self-complacently, "I'm just not to be relied on for anything in time of trouble. —And what about me? The least little thing and I just— And me? Perfectly useless. Have to be put to bed and looked after myself." These contests usually ended in agreement all around that they were lucky

Amy was there for all of them to fall back upon. But some-body had to do it. It was pointless, but they could not just all sit there shut up inside the house. They had to show the world they still cared, were still trying. So Lois, as the fam-ily's representative, went out and made the climb up the cellar mound to plead with her once again.

It was just a damned good thing *she* hadn't known that the TV crew was there or else she might have repeated her farewell speech. Those newshounds were perfectly capable of climbing up there and dropping a microphone down the pipe on a wire to her—in fact, he wondered that they had not thought of that. Then the whole world might have been treated to her saying how she cared nothing for any of her family and wanted only to be left alone and how she had killed their mother.

It had been done just to be seen, done just because it had to be done. There was no earthly use in it any more. They had all taken turns and had gotten nothing but silence and groans and growls for their pains. And for poor Lois there was much that was embarrassing, irritating, painful: to allow that TV technician to hang that microphone around her neck like a halter and with the cord of it trailing behind her to mount the steps cut into the mound and kneel to the pipe while all those strangers watched and prayed that she would fail in her purpose and need not have prayed, for she was doomed to fail, and she knew it. Yet Lois, maybe because she knew how hopeless it was, pitched herself heart and soul into the plea she made to Amy on the family's behalf. De-spite the staged air of it all, despite the intrusion of vulgar and vast curiosity into the family's private misfortune, or perhaps just because of this, Lois had been moved by her mission, and it moved her to tears now to see herself on the TV screen dropping to her knees at the mouth of the pipe and looking down into that blackness where her poor grief-crazed sister had sequestered herself. He had been in that spot himself. He had looked into that void, listened to that silence. Or rather, to that everlasting sigh, and felt the dankness emanating from the pipe, without current behind it—stillness itself—yet with that steady emanation, cool and dank, and with a smell to it like toadstools.

He could picture his sister where she sat, or rather, he could not picture her, it was too dark down there ever to see anything, for the bench ran around the wall and what little light there was was funneled down the pipe and fell like the beam of a flashlight in a circle in the center of the floor. Yet he could see her sitting there in the dark, for he had sat there himself many and many a time, had passed the most frightening hours of his life there—once an entire day while waiting for the end of the world.

He remembered the clamminess of it even on the hottest day and the dank, moldy, mushroom-y smell, and in the fall, cyclone season—right now: and he just wished one would spring up and catch them all out there and whirl them off to the kingdom-come they believed in and yearned for—the smell of potatoes, and the sweet putrid smell of rotting potatoes, and of carrots and apples and pears laid down for the winter on the shelves over your head above the bench. But he was wrong: you could see in there sometimes—whenever a bolt of lightning breaking overhead sent a momentary flare down the pipe and you saw the white faces around the wall with eyes as wide and dark and deep as the eyeless sockets of the skulls on the shelves in the catacombs. He remembered how they sang songs at his mother's urging to keep their spirits up and played guessing games, recited poems and told stories and asked riddles in voices unnaturally high with forced gaiety. The winds of the storm would moan over the mouth of the pipe like someone blowing across the lip of a jug, and you knew when the eye of the storm was directly overhead not just because the hole in the ceiling had blacked out but because the atmospheric pressure outside had dropped and inside it was hard to draw your breath, so hard there were moments when you feared you would surely all suffocate and be found sitting upright in your places around the wall like in a tomb in Pompeii. Hailstones would rattle against the pipe and sometimes come down the pipe and strike the lighted circle on the floor and scatter like popcorn in a pan.

The time he remembered best, or rather worst, was the day he spent there waiting for the world to come to an end. His grandmother was alive then, ancient, senile, superstitious —an easy convert for the wild-eyed itinerant millenarian minister who passed through the district preaching damnation, destruction and doom. Doomsday was nothing new, of course; it had come and gone before, came periodically to this district. But usually it stayed outside the city limits, in the tabernacles of country crossroads tent revivals: the brimstone creeds of the religious underprivileged. The Renshaws were of a caste to find such cults not only crazy but common and comical. But somehow this particular prophet got to Grandma and managed to convince her that he really had been shown God's calendar and that on it the second Thursday of next month was marked with a big red X, and that after that there was no more calendar.

The minister convinced Grandma and Grandma convinced him. Her only convert. Whether she had tried to convert the others and been laughed at or whether she knew she would be laughed at by anybody else over twelve and had not tried, he did not know. In any case, she pledged him to secrecy while, in preparation for Judgment Day, they provisioned the storm cellar, their refuge. She was not sure how long they would have to stay down there before it would be safe for them to come out—they would be given a sign—so he laid in plenty of peanut butter and graham crackers and she an ample store of condensed milk and the cigarettes for her asthma that smelled like feathers burning.

Maybe some of what was wrong with him still, all these many years later, was owing to the terrors of that day. They closed and bolted that huge heavy door upon themselves when the dawn sky was streaked with red—it really did look like the dawn of earth's last day—and there they stayed until found by his frantic mother after sundown, by which time he was tonguetied with terror. For something like sixteen hours he had sat on the bench beside the crazed, incontinent old woman who smelled of stale pee-pee and who, serenely confident of her own salvation, and maybe that minister's—he did not count, he realized about halfway through the afternoon—and enjoying the thought that outside the sinners were being toasted at God's bonfire like marshmallows on a fork, sat grinning a self-righteous grin that did not have to be seen to be felt.

"I'd have sworn he said Thursday," was her comment when they came out to find, to her visible disappointment, the world still there.

It was not long after that day that a cyclone had struck. He saw it coming, for he kept himself constantly alert to the signs, and hid himself beneath his parents' bed, shaking with terror alone in the house as lightning which seemed aimed directly at him crashed and crackled all around and thunder shook the floorboards underneath him, but preferring this, preferring death itself, to the clammy claustrophobia of the storm cellar. It was years before the family could induce him to take shelter with them there from a storm.

At least he had had company; Amy was all alone. No she was not. She was anything but alone. She had gone there to be alone but she was not. She shared her narrow cell now with a prisonful of uncaught criminals. Her living tomb was now a graveyard of unquiet ghosts. She had retreated from the world judging herself unfit for it, and the world, coming to convince her that it was unfit to live in, had worn a path to her retreat. Sin, like misery, seeks company. Amy's sin was not having loved her mother enough. Unlike many who have sinned grievously (or think they have, which comes to the same thing) and been found out, Amy had not succumbed to the temptation to believe that the only difference between her and other people was that she had been found out. To spare the world the sight of her she had taken to her cellar; now the whole world seemed to be trying its best to get in there with her. Around that bench beside her sat ghosts whose wounds for half a century had never ceased to bleed because their deaths were still unpunished, undetected, and yoked to them, like Siamese twins, their killers, the former alive in death, the latter dead though alive. Together there sat a family of three: the father, the mother who was his daughter, and the drowned infant who was her grandfather's daughter and her mother's sister. His own lurid imagination? He had seen the man, if what he had seen might be called a man, had watched him climb the mound and sink to his knees and pour his confession down the pipe, and if not what he imagined, it was something equally depraved. And that one was only one of many.

Not all who, because of their moral leprosy, ought to have been, were social lepers. Not all came shambling on foot wrapped in two cast-off overcoats and confessing endlessly to themselves. The man who pioneered what had now become the rite was said to have driven away afterward in a chauffeured Cadillac. Jonah at Joppa taking passage clean out

of God's world could not have worn a more furtive and
guilty look than that well-tailored customer. Even in his
Cadillac he could never get away from what he was running
from. He carried his pursuer with him like his own shadow
wherever he went, a fugitive from himself.

The last man on earth (or so you thought at the time,
not yet having seen some of those who were to follow this
one) to want to draw attention to himself, he had, notwithstanding, been moved to rise from his place on the ground
and work his way among the tangle of outstretched legs and
down to the mound as though to the stage in response to the
hypnotist's call for a volunteer from the audience, and while
at least four hundred eyes watched, climb it and lower himself to his knees before the culvert pipe and, laying his fine
felt hat on the ground beside him, speak into it. Vomit into
it, was what it looked like he was doing, said those seated on
the side where his face was visible—vomit up something he
had had on his stomach for thirty years. Whatever he had to
confess to, it was enough to keep him there on his knees for
some time. When he came down, bareheaded, hat in hand,
and made his way through the crowd, which, either out of
revulsion against the man he had been or out of respect for
the man he had just become, drew back all along his route,
his eyes were shining bright with tears.

To see their self-sick faces was to know what soul-sickening confessions they were pouring in upon the head of
their captive confessor trapped in her narrow cell. Unspeakable crimes, undiscovered, or for which an innocent person
had paid in their stead, perhaps through their connivance, or
else with hearts deformed by self-hatred for some monstrous
wrong that had been done to them. He could picture his sister sitting on that which was to have been her mourners'
bench, and the ghastly mockery of it: there forced to listen
to the sins of others. It must have been for her like it used to

be during a cyclone when the eye of the storm hung overhead and shut out the meager light and took your breath
away, whenever one of those put his head inside the pipe and
breathed down upon her the breath of his corrupt conscience. He could picture her in her vain efforts to escape it
holding her hands over her ears while in that megaphone of a
pipe and in that closed and narrow space it was magnified
until it came to seem like the very voice of the earth, the
dead in all their graves in all the world, victims and victim-
izers, relaying to her, as through a network of nerves, their
pitiful and horrifying histories. Listening to confessions had
always been Amy's second career, and he could see her, out
of a sense of duty—misplaced—and out of her own sense of
guilt—mistaken—taking her hands from her ears and forcing
herself to listen and in her horror and disgust feeling her way
in the dark around the clammy continuous wall as though
to avoid a pile of excrement or a rotting corpse thrown in
with her and lying in the center of her cell. And he could
picture her when her hand touched the wood of the door
drawing back in revulsion against re-entering a world where
such things lay moldering in the cellars of human hearts.

"Amy, this is Lois," said she, her voice choked with
tears. "I hope you will listen to me. Please, listen. I've come
to beg you again to come out and rejoin your family who
love you and let us try to comfort and take care of you. I
know what you're feeling, Amy, hon. Like you just never
want to set eyes on another human face, knowing you'll
never see Ma's dear loving face again." Lois had touched the
nerve that was exposed: the groan that arose from the pipe
and was picked up by her microphone confirmed it. "I know.
I know. It's how I feel, too. How all of us feel. But, sweetheart, you're not helping things any by hurting yourself.
You're only making it harder on us all, worrying over you
like we are. Open the door, Amy, dear sister, please, I beg of

you, we all beg of you, and come out and let us look after you. Come out where we can all be together and comfort one another."

She had told them, or rather, had relayed to them through her chosen messenger, that she had said her last, and she was true now to her word. From the cellar now—or rather, yesterday, when this had been filmed—came no sound. Lois sighed and got up off her knees and with tears glistening in her eyes came down the steps of the mound. She rose now from her armchair and quit the room, shaking with sobs. Clifford followed her.

As though to add to the insult, it was Jug Amy chose through whom to convey her last word. He was on guard duty beside the pipe. It was night, four hours before he could expect to be relieved. He was groaning inwardly but did not know he had groaned aloud until he heard a voice from beneath him say, "Who is there?"

Speaking into the pipe, he said, "Me, Miss Amy. Jug."

"What are you doing here?"

"Watching out over you. I'm here to see that you don't do yourself no harm."

"I'm doing myself all the harm I know how."

"Yes'm, you surely are taking it mighty hard. How much longer you reckon on before we can expect you to get feeling better in your mind and come out?"

"The rest of my life," she said.

To the family, Jug said, wetting his lips, and having primed himself with drink, "Now don't blame me if yawl don't like this. I'm only saying what she told me to say."

He shut his eyes and kept them shut throughout his recitation. The effect was as if he were a medium at a seance transmitting to them a communication from beyond the grave.

"She say she gone stay right where she is and for all the

world to just go about their business and forget about her. She say anybody try to bust down the door and get her out they gone have her blood on their hands."

"Just like I said," said Lois.

"She say tell yawl to keep your preachers and your psychatrists cause she don't care to hear nothing they got to say. She say she know her own soul better than any preacher and her own mind better than any psychatrist. She say she is where she belongs and where she wants to be. She say she the meanest woman alive and not fit to look nobody in the face nor see the light of day. She say she killed yawl's mother. She say to say that again: 'I killed my mother.' She say for yawl not to come talk to her no more. She say she not interested in anything any of yawl got to say, either. She say, tell them if they knew how little I care about any of them they wouldn't care no more what becomes of me. I told you yawl wasn't gone like it but she made me swear and that is what she told me to say. And that, she say, is all the more she ever gone say."

Now the preliminaries were over; the feature attraction could begin. She had had her daily bread and water, had heard the family's daily plea; now she belonged to them. The camera roved over the crowd; faces appeared on the screen as in the sights of a rifle. For TV this coming interval would have to be shortened. Sometimes it took so long before anybody mustered the courage to go first that everybody there seemed to be saying to himself, if somebody doesn't do it soon then I will have to. As over the faces of the suspects in a police line-up, the camera roved over the crowd, seeking the one ready first to break and confess his guilt.

Time now for a commercial.

On the other side of that coin of which Heads, I Win is the ideal old age he imagines for himself, there is for every man Tails, I Lose: the worst old age he can imagine befalling him. The future the man dreads may be remote from his circumstances in life, as remote as—heads and tails: opposites, but not separated from each other by very much. The rich man may see himself winding up a pauper. The man with a family as large and as close as Clyde Renshaw's may see himself a lone and homeless old tramp sleeping in a doorway on Skid Row. In fact his, Clyde's, familiar vision of the worst old age that could be his lot was to become one of those homeless old men in two tattered overcoats who, always going from somewhere, never to anywhere, ply the nation's highways on foot in all weathers. Perhaps, in fact no doubt, part of his resentment against those of them who had lately begun to show up here on the place came because they brought to mind his old fear of winding up just such a one himself—though not, of course, with so many outward marks of the outcast upon him as these bore. Surely to be a homeless old man bad luck was enough; it was not necessary to have committed whatever things these had done to set them on the road and muttering to themselves.

Now—the ads over and the program resumed—seeing one of them get up from his seat on the ground and make his way down to the cellar mound (rather as if he needed to relieve himself, and was about to do it in public, Clyde thought) there came into his mind a picture of himself doing that very thing. He saw himself some years hence, though not so many as to account for that shuffle to his gait, the slouch to his shoulders, the silent movement of his lips and that look in his eyes hungry for home, as he came along the road. For it was the road home. The road to this place which had always been home to him but from which he had been gone for a long time, having left it for some reason he could not find, or rather, having had to leave it for some reason, something that had caused him not just to leave home but to expect never to see it again. What was this? Was it just this beard and the long hair which made him feel like one of those old tramps—look like one, too, he expected—along with that foolish old fear of his of being left old and homeless and a wanderer, and added to that, his thought of his self-exiled baby brother and his inability ever to come home again? He could not say, but in this vivid vision he saw himself trudging up the road, unknown and grateful to both his overcoats for hiding his identity, unrecognizable in his rags and behind his beard and the premature whiteness which had settled upon him like an early winter, even to his close kin. He saw himself come among that crowd, mount the cellar mound, up those steps he himself had ordered cut there years before not knowing he was cutting them for himself, and to his sister—still there, still faithful to her vow of seclusion—pour down the pipe his history. His history? What history? He did not know. He only knew he had one, and that he had come home, to Amy, hoping by telling it to her to gain readmittance not just to his own family but to the human family, if only as the poorest of poor relations.

It was the beard and this long hair. Two cast-off overcoats one on top of the other was all he needed now to make him look like another of those old tramps. Were there white whiskers in his beard? he wondered. Of course there were. There were in Ross's, and Ross was younger than he. He would soon know, even if the mirrors were not washed off. If things went on as they were much longer it would be grown out long enough for him to see it without a mirror. Already they—the men—looked like castaways, with these whiskers, with hair beginning to straggle over their collars. The women, without make-up on their faces, were faded and dim and looked like ghosts of themselves.

On her return from taking the boys their lunch today Gladys reported more spots on the walls of the cold storage vault where chunks of ice had loosened and fallen to the floor, leaving the pipes bare. Beneath the thick coat of frost still sheathing the walls a steady dripping could now be heard. It was still like an igloo in there, but who knew how long the thawing had been going on before they noticed it?

It was cooler weather now and the town not quite so dependent upon the ice house. Even those who would have liked to resume their use of the cold storage vault, the butchers and grocers and cafe owners, forebore under the circumstances to press. The crowd that gathered daily outside the ice house was definitely with them. Respect for parents, alive or dead, family feeling to the point that made the family a law unto itself: the Renshaws were not alone in that. Observance of the proper form, not wanting to bury their mother without all her children present, or at least until they had done all in their power to bring the last one home: all shared that. The Renshaws' audacity in commandeering the ice house out of respect for custom commanded universal admiration. Well, almost universal. When they stood off the U.S. Navy the crowd was with them to a man. That was when the two MPs came from Waco to arrest Derwent for being AWOL. When Derwent announced his refusal to go back until his grandmother had been buried, the crowd formed a living wall around that Jeep.

"You see that crowd?" the Sheriff had said to Mr. Tom Gibbs, who was pressing him to go in shooting if necessary and evict the Renshaws from his cold storage vault. "Every one of them has got, or had, a mother."

"Every one of them's got a vote, too, haven't they?" said Mr. Gibbs.

"They got that too," the Sheriff cheerfully conceded.

The generating plant which supplied the power, a complex of turbines and louvered cooling towers, stood detached from the ice house, enclosed by a high cyclone fence with a padlocked gate to which Mr. Gibbs had the key. No knowing how long ago he had pulled the switch. The vault was steadily defrosting. It was still cold in there but not as cold as it had been.

In this TV reporter, the Devil had an advocate. A town man, he was embarrassed by the hillbilly holy-roller mentality here on display. That psychiatrist would have found an ally in him. Upon a number of members of the audience, especially those who had come from afar to get here, he had tried out his line that the woman in the storm cellar was simply sick. It was well known that she had done what she claimed to have done. She was sick.

Well, yes, uh-huh, they had heard something like that said. And they tried to see around him to the cellar mound.

Now he was beginning to lose patience and to show his annoyance with them for not giving him any argument. "Don't you believe that if she was guilty of killing her own mother the authorities would come and take her out of there and prefer charges against her?"

"You would surely think they would do that, wouldn't you? Yes, sir, you would surely think they would."

Now he had stopped the man who had just come down off the mound. This was the second one of those whom he had tried to interview. The first one he had approached as he reached the ground and, holding out his microphone, had chased him clear to the edge of the crowd. The man was not refusing to be interviewed; he did not know that anybody was trying to interview him. He was in a trance. So was this one now: in a trance, a transport, exalted by the experience of having disburdened his conscience down that culvert pipe. Which so exasperated the reporter that he said, "Listen here. That woman in there is sick. Mentally sick. She no more killed her mother than you did." The camera was on him. And what the viewer saw was the face of a man who might have just been talking to a man who had killed his mother.

It was not that any of the family expected Ballard and Lester to succeed in their quest. Even Clifford knew the world better than that. They would have been insulted by the suggestion that they were so backward as to believe their brothers were going to accomplish their impossible mission. Except that anybody who made such a suggestion would deserve rather to be pitied for his own backwardness. And for having so entirely missed the point. Ballard and Lester were not there to succeed but just to do their best. And yet the others, all but him, did at least half believe they might succeed, and such devices as the sky-writing raised their hopes. Although Lester admitted their having gotten the idea from an ad for Life Savers, it was smart of them to adopt it, and their having chosen the lunch hour, when workers were out of their offices and on the streets, showed that while they might be two country boys in the big city for the first time, they had observed its ways pretty closely. It was attention-getting—it had even gotten a write-up in the next morning's *New York Times*—Lester had sent them a clipping—and where could you buy more advertising space than the skies of New York City? For over two hours, according to Lester, it had hung there, growing bigger all the while as the letters lengthened. But although it may have sent others with the same Christian name hurrying home, to Kyle Renshaw, if he was there, and if he had been out on the street that day at lunchtime, and if he had looked up to see what everybody was looking at, the message KYLE COME HOME MA IS DYING was not a call but a warning. Clyde alone could have told them all this but he could not tell them because he would have had to tell them how he knew.

He had traveled. He had seen the world. He had seen just enough of Cardiff and London, Casablanca, Algiers, Palermo, Naples, Rome, Paris and Berlin to dislike them one and all. In none of these, though, had he felt more out of place, and of none did the memory tease and torment him more than New York City, where he went on a three-day pass just before being shipped overseas.

So of all the Renshaws none was more ashamed than he of his baby brother's leaving home. To the feeling that Kyle was an unnatural son and brother they had all superadded the belief that he was a traitor to his birthplace, which they would not have felt if he had left home for New Orleans or Memphis or even San Francisco. An odor of implication clung to the entire family which had a member "up North." None, though, was as scandalized by Kyle's choice of his place of expatriation as Clyde. For, remembering the things he himself had done during his three days there—or able, that is to say, to remember some of them and from these to guess at the rest—Clyde knew as none of the others could know what their brother was up to, what had ensnared him and kept him from ever returning home or communicating with the family again. Some of the others, who disapproved of New York City no less for this, thought of it as a place where their brother might have risen to a station in life from which he could look down upon them. Clyde knew it as a place where a man might sink completely out of sight.

Clyde knew that Ballard and Lester were never going to find their brother, and he dared not tell the rest why. He could not tell the others because against that suspicion they would have defended even Kyle, and from the person who had voiced the suspicion, even their own brother, they would have recoiled in disgust. Acting upon the same prejudice, Ballard and Lester were going to look everywhere except the one section where Kyle might be found, and this section they were specifically going to rule out of consideration. Whatever else he might be—undutiful son, renegade brother, traitor—Kyle Renshaw was still a white man and a Southerner.

Clyde had penetrated regions where neither Ballard nor Lester nor any other Renshaw had entered. Among the sons of—and with one dusky daughter of—Africa, Clyde had explored the jungle in the depths of his own soul. And he envisaged in darkest Harlem a vast preserve where a man might raven unrestrained. Lost in there and gone native, probably under an assumed name, was Kyle Renshaw. . . . Those thick lips, pouting with passion, those heavy-lidded liquid eyes, the white shading off into ivory, those broad nostrils dilated with desire, firm bodies smooth as onyx, redolent either of provocative perfume or the quick musk of their responsive glands—white women, after a man had known the other, were as dry and insipid as the white meat of chicken compared with the dark juiciness of the thigh.

That until recently was how Clyde had explained his brother Kyle's long absence from home. Now he had another explanation, similar but different. You could enjoy all that up there and, by detouring around your conscience, still come back home. You could stay at home and do it. He had. There was no place of exile from which there was no way back home—if you were alone. Even to himself Clyde had to say this in a whisper: Kyle had married one. Maybe was raising a family.

"Naw, sir, excuse me, not meaning to give you a short answer, but no, I won't tell you my name nor where I come from nor just what I said to that little lady down there in that cellar." At last the TV reporter had managed to stop one of the mound-mounters as he reached ground. One he could not get the mike away from. "But I will say this. I am a man that did wrong. I give myself up and was tried and found guilty and sentenced to life. After making license plates for twenty-one years the new governor pardoned me. I had paid off my debt to society. Trouble was, I couldn't pardon myself. I still didn't feel purged. I joined one congregation after another. Watchtower, Churchachrist, Pentacostals: I tried them all. Whenever I heard of some new preacher I'd throw up my work and go a hundred miles. What I could never find was one I could say to myself, he knows what I'm talking about because he's been through it. Ask God's forgiveness, that's all any of them had to say to me. He will forgive you. And that's a fact, He will. It's about like pleading guilty by mail to a parking fine. Today's preachers have gentled God down to where He's about on a par with Santa Claus. To get you into church these days they're ready to give you Green Stamps at the door. What I would like to say to all the folks watching out there on their TV sets, if you have gone from denomination to denomination and preacher to preacher and had them all put you off with words like they done me, then here is the place for you. I got more relief from telling about myself to that little lady down there all alone in the ground than I ever got from all them preachers put together. What did she say to me that give me such comfort? Nothing. Not a word. Not one word. What a comfort there is in silence! Not one lying cheerful word come up that drainpipe. Just a kind of steady low moan. More understanding in that moan, Mister, than in a month of Sunday sermons! Jesus wept, but that was a long time ago. We need somebody to weep for us now. All of us, I ain't the only one. Mister, if poor suffering sinful humankind is ever to learn to live on this earth it'll be when a living saint comes among us that instead of suffering for us or because of us, suffers with us. I say we have got just such a saint among us right now. I say she's sitting right this minute down there alone in her living tomb."

That would do it. That would draw them. That was all

that was needed. Billy Graham might as well go back to peddling Fuller brushes. He could see them already, coming up the road like a line of ants: every faith-faddist, every chronic cultist, every spiritual hypochondriac—everybody!—in the land. It was what the world was waiting for—a faith for the times—and here was its Jerusalem. A faith for our times: confession without absolution. Group guilt. Nobody believed in absolution any more but everybody had more of an urge to confess than ever—maybe that was the reason. Everybody was simply busting with things to confess. Ride on an airplane to anywhere and you were barely off the ground before the person seated next to you was confiding everything you hadn't asked about himself. First class or economy—made no difference. And never make the mistake of trying to cheer one up by making light of his self-indictment. Nothing offends a man more—though your aim was to help ease his conscience—than to have his sins belittled. Of nothing is a man more vain than of a bad conscience—so long as he has got nothing really bad on it. Their sins were the only thing that made them interesting to themselves. Absolve them and they would have nothing left.

Not hope, but release from the fretfulness of hope: that was what people came here seeking. A strange new kind of cult, this that had sprung up around his deified sister. One that worshiped a god who instead of rising preferred the tomb. Who instead of offering her followers hope and life offered them despair and death. It must suit the longing of the times: in this short while they had multiplied like a mold around that mound. The hordes of the hopeless, that was what they could look forward to having descend upon them.

Shug's face appeared on the screen and just as quickly was gone.

It was as if he had never seen her before. Was that just the surprise and the novelty of seeing her on the television screen? Was it because she was unconscious of being seen? Or was it her expression that made the sight of her so poignant, an expression of sorrow which he had never seen on her face before and which he could still see in his mind? Perhaps it was all these things. In any case, it was as if he were seeing her for the first time.

Had none of the others, not even watchful Wanda, heard his gasp? His panting, the hammering of his heart— how could they sit there watching television and not rush to his aid? Surely he was dying. No, he was not dying, though he might be better off dead. He was not dying. Just that when a man rounds a corner and collides with himself going full tilt in the opposite direction, he does get the wind knocked out of him.

He felt like crying, "Foul!" Only where would he find a referee who would rule that a foul blow was one above the belt, a blow to the heart?

In that instant his doubts about whether Shug was deceiving him were resolved. She was. You learn that you want something when you learn that you cannot have it. She was not his; the breaking of his heart told him so. He put his hand upon it, and he felt the grim reassurance of his razor.

He saw then what was so engrossing to the others that they had not heard even his stricken groan. They were watching as he, on the screen, got up from his place in the crowd and made his way down to the mound. Not "years hence." Not "hence" at all. Not even now as he watched, but already—yesterday, when this was filmed. Just as he had always feared, always known he would, he had done it without knowing it.

He watched himself mount the steps of the mound, as in a trance, and sink to his knees before the culvert pipe. Useless to hold his hands over his ears. Had he had as many hands as a Hindu statue they would not have been enough to keep

him from hearing himself say down that pipe that he loved a
nigger. No getting off light; he must confess it all. "Don't
think I mean just—" And for a moment he had not known
how to put it, he who had never been at a loss for a word
for that before. "Just that I go to bed with her," he said, his
head bowed with shame. It took all his breath to say it, but
he said it. "I love her." Horrified silence came up the pipe
from below, and he nodded in assent. "The joke's on me,
Amy," he said. "A little black slut that I took without so
much as a by your leave, who isn't even faithful to me but
deceives me with one of my own fieldhands, and I have to go
and fall in love with her." Before rising to go he said, "I
know I don't deserve any pity. I don't ask for any. I don't
want any. I'm here to confess, not to complain. But, Sister,
isn't it a rotten piece of luck!"

There was nothing left for him to say. He wondered
whether he would ever say anything more. He had said everything. He stood up and turned to face the camera and come
down the steps. It was like looking into the mirror and seeing
somebody else: the man on the mound was not himself but
some stranger from out of the crowd. He had not even been
in the audience yesterday when this film was shot. His secret
from the world was still his. It was his secret from himself that
he had given away.

Following the commercials, a silhouette of the cellar
mound against the setting sun, the day's last penitent on her
knees, her head bowed over the pipe. Not just yesterday.
Not just staged for pictorial effect by the television cam-
eraman. By turning around in his chair and looking out the
window he could have seen the same sight outside now. A
part of the rite, one that like all the other parts had become
ritualized without ever having been set down, a tradition no
less rigid for being recent: that with the setting of the sun
the time for confessions was over. The woman on the mound

stood up and turned from the pipe and slowly descended the
steps to the ground. Between sundown and darkness was the
time allotted for what in orthodox church services would
have been the reading by the preacher of the prayer and the
response of the congregation but which in this gospelless
church dumb with despair was a wordless wail.

It began low, like a wind sweeping over a waste. oooo
oooooooooh. Then like a wind it quickened: ooooooo-
OOOOOOH. Like a wind over some desolate waste it rose
to a howl, a shriek: aaaaaa AAAAEEEEEEEH. It fell
away in a series of dying gasps: AAAH aaah aah ah a . . .
Only to rise again. And again. And again.

Some—as though her message were not clear enough!—
strained, like listening into the wind, for words in it; but
none could ever agree on what these were. Some said she
was begging God's forgiveness for herself and all of them;
others said she was calling down His wrath upon them all.
One old man maintained that it was Gaelic she was speaking; he had heard it spoken when he was a boy long ago in
Ireland. Told that the woman knew no Gaelic, he said she
did now; she had been given the gift of tongues and could
speak them all. On the contrary, said others, the faculty of
speech had been taken from her. As punishment for her
crime she had been shown a vision of the world's coming
doom and condemned to warn the world in words which no
one could interpret. Others said she was not saying anything,
it was enough that she was simply lamenting. Even here
there was disagreement. Lamenting her mother's death, said
some. The death of God, said others.

Now came the first response from the crowd. Somewhere someone—generally a woman—released upon the air
a long-drawn, broken groan. It was the signal all were waiting for, and throughout the crowd, as though a baton had

been brought down, other voices joined in the lugubrious chorus.

And now came the separation of the sheep and the lambs. Now began an exodus from the grounds and from the parking lot that on some evenings tied up traffic along the road as the fainter-hearted fled with their faith intact, or in tatters, from this prairie Golgotha where the buried god did not rise radiant from the sepulcher promising redemption and life everlasting but remained stubbornly entombed. Those fled, the ones made of sterner stuff stayed on. Old Testament types, these: believers in damnation but not in salvation, of too little faith, or too much pride, to accept redemption through any god made of mere flesh and blood the same as themselves.

They were lost, and had abandoned hope. They were not calling to that empty sky above to hear their cry and forgive them for their sins. They were not even appealing to that distant dome to come crashing down and flatten them to earth for their unforgivable offenses. They were simply calling on night to fall and hide them one more time from themselves and from the sight of others like themselves. He could feel rise in his own throat a kindred cry. . . . aaaaaaaa aaaaaaaaaaaaaaaaa AAAAAAAAAAAAAA aaaaaaaaaaaaaaaaa ooooooooooooooOOOOOOOOOOOOOOooooooooooooooo aaaaaaaaaaaaaaaaa AAAAAAAAAAAAAA aaaaaaaaaaaaaaaaa ooooooooooooOOOOOOOOOOOOOOooooooooooo. . . .

On and on it went, and when one could carry the lead no longer, another, others, in the crowd took it up. And when all fell silent, the voice from underground went on, urging them to it again. Words? What could words add to that woeful wail? If the world could have concentrated the sickness of its soul and the depth of its despair into one cry it would have chosen that voice and it would have uttered that inconsolable lament. Uttered in that close space and with the pipe its outlet, even what had been a loud cry, even a shriek, came out muffled, low, sometimes so low that it could just be heard or not heard at all; yet even at those times you knew it was going on—the voice of the earth itself and of all the suffering souls interred in it since time began, those yet to come for all time to come. That even when you did not hear it it went on, like the sigh of the sea inside a sea-shell, always there whenever the shell is picked up and held to the ear, though generations might elapse between times.

The scene on the screen slowly retreated and the sound retreated too as the camera backed off for the fadeout. He got up and switched off the set. The switch-off light contracted with a concentrated gleam to the center of the screen, winked out, yet the sound seemed still to come from the set as, outside, the wail went on.

He went to the window, a man crushed by a confession made to himself alone. He had admitted the inadmissible. He had condemned himself, he had exiled himself. Of all degradations, what more shameful than a forbidden love?

The cows came up the path to the barn, bending slow incurious glances upon the wailing throng seated around the cellar mound. Now was the hour when bullbats and barn swallows, martens and chimneysweeps and presently bats appeared low overhead to bank and dip and to add their squeaks and hurt little cries to the human chorus below.

Another day was done. In Amy's cell the pale circle of light in the center of the floor would have failed, leaving her in darkness. Up from the pipe came no further sound. She had cried herself out and the crowd now followed her lead, like a distant, dying echo. The last wail subsided into a sob, the sob into a sigh, the sigh into silence. Another day with evil sufficient unto it was done; all too soon another would be here.

▫▫▫ FOUR ▫▫▫▫▫▫▫▫▫

O'Toole winds. Kicks. Delivers. High and outside and the count on Lopez is three balls, no strikes.

Again O'Toole looks down to Hubbard for the sign. Nods. Cranks. The pitch. It's over for a called strike with Victor taking all the way, and the count goes to three and one.

O'Toole goes to the rosin bag. Taking his time. Now he steps back onto the rubber. Gets the sign. It's a slow curve breaking just inside for ball four and Lopez is on with the fourth pass issued by the visiting young left-hander here today. That brings up Deron Reynolds, Mets third baseman. Reynolds batting .265 for the season, one for two here today.

Lopez leads off first. The pitcher checks the runner. He serves. Reynolds swings. It's past Hollachek, a sizzling line drive going deep into left center field, that brings the crowd surging to their feet. Turley off and running with the crack.

And Turley has it! A spectacular one-handed running catch by Leo Turley, his second of the inning, and the side is retired. One run: Clemson's homer into the left field stands; one hit, no errors, and at the end of six it's the Mets 2, Cleveland Indians 0, here in the fifth game of the World's Series being played in Shea Stadium before a crowd of . . .

The youth with the portable radio slouched around the corner into Mulberry Street. Maybe that was where his runaway brother was today, thought Lester Renshaw, feeling a sneeze coming on and lifting his nose with his forefinger, sneezing anyway: among the fifty-one thousand three hundred and some odd out at the ball park.

He rang the doorbell again, and as he waited for the buzzer to sound, looked across the street. Out of a doorway at the far end of the block Ballard emerged, doubled over in a fit of coughing, but staggering on, unheeding, grim, intent, his face set in a scowl that carried a city block, into the next doorway beyond. Ballard was already finishing the block on his side of the street; he, Lester, was just starting in on his.

The buzzer razzed as Lester was stifling another sneeze. He grabbed the door handle, just in time, and stepped inside. The air of the hallway tasted of yesterday's fried onions, of last Tuesday's boiled cabbage, of (though this Lester was unable to identify) of Friday evening's tallow candles. He found himself at the foot of a long flight of stairs. He was climbing stairways in his sleep these nights. Heaving a sigh he grasped the gummy handrail and hauled himself up. The air thickened as he ascended into the gloom.

He could hear behind the door the shuffling of felt slippers along the floor, accompanied by a querulous mutter. The door opened of itself, until, looking down, he saw her. She reached hardly above his waist, a stooped and frail, tiny creature, snuff-colored, crinkled as an autumn leaf.

"Excuse me, Ma'am," said Lester, removing his hat. "Sorry to disturb you. I'm looking—ah-choo! Beg your pardon. I—ah-choo!"

She held up a twisted brown finger, one of a bunch like dried roots, then turning back, disappeared into the darkened room and he heard a shuffling of papers and the noise of something knocked off a table to the floor, then she returned with a sheet of gray cardboard in her hand, the kind that comes back from the laundry inside a shirt. At first Lester could see nothing. Then he made out these words, in pencil, gray on gray:

COME BACK NEXT WEEK WILL HAVE SOME MONEY THEN

The old woman looked at him from underneath the board, her head cocked, her black eyes glistening with rheum. "Ho keh?" she said.

He had been taken now for a process server, the truant officer, the parole officer, a bill collector, the meter reader. For an adoption agency investigator, for a respondent to an ad seeking a home for a kitten, for "a friend of Maury's," for the alienator of a wife's affections by her husband. He had been shown inside and told the patient was in the next room, and he had twice been asked whether he couldn't read and shown the plaque that said, "Service entrance in rear."

Lester shook his head. "No, no, lady," he said wearily. "I'm not the rent collector. I'm here looking for a man. He's my brother. Can you tell me if Kyle Renshaw lives in the building? That's Renshaw. R-E-N—"

She pointed again to the message on the cardboard. "Ho keh?" she said.

So that when Lester tried again he shouted, thinking she was hard of hearing. And when she shook her head he took the card from her and the pen from his pocket and wrote, or rather printed:

"Ho keh," she said, and shut the door in his face.

He knocked again. The door opened. In Spanish that sizzled like something frying in a pan, the old woman told him off, slammed the door, and he could hear her slippers shuffling away across the floor.

When Lester came out again on the stoop, Ballard, wracked by coughs, was ringing the bell of a doorway down in the next block. Ballard's way of ringing a doorbell was to lean on it until the door was opened. That brought many people to the door in a bad temper. One look at Ballard, however, was enough to cow them. A scowl had always been more or less Ballard's natural expression, but now his face was enough to frighten children and when he spoke he snarled. If one of his coughing fits should seize him just as the door was opened, he might, in the case of a woman, grab her arm, or in the case of a man grab his lapels and hold on until the fit was over and he could speak.

With Ballard everything had gone wrong right from the first morning when, at the automat, he had put his coins in the slot and pulled the lever and watched his coffee go down the drain because he had neglected to set his cup under the spout, and the customers waiting in line behind him, and Lester too, had snickered. Ballard's fears of being taken for a rube were well founded and he soon developed on his thin skin a raw spot like a gall. If he had worn a sarong—or a ten-gallon Stetson and a pair of high-heeled boots—they could hardly have spotted him sooner: the various leeches and panders who patrol the streets of mid-Manhattan on the lookout for greenhorns. In a single day he had had his picture snapped so many times by those men who jump out at you, if you are a tourist, near the library on 42nd Street, draw a bead on you with an ancient bleary-eyed Leica, and force a claim check on you, that soon he was walking four blocks around to avoid the spot. Those fellows in porter's caps who haunt the corners of Times Square recruiting for Manhattan sightseeing tours would let a whole stream of native pedestrians flow past, then pounce infallibly upon Ballard. Panhandlers recognized him. Even called him "Tex." He was offered in raspy whispers wrist watches guaranteed hot, fountain pens, lottery tickets, rubber goods, filthy photos, women. Even urchins identified him at a glance, and every little boy in Greater New York seemed to have lost his subway fare home. One thing only made him madder than all this: that was to be taken for a New Yorker. This error was usually committed by another out-of-towner, who stopped Ballard on the street to ask directions. He never asked directions himself, not of anybody, citizens or policemen. A Texan, and therefore accustomed to taking the car whenever he had to go around the block, he trudged the streets of New York, lost, for hours, sooner than reveal that he was from out of town by asking anybody how to get to wherever he wanted to go.

Ballard did not dislike the people of New York City because of anything they had done to him. He disliked them because they were strangers and because there were so many of them. It angered him to find how many people there were in the world who neither knew nor cared anything about him and his concerns.

Ma's death and burial, instead of being the time to discontinue their search, was for Ballard the time to press it. Ma's dying and being buried without Kyle there made Ballard all the madder at him. He held it against him for having made him and Lester miss it. And New York City's harboring Kyle at such a time was a reason for being all the madder at it and everybody in it.

He could no longer be reasoned with. Lester had tried

again as they were starting in on this street. "Ballard?" he had said. "Bubba? Buddybud? Listen to me, Ballard. Ballard? Ballard, you're not listening. I'm talking to you, Ballard, listen to me. You hear? Ballard? Listen. Listen, Bubba. We can't go on like this, hear? Ah-choo! This is crazy. You hear me, Ballard? Can't go—ah-choo! Crazy. You know how long we've been doing this? You know what day it is? And we're not even up to where they start numbering them. And there are two hundred and fifty numbered ones. And they get wider all the time. This island gets wider all the way up. And there's two hundred and fifty numbered streets after the ones with names to them give out. And after Manhattan there's the Bronx, Brooklyn, Staten—Ballard! Ballard, you're not even listening."

"I heard every word you said. You through now?"

"No, I'm not through! Listen, Ballard, you know I love Ma every bit as much as you do, and I'm just as anxious as you are to—"

"Nobody's asking you to stay. Go if you want to. I can get along without you. Go. But not me. (cough) I'm staying. See? (cough) Son of a bitch if this goddamned town is going to make a monkey out of me."

A Note on the Type

This book was set on the Linotype in JANSON, a recutting made direct from type cast from matrices long thought to have been made by the Dutchman Anton Janson, who was a practicing type founder in Leipzig during the years 1668–87. However, it has been conclusively demonstrated that these types are actually the work of Nicholas Kis (1650–1702), a Hungarian, who most probably learned his trade from the master Dutch type founder Dirk Voskens. The type is an excellent example of the influential and sturdy Dutch types that prevailed in England up to the time William Caslon developed his own incomparable designs from them.

*This book was composed, printed and bound by
The Kingsport Press, Kingsport, Tenn.*

*The typography and binding design
are by Christine Aulicino.*